Raining Tears

by

Laura Freeman

Raining Tears

Cover Art by *Tina Lynn Stout*

The Wild Rose Press, Inc.
PO Box 708
Adams Basin, NY 14410-0708
Visit us at www.thewildrosepress.com

Publishing History
First Edition, 2023
Trade Paperback ISBN 978-1-5092-4729-5
Digital ISBN 978-1-5092-4730-1

Published in the United States of America

She was wasting time. She needed to get out of the alley now. She waved the gun sideways to send the man on his way. "Forget it."

He held out his wallet, waiting for her to claim it. A loud crack made her look above at the overhang of the building. The rusty gutter, filled with rainwater, broke away from its neighboring section and crashed onto Claire's outstretched arm and hand holding the gun.

The weight of the water inside the aluminum frame was like a brick being slammed down on her forearm. She screamed and dropped the gun. A spasm shook her arm, and a sharp stabbing pain shot through the muscles up into her shoulder and down to her fingertips.

The gun lay on the wet pavement between them. The man gazed into her eyes for the briefest moment before he leapt. Claire dove onto her knees to reach her revolver, but the man snatched it in his left hand and stood over her. He pointed the barrel down at her head as she knelt on the wet pavement.

"I think I'll keep my money." He still had his wallet in his right hand and gripped the gun awkwardly in his left.

She looked up at him towering over her and debated whether to challenge his possession of her weapon. "Do you even know how to use that?"

Dedication

To everyone who forgives those who trespass against them.

Chapter One

Claire Batton recognized the old woman seated at the Newtown bus stop as an easy mark. Edith Merryweather was a regular in the pain management program at the hospital where the doctor prescribed her oxycodone medication. Although the opioid painkiller was highly addictive, it provided comfort care to octogenarians like Edith. Many patients kept their pills handy when away from home. If Claire was lucky, Edith had her meds in her outdated leather purse left unattended on the bench beside her. If nothing else, she'd net a few dollars.

The clouds on Ohio's May evening were leaking a misty drizzle, and Claire pulled her backpack from her shoulders and removed a small bag. The hospital had given out the one-size-fits-all rain gear in assorted colors at the chamber of commerce expo in February. She shook out the black one and slipped it over her head, pulling the large hood forward to obscure her face. The raindrops fell steadier. The poncho's thin plastic blended with her black stretch pants and battered running shoes and created a dark mass of nothing identifiable to any witness of her anticipated acquisition.

After slipping on latex gloves, she removed a small revolver from her bag. As a nurse, her fingerprints were in the system for background checks, and she was careful not to leave any on the weapon or ammo in case she had to ditch the gun. She was a fan of mystery stories and paid attention to details. She pulled her backpack onto her shoulders and took a deep breath as she surveyed her target. Her right hand gripped the molded handle beneath the folds of the poncho. She didn't want to hurt anyone. The doctor could prescribe Edith more medicine, and she would return to a feeling of normalcy the pills produced. She'd be able to function again without the panic and anxiety that haunted her. It wasn't a crime to feel like a human being.

Claire dashed across the street as the gentle sprinkles morphed into an intense downpour. The rain pelted against the plexiglass enclosure around Edith. A wind blew an empty coffee cup out from under the raised walls and into the street. The trash can outside the enclosure overflowed like a scoop of melting ice cream on a cone, and the ground was littered with soggy clumps of cigarette butts and crumpled food wrappers.

The change in the weather had come on suddenly, and unprepared individuals scattered for cover, but no one joined solitary Edith. The bus traveling toward the stop was a half-dozen blocks away, delayed as a mob of wet boarders pushed and shoved to escape the rain. Claire had to make a decision while the timing was right. She could snatch the purse and dash off before the bus arrived and Edith realized she had become a donor to the Claire Batton Foundation, or she could do nothing and continue on her route.

Claire hesitated. What if Edith recognized her? What if she grabbed for her purse? She saw the bus closing its doors. The vehicle wouldn't take long to cover the distance. It was now or never. She stepped inside the shelter. The rapid fire of heavy raindrops was deafening in the small enclosure, but there was no need to talk. Edith's arthritic hands struggled to tie a plastic hat over her fluff of white curls.

Claire tugged her hood forward and pointed the gun in Edith's face. Before the elderly woman registered what was happening, Claire snatched the purse off the bench and dashed out into the rain. She fled behind the bus stop, along the brick wall of a Mexican restaurant, and turned into the alley that ran behind the eateries and small businesses of downtown.

The cloudburst continued an angry assault on the rooftops and roads, filling gutters and potholes. Newly formed rivers flowed along the edge of the sloped asphalt pavement, seeking storm drains. She splashed through the virgin rivers as the water soaked her exposed clothing.

Claire hugged the backs of the retail buildings, hiding in the shadows, listening for any pursuers. The darkness was broken by an occasional streetlight attached to a telephone pole.

Her heart raced, the rush of adrenaline from obtaining Edith's purse rivaling any feeling of opioids when they coursed through her body. She slowed to a walk, savoring the natural high. Ahead was a large metal trash dumpster with two plastic flip-up lids. She stepped beneath the overhang on the back of the building for protection from the steady rain and opened Edith's purse to search the contents. She pulled out a prescription bottle of oxycodone and shook it. Nearly full. It had been worth the risk. She slipped her backpack off one shoulder and transferred the plastic bottle inside along with her revolver.

She glanced around. Alone. If Edith had raised the

alarm, they weren't after her yet, and she could make her escape. She pulled out Edith's wallet. The bills were arranged from ones to twenties all facing the same way. Claire didn't have time to count it. She folded the stack in half and shoved it deep into her bag. The remaining items inside the old handbag were useless. She tossed the purse and wallet into the trash container.

The rain eased into a gentle pitter-patter, but the cloud clusters bathed the alley in dark shadows even though it wasn't yet nine o'clock. Claire searched her surroundings to find her bearings. Edith's bus stop was behind her. The hospital and her nearby apartment were north on the other side of Main Street. She'd have to use the crosswalk a couple of blocks ahead. The police would be looking for someone in black.

She searched for another poncho. Neon yellow would work. No one would think a thief wore a bright color. She removed the black one and debated whether to toss it in the trash. It had the hospital name printed in small letters near the neck. *Leave no clues* was her motto. She took time to fold it over and over until it was small enough to fit into the storage bag. She shook out the yellow poncho and slipped it over her head. It was like transforming from notorious Ms. Hyde into sweet Nurse Jekyll.

Claire's shoes were soaked, and a chill in the air made her shiver. She had an hour to run home, take a hot shower, and put on dry clothes before reporting for her ten-hour shift at the hospital. She kept her latex gloves on to keep her hands warm and headed toward the intersection.

She paused. The sound of footsteps, softened by the splashing of water, approached from the opposite direction. Who else would be in the alley? A police officer wouldn't be on foot. She moved against the back of a building, searching for the closest alley for an escape. Claire wasn't afraid of the dark. She had her gun. No one was going to mess with her. She searched her bag, glad she hadn't removed her gloves, and withdrew her revolver.

A man whistling a jingle stepped into a circle of dull yellow from a light fastened to the back wall of the next building. He wore a fancy raincoat and a floppy hat.

Claire remained in the shadows. Water dripped in a steady plop-plop beat as it overflowed a sagging gutter overhead, splashing in a puddle at her feet. It hit the barrel of her gun, and she jerked it out of the water's path to protect her weapon.

He stopped and stared at her. "What do you want?"

She extended her arm, and the metal of the barrel reflected in the dull glow of the light's outer edges.

He gasped in a sharp intake of air but didn't run. "You have a gun."

She laughed at his statement of the obvious.

"You're a woman." The man's voice squeaked with surprise.

Claire had made a mistake revealing her gender. "Don't let that fool you." She jabbed the gun in his direction. If he wasn't going to flee, she'd use his stupid bravado against him. "Give me your wallet."

"You can have it." He reached into his coat pocket. "I don't want any trouble. My boy is sick, and I need to return home with his medicine."

Medicine? "What kind of pills?"

"Penicillin drops. He's eight months old and has an ear infection."

Drops for a baby were useless to her. A police car's siren echoed in the distance. Edith must have told the bus driver about the robbery, and he'd called it in. An old friend worked at the local dispatch center and had shown her the screens she monitored every shift. The mapping system allowed dispatchers to track patrol cars and calculate distances to crime scenes, sending the closest officers.

She was wasting time. She needed to get out of the alley now. She waved the gun sideways to send the man on his way. "Forget it."

He held out his wallet, waiting for her to claim it. A loud crack made her look above at the overhang of the building. The rusty gutter, filled with rainwater, broke away from its neighboring section and crashed onto Claire's outstretched arm and hand holding the gun.

The weight of the water inside the aluminum frame was like a brick being slammed down on her forearm. She screamed and dropped the gun. A spasm shook her arm, and a sharp stabbing pain shot through the muscles up into her shoulder and down to her fingertips.

The gun lay on the wet pavement between them. The man gazed into her eyes for the briefest moment before he leapt. Claire dove onto her knees to reach her revolver, but the man snatched it in his left hand and stood over her. He pointed the barrel down at her head as she knelt on the wet pavement.

"I think I'll keep my money." He still had his wallet in his right hand and gripped the gun awkwardly in his left.

She looked up at him towering over her and debated whether to challenge his possession of her weapon. "Do you even know how to use that?"

His shoulders snapped back, and he cocked the hammer before she could warn him. It took skill to safely uncock the firing mechanism of the old gun, and in his inexperienced hands, it could go off and kill her with the slightest touch on the trigger.

Claire huddled close to the ground, watching a vehicle as it entered the alley at a slow crawl behind the man who now held her captive. The suburban utility vehicle flashed no lights and echoed no siren, but the reflective white letters on black paint declared it was the police. It had to be a second car from the one approaching with sirens blaring from the opposite direction. They were trying to trap her in the alley. How would she escape? Maybe she could dash for the narrow opening between the next two buildings and cross Main Street. She raised one knee and put her foot beneath her.

The driver of the police car turned on the spotlight and lit the man's figure from behind, outlining him above her. They'd see her escape if she ran, especially in the yellow rain poncho.

Claire crouched down and covered her head as she screamed, "Please don't shoot me! Please don't shoot me!"

"What?" The man gasped. "I'm not going to hurt you."

She raised her head, trying to decipher the figure in the bright blinding light. He fumbled with the gun.

"Police! Turn around!" a female officer ordered. Her voice was from the other side of the alley on the passenger side of the cruiser. That meant two police officers and less chance of escape. What was the deal? All she had done was steal an old woman's purse.

"Show me your hands!" The masculine voice of the

other officer sounded closer.

"What?" The man above her turned. The metal of the gun in his hand reflected in the bright spotlight as he rotated to his left and the voice.

"Gun!" the male officer shouted from the center of the alley. "Drop it! Drop the gun!"

The first shot was from Claire's revolver. She'd practiced shooting enough to recognize the high pinging sound. The shots that followed were from a different gun and rang out deeper and louder above her, one after another. She covered her ears as the barrage echoed off the buildings in the narrow alley.

She watched as the man fell backward from the blows of the shots, and his body crumpled to the ground, sprawled out on the pavement. He was on his back, his face turned toward her, his eyes open in shock and pain. Ribbons of red swirled in the puddles of water around his body. His mouth opened as if to speak, and he gave a final gasp as life left his body.

She heard footsteps approaching and snatched the latex gloves from her hands, stashing them in a pocket. Freed, her damaged hand throbbed, and tears filled her eyes. She blinked to make them fall.

After kicking her gun away, the male officer knelt by the body and checked for a pulse. He walked toward her and extended his hand. "Are you all right?"

She sobbed and placed her left hand in his as she planned her escape.

Chapter Two

Detective Sydney Harrison parked her unmarked cruiser on Main Street away from the emergency vehicles gathered in the alley. Officers had responded to an armed robbery at a bus stop, and shots had been fired.

Sydney had been on the force for nearly ten years, but this was her first fatal shooting investigation as a detective. She needed to stay focused and gather information on the death of the alleged criminal. His guilt would exonerate the officer's actions. She put on her bulletproof vest and checked her gun holster on her hip. Her belt contained a stun gun, handcuffs, mace, and her badge. Her other equipment was kept in the pockets of her coat and cargo pants. She identified herself to the auxiliary officer and passed through the blockade that had been set up to keep reporters, photographers, and the morbidly curious at bay.

The alley stretched for several miles behind the restaurants and shops making up the commercial district of Newtown's downtown. It was Saturday night, and most of the places would stay open past midnight for those lucky to have the weekend off. All her personal plans were on hold until the case was resolved.

Sydney strode past the medical examiner's van and stepped into a deep pothole filled with water, a remnant of the cloudburst that had passed as quickly as it had arrived. She paused long enough to shake the water off her boot and pant leg. Paramedics unloaded a stretcher from the back of an ambulance. She passed between it and an empty police vehicle. She stopped at the yellow ribbon marking the crime scene and surveyed the site. Across from her, battery-operated lights illuminated the motionless form sprawled on the asphalt. A medical examiner's investigator knelt over the body and recorded observations in a computer notebook.

Back and to the left of the body, Sergeant Rick Faris paced back and forth along the length of his patrol vehicle.

She blocked his return path. "Sergeant Faris."

He stopped and stared. "What happened to your eye?"

Sydney touched her tender cheek. She had learned the hard way not to share personal information with Rick. "This little thing? You should see the other guy."

"No man ever got the best of you." Bitterness coated his words. They had both applied for the detective position four months ago. Even though Rick had more years on the force, she had a college degree, a higher test score, and no black marks on her record.

The detective position was a lateral move in the Newtown police force, but beating him out for the job had rubbed salt in the wound left from a brief affair she had called off before it went beyond a few stolen kisses and whispers of endearment. She had ended the game before the final chapter of infidelity when she wisely came to her senses. She wasn't going to fix her marital problems by sleeping with another man.

Sydney looked around. "Were you first on the scene?"

"We were." Rick pointed to the young female

officer sitting inside the patrol cruiser. "Officer Beth Moreno." She was pale, quiet, and her gaze strayed to the body sprawled on the pavement where the forensic investigator was documenting the scene with photographs. The paramedics set up the body bag on the nearby stretcher.

Sydney turned from Beth to Rick. "You were on patrol together?"

He chuckled. "You sound jealous."

"You're the one with a commitment issue, Sergeant."

He looked baffled. "Commitment issue?"

"You keep forgetting you're married."

He lowered his voice to a deep growl. "You knew I was married when you wanted a shoulder to cry on."

She met his gaze. "You took advantage of my vulnerability when I needed a friend."

"Men and women can't be friends." His face cracked with laugh lines. "Sex gets in the way."

"You made that clear, Sergeant, so let's keep this professional." She waved him up the alley away from the vehicles and flashing lights. A dim streetlight bathed them in its glow. She attached her video camera to her coat and took out her notebook and pencil to jot down information she deemed important. She nodded at Rick and activated the camera. "This conversation is being recorded. Detective Sydney Harrison interviewing Sergeant Rick Faris." She looked at him. "What happened?"

"We were responding to an armed robbery call."

"For the record. You and…"

"Officer Beth Moreno. She was on rotation with me." He raised an eyebrow, and a crooked grin conveyed more. She had once thought the smoldering gaze charming. Now it came across as trying too hard and a sad commentary on a middle-aged man in an unhappy marriage.

"Wasn't the robbery at a bus stop on Main? Why drive this way?"

"I figured he might use the alley to get away from the bus stop, so I came in quiet with no sirens or flashing lights. I was right." He paused, waiting for a comment.

His need for praise was obvious. "Good call, Sergeant. What happened next?"

"I put my spotlight on him. He had a woman on her knees begging for her life. When Officer Moreno ordered him to turn around, I saw the revolver in his hand and shouted, 'Gun,' and ordered him to drop it. He fired. Moreno returned fire and resolved the situation."

"How many shots fired?"

"I lost count. An investigator from the medical examiner's office has her gun. They'll have a report."

"Did you fire any shots?"

His voice deepened, and he raised his shoulders, his stance rigid in defense. "I was in a bad position. Moreno had a cleaner shot of the man."

She looked at the position of the vehicle and the body. "Show me where you were standing."

They returned to the vehicle, and Rick stood next to the driver's door. "Moreno had exited and stood behind the front of the cruiser," he said.

"Show me Moreno's position." Sydney took his position and then moved to the other side of the car. She leaned into the open window. "Is this where you stood?"

Beth nodded from inside. "Yes," she whispered.

"I'll talk to you next." She moved back to the

driver's side. Who had the better angle? "You said there was a woman in the alley. Where was she standing?"

Rick pointed beyond the body. "I placed a cone where she was huddled on the ground while he stood over her with a gun in his hand. One victim wasn't enough for this guy."

"His career in crime is over." She stood in his spot. "Could you see the woman from here?"

"She had on a bright-yellow rain poncho, but she was behind him, so I didn't have a clear view of her. I let Beth take the shot." His voice deepened. "It was a clean shooting."

"I'm not here to judge anyone." Sydney spoke in a reassuring tone. "I'm here to investigate the diffusion of the situation. I have to interview witnesses and piece together what happened and why."

"He had a gun and fired at us. That's the what and why."

"You know as well as I that we have to investigate every discharge of an officer's weapon whether there's a victim or not." She studied her notes and searched the crime scene. "Where's the woman who was in the alley?"

He looked around and shrugged. "After I checked on the body, I helped her to her feet. Officer Wilson had arrived, so I escorted her to his car. Then I took care of Beth. She was pretty shaken."

"Most officers are after a shooting." He liked to console female officers. She'd been one of them.

"Once she was settled, I checked the perimeter. People were coming into the alley to have a look, and I needed to secure the crime scene. When the auxiliary car arrived, he added barricades, and I returned to my squad car but stayed outside. That's when you arrived."

She looked north and south. "Which end were you securing?"

He pointed in the direction of the other police car.

"Near Third Street." Sydney checked her notes. "The robbery was at Third and Main." Like Officer Wilson, the paramedics, and medical examiner team, she had come in near the scene of the crime. Only Rick had come in from the north. She recreated the scene in her mind. "Which way was the man facing when you arrived?"

"His back was to us. We didn't know he had a gun until he turned."

"You saw it first?"

"Yes, and I shouted gun." He ground his teeth. "I told you that. He was committing another robbery. He was the bad guy."

"Once I'm done interviewing Moreno, stop by the hospital for a blood draw."

He scoffed at her suggestion. "Me, too?"

"You and Moreno."

"Neither one of us was drunk."

"I know that, but if he has family and lawyers get involved, you're going to want proof you weren't under the influence. After the test, return to the station and write up your reports. Chief Mills is coming in. He'll probably want to talk to both of you before you go home."

"Anything else?"

"I know you said you didn't fire your gun, but turn it over to a medical examiner's investigator to verify it."

He opened his mouth as if to protest, but instead of speaking, he turned and headed toward the ME's van.

Clouds moved in a lazy withdrawal, signaling the end to the rain, but dampness hung in the air like an annoying guest. Sydney sat in the driver's seat next to Beth. She had rookie written all over her with the new uniform and the academy short haircut. "How long have you been on the force?"

"It'll be a year in June. I'm on my final rotation." Beth's eyes widened. "You have a black eye."

Sydney waved her concern aside. "It comes with the job."

"I have an ice pack in the back. Would you like it?"

"Thank you for asking, but I'm fine."

Beth shivered.

"Are you cold?"

"The temperature dropped after the rain."

She could be in shock. "Do you want the windows up?"

"No, I like the fresh air. It's always cleaner after a rain." Her hands trembled, and she folded them in her lap to control the movement. "I heard you made detective. Officer Faris has spoken highly of you."

That didn't sound like Rick. He had openly criticized the chief's choice of a woman and had spread nasty rumors after her selection over him. She had ignored the gossip, hoping his anger would pass. She needed to do her job, but it was easier with the support of fellow officers. Sydney spoke her name and Beth's for the record and leaned toward her. "Tell me what happened."

Chapter Three

Beth inhaled a calming breath and closed her eyes to visualize the events from the evening. She wanted to get every detail right. "Dispatch called us about an armed robbery at the bus stop on Main Street near Third. The victim identified a man with a gun wearing dark clothing and heading west between buildings."

"Why did you come down the alley?"

"Sergeant Faris chose the route. He said trash collectors and delivery trucks use it for the businesses." She glanced out her window where a six-foot barbed wire fence separated the alley from low-income apartments. The activity had sparked the barking of a large dog chained in the barren backyard opposite her. The bleak poverty reminded her of the life she had fled. She had attended more funerals than weddings of hometown friends and wanted to make a difference by joining a police force and fighting crime. But she didn't talk about her past. No one bragged about being poor.

She turned to Sidney. "He said the fence all along here would limit his escape from the alley."

"When did you see the suspect?"

She pointed to the far side of the street. "The sergeant saw movement in the shadows of that building, stopped the squad car, and turned on the external search light. We could see a man standing with his back to us." She put her hand on the door lever. "I jumped out of the car and took a stance by the front wheel."

"Show me what you did when you arrived." Sydney joined Beth on the other side of the car.

Beth moved to the front of the vehicle and recreated her actions. She overlapped her hands as if gripping her gun in a shooter's stance.

"Where was the man?"

Beth pointed toward the form surrounded by *do not cross* crime tape. "About where his body is now."

"Where was Sergeant Faris?"

"Standing behind his opened door."

"That would make him closer."

"I was first out of the car," Beth said. "I had my weapon ready to fire. The man stood over a woman kneeling on the ground."

Sydney pointed to the body. "Could you see both of them from your angle?"

"Yes, but his back was to me, and she was crouched down."

"How did you know it was a woman?"

"When we drove up, I could hear her shouting, 'Don't shoot me.' "

"From inside your car?"

"Raindrops were on the glass, so Sergeant Faris had rolled down his window to see better, and I did the same. She was screaming the words. The woman was terrified." Her voice shook, and she paused to calm herself. "I identified myself as police and ordered him to turn around."

"Which way did he turn?"

Beth moved her shoulder as she recreated the man's actions with her body. "He turned to his left."

"Did you see the gun?"

"No, but the sergeant did. He ordered him to show his hands and drop the gun. He fired instead."

The shot had startled her, but her training had immediately kicked in. She'd graduated at the top of her class at the police academy and had taken a vow to serve and protect. The man was armed and dangerous. It was her job to prevent him from harming civilians even if it meant using deadly force. "I fired in response." She had fired high to keep from hitting the woman cowering at the suspect's feet and aimed for the largest mass visible, a rule for any shooting. His body had spun and jerked as each bullet hit its mark. His hat had fallen first, followed by his body, collapsing in a twisted puzzle. "I fired until the threat was no longer imminent."

"Then what happened?"

"Sergeant Faris asked me to cover him while he checked on the man. He was dead." Beth's body shook in a spasm. She'd killed a man. Why hadn't he dropped the revolver? Why had he fired his weapon? She'd had no choice. The contents of her stomach churned. She turned toward the fence and gripped the wire in her hands as she bent forward and emptied her belly.

Sydney offered her a tissue.

"Thank you."

"Can you continue?"

She straightened. "What more is there?"

"Do you remember how many shots you fired?"

"I don't know." She ran her fingers through her spiky hair, smoothing it back away from her face. "I never shot anyone before." She stared at Sydney. "Does it get any easier?"

"When it gets easy, it's time to quit the force."

"I joined the police force to save lives. I never

thought I'd take one."

"If you hadn't discharged your gun, you might be dead." Sydney looked around. "Do you know what happened to the woman in the yellow rain poncho?"

The color had been a sharp contrast to a death scene. "The sergeant helped her up and led her to the other squad car. Officer Wilson talked to her while I waited in this car. Is she all right?"

"Why do you ask?"

"When she passed my car, she was holding her wrist."

"Do you remember which one?"

Beth concentrated on the image. "She was supporting her right wrist."

Sydney scratched something into her notebook. "After the shooting, did you touch the body or the gun?"

Beth shook her head side to side. "No."

Sydney pointed to her waist and the empty holster. "What happened to your weapon?"

"The woman from the medical examiner bagged it and put it in her van." Her eyes widened, and she gasped. "She said it was protocol after a shooting. Was I wrong to give it to her?"

"No, I just want to verify you gave her your gun directly. It didn't pass into anyone else's hands before the investigator's?"

"No."

Sydney handed her a card. "If you remember anything or want to talk, call me."

She signaled for the sergeant to approach. "You'll need to go to the hospital for a blood draw. Inform dispatch you're off patrol. Then report back to the station and write up your reports."

Chapter Four

Sydney headed toward Officer Sam Wilson. He leaned against his vehicle parked on the southern end of the alley and scrolled down his phone. His cruiser had been empty when she walked past it on her arrival. She scanned the crime scene. Where was the witness?

She'd heard good things about Sam from other officers but had never worked with him. She introduced herself. "I'm Detective Sydney Harrison."

He stood at attention. "Officer Sam Wilson. How may I help you, ma'am?"

Sam saluted, which made her smile. He was in the Ohio Army National Guard and had returned from military duty in the Middle East about six months ago from his second deployment. He'd helped with evacuations and the casualties from a suicide bombing. His youthful face held captive the eyes of an old man who had seen too much of the world in a short span of time.

She looked inside his vacant squad car. "Sergeant Faris said he escorted the witness to your car. Did you interview her?"

"Yes, ma'am. I wrote up my report."

She nodded toward the empty passenger seat. "Where is she?"

He hesitated. "She left, ma'am."

"What?" She had expected the woman to be in the

ambulance receiving medical treatment or the comfort of a warm blanket after witnessing a shooting. She didn't expect her to be gone. "I was on my way. It would have been nice if she could have waited until I arrived." She strained to control her reaction, but her voice had an annoying ring of disbelief and irritation.

"I stepped away for a minute, and she disappeared." He looked embarrassed.

Her bruised eye began to pound, and she blinked, hoping the pain would ease. "Tell me you have her information."

"I interviewed her and put all her responses in the computer." He motioned her to enter on the passenger side before he sat in the driver's seat and pulled up the data.

Sydney took a deep breath and forced herself to relax before adjusting the screen so she could view it. "What's her name?"

"Abby Keller." The blanks were filled in with standard report data and personal information. A paragraph described what had happened. She activated her camera and asked Sam to state his name. "What did you observe when you arrived on the scene, Officer Wilson?"

He paused. "I entered from Third Street where the robbery was reported and heard gunshots. They ended before I stopped my vehicle. The man was on the ground, a woman was crouched beside him, and Sergeant Rick Faris was leaning over the body."

"Where was Officer Moreno?"

"Standing by her vehicle. She had her gun drawn until Sergeant Faris told her the man was dead. She didn't go near the body." He looked around. "They're gone."

"Blood tests," Sydney said.

"I didn't see the shooting." Sam sighed as he shook his head. "A couple minutes sooner and I would have been a witness, but it was all over by the time I arrived."

"What happened next?"

"Sergeant Faris helped the victim to her feet and escorted her to my car."

"Abby Keller." The victim had a name. "What were your first impressions of her?"

"She was pretty shaken and kept crying. She said she was on her way home when the man stopped her. He pointed his gun at her and wanted her money."

"Did you get her driver's license?"

"Yes, ma'am." The squad computers could retrieve any information in the Department of Motor Vehicles' files. The driver's license number provided a home address, phone number, and an unattractive picture of the person.

"Email all of it to me." She handed him a card with her email and waited for the report to show on her phone. She stared at the DMV photo. "Describe Abby."

Sam frowned. His fingers played on the keyboard.

"Without looking at the picture in your report." She softened her tone. "What do you recall?"

He shrugged. "She kept her face down and sobbed into a handful of tissues."

"What was she wearing?"

"A big yellow rain poncho."

"What color hair?"

He motioned around his head with his hands. "She had a hood over her head that blocked my view of her hair and face."

"You didn't get a good look at her?"

"No, I turned on the heat to high, but she left the hood up. She kept telling me she had a sick kid at home and had to leave."

"Did you offer to drive her home?"

"Yes, but she refused. Then I offered to get a paramedic."

"Was she hurt?"

"I noticed when she signed the screen that her hand looked swollen, and she barely scribbled a few letters. I asked her about it, but she said it was nothing and hid her hand beneath her poncho. I told her it wouldn't take long and walked to the back of the ambulance parked next to my car to find a paramedic. When we returned, she was gone."

Sydney made a note of the sick kid excuse and checked the personal information on Abby. She was twenty-one, a couple of inches over five feet tall, and weighed a hundred forty pounds. "How long before you realized she was gone?"

"I returned within a few minutes. She didn't come past me. I was at the back of the transport bus and would have noticed that yellow poncho. When I realized she'd gone AWOL, I searched but found no sign of her. I wrote up what she told me." He pointed to his screen.

Some officers took extra space to write a detailed report. Sam's interview was sparse.

Abby Keller, white female, age 21, had been walking in a northern direction in the alley parallel to Main Street when a white male with a gun stopped her between Sixth and Seventh streets and made a demand for her valuables. Car 2 with Sergeant Faris and Officer Moreno arrived and confronted the suspect. Keller fell to the ground and stayed there until the confrontation was resolved.

Sydney looked at the alley and the position of the cars. "Are you sure she was walking in a northern direction?"

"That's what she told me."

The bus stop where the purse was snatched was south of them. Abby was walking north. The robber must have come up behind her, surprised her, and then police had arrived. Beth had said the woman was on the ground when they drove up, but Sam reported Abby didn't go to the ground until after the police arrived. Errors were common in memories, especially in stressful situations. She needed to resolve the discrepancies and interview Abby again. "Did you get her employer?"

"Newtown Hospital," Sam said. "Maybe that's why she didn't want a paramedic. She has health insurance through work."

"But she was going home to a sick kid. Why not have her hand looked at?"

Sydney didn't like loose ends. Why was Abby in such a hurry to leave? She'd taken courses in psychology, learning how a person reacted to stress or unusual situations. Abby wasn't acting like a woman who had witnessed a violent death. The shock was expected, but running off as soon as the officer's back was turned signaled she had something to hide. Especially since she had chosen to walk past the body instead of the ambulance where Sam would have seen her, and she could have received medical care.

"Do a search for any criminal record for Abby Keller."

Sam tapped on the screen until Abby's history

appeared. "Ordinary. She had a speeding ticket two years ago and reported a theft at work three months ago."

"What was stolen?"

"Her purse from a locker."

Sydney believed in intuition. It had led her in the right direction too many times to ignore. The facts weren't adding up. What was Abby doing in a dark alley alone instead of walking along well-lit Main Street? Why had she refused medical care? And the report of a stolen purse nagged at the back of her mind. A purse contained a woman's driver's license. But she was trained not to jump to any conclusions. Uncover the truth and follow the facts where they led. She had a lot more questions before the picture would focus into clear view.

She shifted gears. "Do you have anything on the first victim at the bus stop?"

Sam pulled up the information. "Edith Merryweather. The bus driver called in the robbery after arriving at the bus stop and picking up the woman."

"Did someone respond and file a report?"

"Car 8. The officer talked to the driver and victim." He tapped on the keyboard. "She lives at 115 Broadway."

Broadway ran parallel to Main Street, and the number meant she lived between First and Second streets. The picture showed a woman with white hair and a soft smile as if caught off guard by the DMV camera.

"Is that right?" Sydney pointed at the birthday. "She's eighty-five years old?"

Sam grunted. "I hate criminals who take advantage of the elderly."

She looked toward the body on the ground. "She doesn't have to worry anymore. Send her information to me with a copy of your report. The chief will want a copy, too." She looked at the report on Edith. "Did you find a purse?"

"Purse? Do you mean the one Abby had?"

She meant Edith's purse, but the information might be helpful. "What did Abby's purse look like?"

"It was more of a backpack than a purse. The bag had straps to wear over your shoulders and a flap. She took it out from under her poncho to remove her driver's license."

A phony driver's license. She'd bet the woman wasn't Abby Keller, and she didn't have a sick child.

"Anything decorative on it?"

"No, it was plain. She was plain."

"I thought you didn't see her face."

"I didn't, but when she handed me her identification, I noted her hand was plain. No jewelry. No nail polish." He shook his head. "That's no help at all."

"Yes, it is. Not wearing jewelry is as important as noticing a ring or watch."

He snapped his fingers. "She was wearing a watch on her left wrist. I thought it was odd. Nobody wears a watch these days."

Sydney made notes of his observations. "What about the purse stolen from Edith Merryweather, the woman at the bus stop? Was it found?"

"I don't know."

She opened the door. "Come with me."

Chapter Five

The dark netherworld whispered on the wind, claiming a soul, as Sydney watched workers tend to the dead man. Who was he, and what had brought him to this end? She splashed through several small puddles, but her leather boots kept her feet dry. She was a practical woman with no spiked heels, no heavy makeup, and no stifling perfumes. She'd always been athletic and had been drawn to the physical aspect of police work as well as the mental challenges.

A woman with *Dept. of Medical Examiner* printed on the back of her coat circled the body. The long black braid with a big pink bow meant it was Irene Enrich, one of three forensic investigators who worked for the county. The medical examiner didn't always respond to the crime site. His job was to do an autopsy and determine cause of death at the lab. He sent his assistants to the scene.

Sydney had worked with Irene before, and she had proven to be a good crime scene investigator. She gathered evidence to prove how the person died, and the police would figure out who and why. Irene's evidence bag was open on the ground near the body.

"Did you find a purse with the body?" Sydney checked the description. "It's black leather with a small strap."

"No purse."

"He could have ditched it." Sam looked toward a dumpster near the back of a brick building. "I'll start searching."

"I'll join you when I'm done here."

His eyes widened. "You're helping?"

"Why not?"

He shook his head. "The Army leaves all the dirty jobs to the grunts."

"We can't let you have all the fun."

He chuckled and headed for the dumpster.

Sydney withdrew latex gloves from a pants pocket and covered her hands. "Lousy night for this."

"The rain helps to wash away the blood." Irene met her gaze. "What happened to your face?"

"Family ruckus."

"Professor Blackwood hit you?" Her voice rose in disbelief.

"Gordon?" She dismissed her concern with a wave of her hand. "You know him. He doesn't believe in violence."

"I took your husband's anthropology class. Every civilization rises to wealth and power on violence."

"This was not a power struggle. I was sneaking up behind my nephew to tickle him and whack!"

Irene frowned, and for a brief moment a small line creased her forehead. "How old is he?"

"Four, but that's not the point," Sydney dismissed. "He had a truck in his hand. It was a birthday gift."

She examined the damage. "He clobbered you with a toy truck? How big was it?"

Sydney held her hands apart to demonstrate the size. "It was a big truck." She pointed at her eye. "This isn't funny."

28

"I bet Gordon laughed."

"You'd win." His laughter had caught her off guard. Spontaneity was rare as they labored to recapture the love both cherished before the accident.

"It's been nearly a year since the hit and run. How is he doing?"

She had learned not to share the physical pain, the countless setbacks, or the personal conflicts they had battled to overcome. She focused on the positive. "He's going to teach a summer class."

Irene paused in her examination. "I bet he's excited. I always considered him my favorite professor."

"Don't tell me you had a crush on my husband?"

"All the women did, but they knew he was married to a cop. You have a reputation, Sydney. We were terrified of you."

She had worried about Gordon straying with a class of young women sitting in his classroom every year, but she had been the one to forget their vows. She nodded toward the body. "Tell me what happened."

"I know how he died." Irene looked around. "What does the scene tell you?"

The body was on his back with his face turned to one side. The man wore rubber boots and a nice trench coat. Gordon had one like it with plenty of deep pockets and a back flap. It was a required garment for professors and businessmen. His pants were covered in penguins. Penguins? She pointed. "What's he wearing?"

"Pajama bottoms." Irene squatted near the body to keep her knees dry.

Sydney did the same.

"Looks like he was lounging around the house on a Saturday and pulled on the boots and coat to walk in the rain," Irene said.

"To rob someone?" Sydney touched the wet pajamas stuck to muscular legs. "In penguin pants?"

She shrugged. "Kind of reduces the intimidation factor."

"A bit." Sydney studied the robber's face. "He's young." What had made him turn to a life of crime? "Test him for drugs."

"We always do."

"Where's his gun?"

"Bagged. A snub nose revolver, .22 caliber. Small and compact."

"Anything in his pockets?"

"I was just about to check." Irene removed several evidence bags from her tote. "I'll take this side, and you can take the right."

Sydney moved the coat and saw a wallet. "This was on the ground."

"Could it have fallen out of his coat?"

Sydney examined the deep pockets. "I don't see how." She removed the driver's license. The photograph matched the man on the ground. He was smiling in the photo. "His name is John Lawson. He lives on Fifth Street." They were between Seventh and Sixth streets. "He was close to home."

"Doesn't he know not to commit crimes in his backyard?" Irene pulled out a narrow white prescription bag from his left coat pocket. "Penicillin drops. The patient is a baby."

Officer Wilson had mentioned Abby Keller had a sick kid. "What name is on the prescription?"

"John Lawson, Jr. Eight months old according to the DOB."

"Our witness claimed she had a sick child and rushed off before I could interview her. What are the odds they both had sick kids?"

"Lots of babies in this world." Irene's voice had a hint of disbelief. "You look confused. What's going on, Sydney?"

She flipped through the wallet and found a photograph of John Lawson holding a smiling woman with a baby in her arms. On the back was written *one year married* inside a heart. She shared the family photo with Irene. It was too early for speculation, but now she had a mystery. Why did he have medicine in his pocket for his infant son? She looked around. "Where's the drugstore where he bought the prescription?"

Irene looked at the bag. "Tenth and Main."

"He lives on Fifth Street." Sydney drew a crude map in her notebook. She marked the drugstore, their location, and the bus stop. Rick and Beth had entered at Thirteenth Street and had been traveling south, the same direction as Lawson. He'd been heading home from the drugstore. "Is there a time on the receipt?"

"Eight forty. What are you thinking?"

The armed robbery had been on Third Street at eight forty-five. Even if Lawson ran, he couldn't have been in two places at the same time. *Crap.* Her case was heading into the whole-lot-of-trouble category. "Can you tell if he's left-handed?"

"You found his wallet under the right side of his body." Irene examined his left hand. "No calluses, but he's wearing a wedding band."

"He has a wife and a sick baby."

Irene examined his other hand. "He has a writing callous on his finger on the right hand. He's likely right-handed."

"Some people hold a gun in their non-dominant hand." Sydney circled the body. Rick and Beth had said his back was to them when they arrived. The woman was facing him. She pointed at the cone Rick had used to mark her location. "Did anyone move the cone?"

"No."

"She was closer to the building." Sydney stood by the orange plastic cone and looked around. The only thing on the ground was a broken gutter section. It could have been lying in the alley for weeks, or the break was fresh.

She looked up at the roof eave. A small addition had been added to the back of the building with gutter sections pieced together. A short piece was missing. Water dripped from the broken end and splashed into a puddle of water below.

The smell of cigarette smoke drew her attention to a man in a soiled apron leaning against the wall near the back door of the building. She showed him her badge. "Were you out here before the rainstorm?"

He took a final puff and dropped the cigarette to the ground, smashing it with his foot. "I took a break at five."

She pointed. "Was that gutter piece on the ground?"

"No." He looked up at the roof eave. "We had a heavy rain earlier. It must have broke off durin' the storm."

"We're going to have to take the broken section for evidence."

He nodded toward the crime scene. "What happened?"

"It's part of a police investigation. Did you hear anything just before nine?"

"I heard the rain and some loud booms. I thought it was thunder."

"You better go back inside until we're finished." Sydney lifted the gutter and weighed the aluminum piece. It was light, but the quick downpour could have filled the frame with water. The additional weight could have caused it to break free and crash to the ground. Had it hit Abby?

Sydney positioned herself near the building beneath the gap in the gutter. If she was facing north, the broken section could have crashed down on the woman's right arm, causing the injury Sam noticed. Why was her hand extended? Was she handing John her money, or was she holding something else?

The gutter was too far away to hit John, but she needed to make sure. She returned to the body and checked his hands and then pushed up his coat sleeves.

"What are you looking for?" Irene asked.

"Bruising on his arms, but I don't see any."

"We'll have a complete report after the exam."

She studied the body. "Why wasn't his wallet in his pocket?"

"Are you asking me?"

She was thinking aloud. "He was being robbed."

"I thought he was the robber."

Sydney handed the gutter section to Irene. "I need this bagged."

Irene removed a large plastic bag from her evidence kit and dropped the gutter piece inside. She sealed the bag. "What do you want it tested for?"

"Blood, DNA, whatever you can find."

"I can't promise we'll find anything. The rain could have washed away any evidence."

"I'm hoping to get lucky, but this doesn't appear to be a night for wishes coming true."

Irene signaled the paramedics to place the body of John Lawson inside the black plastic bag on the stretcher.

Sydney took John's likely position and turned around and took Abby's position. She straightened her arm and then opened her hand. What if he was handing over his wallet when the broken section knocked the gun from Abby's hand onto the ground between them? What if Lawson picked it up? He couldn't let her have it and use it against him. But then the cops had arrived, and he'd turned.

She blew out a long breath to calm her racing heart. The facts were adding up to a different story than the one originally proposed. John Lawson had been at home in his penguin pajama bottoms, relaxing in front of the television with his family, but the baby was sick. The pharmacist filled a prescription, and he'd volunteered to pick it up even though it was raining. He'd put on his galoshes and raincoat and ran out. Why didn't he drive? She calculated the distance from his home address to the drugstore. About a mile. Why start a car? He was on his way home with the medicine in his pocket when a woman confronted him with a gun. Somehow the revolver had ended up in Lawson's hand, but why did he fire at police?

"Do you know how Lawson was moving when he was shot?"

Irene brought up an outline drawing of a naked man on her screen with three bullet wounds marked on the body. "The first shot hit him in the shoulder, back to front, and spun him around to face the police. The other two were in the chest." She pointed at the one nearest the heart. "This one likely killed him."

He had his back to the police and was turning to his left according to Rick and Beth. He fired a shot. Beth shot back, and he dropped to the ground.

Sydney extended her left hand in the position he had to be for the first shot. "He was aiming the gun up the alley. What was he shooting at?" She turned to Irene. "Did you find the bullet from his gun?"

"No. We might have better luck in the morning, but it could be anywhere. This alley runs for several blocks."

Sam joined her. "I got lucky." He handed Sydney two bags. "The purse and wallet were on top inside the first trash bin I searched. Edith Merryweather's ID is in the wallet."

"Good work, Officer Wilson."

"I hope it makes up for my earlier mistake." He shrugged and headed for his squad car.

Sydney joined Irene at her van. She handed over the evidence bags. "Can I have the penicillin medicine for the baby?"

"Are you paying a visit to John Jr.?"

"My kids have had ear infections. I might as well ease one ache while delivering another."

Irene frowned. "You think his widow doesn't know about her husband's life of crime?"

"I'm positive she doesn't know."

"Let me keep the bag and receipt for evidence. The instructions are on the bottle." Irene removed a small brown bottle with a stopper but hesitated to hand it over. "I don't envy your job."

"Someone has to tell Mrs. Lawson she's a widow."

"Are you going to tell her how her husband died?"

She shrugged. "Gunshot wound during a robbery."

"And who shot him?"

"No." Sydney wasn't cleared for revealing that bit of information. Any time a police officer was involved in a fatal shooting, the incident became a media frenzy. When it did come out, the department would be on damage control. "It's an ongoing investigation."

Chapter Six

After quietly opening the cruiser door, Claire had walked past the crime tape, the other police cruiser, and up the dark alley. The only one who had seen her was the female officer who had shot the man in the alley. She shouldn't have looked at her but had reacted to her voice when she asked if she was hurt. The soft-hearted cop looked like she had been crying. Maybe her tears blurred her vision.

"Gotta go," she had said and hurried toward the hospital on Thirteenth Street to report to work. Normally, she would have gone home to shower and dress for work after her evening run, but the police had delayed her and upset her routine. Before arriving, she had removed her rain poncho, wadded it into a small bundle, and stored it in her backpack to avoid being caught wearing it in any video from the security cameras that were mounted on the outside of the building.

She had clocked in to avoid being late but had a few minutes before anyone would miss her at her station. She removed her sweaty tee and examined the damage to her arm.

The gutter had crashed down on her hand and forearm and left a long welt that had swollen to a bruised mass. She ran her fingers along the radius from her wrist to her elbow and then along the ulna. They felt intact but could be fractured without breaking apart. She wouldn't know without an x-ray. She couldn't have a technician do it here at Newtown Hospital. They'd ask how she hurt herself and whether it was work related. She'd give the injury a day or two to improve before seeking help.

She took an ace bandage from the medical supplies stored in her locker. She had vials, test tubes, syringes, and other items she had taken from the supply cabinets she worked hard to stock. She never knew what she might need for personal use. Like now. She had learned to be prepared for any trouble or challenge after her husband's erratic behavior during their last few years of marriage. When an opportunity arose, like taking Edith's pills, she acted. But how had a simple snatch and run turned into a shooting and death?

She wrapped her arm in case the bones were broken. Her fingers were swollen, but latex gloves would cover them. The young police officer had stared at her hand when she had trouble signing his report, but when he left to find a paramedic, she had escaped. How would she have explained her injury? The poncho had protected her skin from being cut. The edge of the gutter had been rusted, and she couldn't remember the last time she had a tetanus shot.

Claire removed extra clothing she kept in her locker for emergencies. Nurses had the dirty jobs. A patient could throw up, bleed, or pee all over a clean uniform. The ER nurses wore black scrubs with skid-free shoes. No cute smocks like in other departments. She had a long-sleeved top that would cover her injury. She exchanged her wet pants for dry ones and put on dry socks and a pair of spotless white sneakers she kept at work.

She wrapped her stethoscope around her neck and

draped her wet clothes on the hooks in the center of the locker. They would be dry by the time she went home tomorrow morning. Most nurses hated the ten-to-eight-thirty shift, but a nurse in Pain Management had noticed missing pills, and she had transferred to the ER and night shift. Her supervisor left at midnight, and she could do what she wanted without probing eyes.

After checking the hallway for anyone lurking outside, she sat on the bench in front of her locker and opened her backpack. She moved a few items around and found the bottle of opioids she had obtained from Edith. She usually didn't use her pills until she was home, but the shooting and her injury had given her the shakes. She needed a snort to allow her to cope with the plethora of troubles.

She kept her pills sorted by milligrams in a plastic daily dosage container and calculated the number she would need for a feeling of calm without being dazed. She was careful to use the minimum amount, especially when she needed a boost at work, which was becoming more often.

She crushed the tablets, pressing down on the round top to grind them. She removed a square mirror from her bag and tapped out the powder on the glass to form a thick streak. She inhaled through a straw, wiping the residue with her finger and licking the last bitter remnant. She put her mirror, straw, crusher, and pills back in her backpack. She pushed it to the back of the shelf and removed a water bottle the employees were given with the hospital name stamped on it. Hers was filled with water and a healthy splash of vodka.

She took a long gulp and returned it to her locker. Then she sat on the bench, waiting for the dull comfort to kick in.

Claire wasn't an addict. She could quit anytime, but she didn't feel functional without the drugs. How could she cope after her husband died in a car crash while seated next to her, and she had been helpless to save him? She was a nurse, but her own injuries had been too severe for her to offer any aid. It was a miracle she had survived. The paramedics, police, and doctors told her she couldn't have done anything, but guilt gnawed away at her soul. The only cure had been in the prescription pills that dulled reality from the pain that never entirely disappeared.

She stared at the closed locker. She needed to report to her station, but she couldn't forget the look on the face of the man in the alley. His young features had registered shock, then horror as his mind connected pain to the bullets that had torn through his body. He stared at her with eyes filled with accusation and then comprehension of the reality of impending death in the final moments of his life.

He blamed her, but she hadn't expected anyone to cross her path in the isolated alley. She had given him a chance to run. If only the gutter hadn't fallen. Claire had trained herself not to react to pain and death. No one appreciated a hysterical nurse in a crisis, but she could turn on the tears when necessary.

The handsome police sergeant had offered his hand and asked if she was all right after the shooting. He had escorted her to the police car to answer a few questions. That young officer was gullible, and she had acted the shocked and crying female victim. The damsel in distress was a familiar role for Claire. She'd learned the hard lesson that screams and tears reduced the number of blows from a man's angry fists. She had kept her hood up and eyes downcast, sniffling into tissues to muffle her answers. He'd been sympathetic and hadn't pushed her to talk. Besides, she didn't have to act to play the victim. She hadn't shot anyone. She was an innocent bystander.

Did it matter that she had given him Abby Keller's driver's license? She couldn't give him her own identification. Abby was her co-worker. She'd forgotten to close the lock on her locker located a few over from her own. The stupid girl had been inviting trouble. Claire had only meant to take the prescription of pain medicine Abby had received after having her wisdom teeth removed. She no longer needed the pills. Why let them go to waste sitting in her purse? But the wallet had been on top with two hundred and twenty dollars in cash. She couldn't pass up the gift. Abby's driver's license had also come in handy.

The young police officer had barely compared the photo on the license to her face, and she had stayed in the shadows of the police cruiser as he entered the information into his computer. The police didn't have her name, and if they questioned Abby, they wouldn't find any close connection. Abby worked in registration, the entry level job at the hospital, and the girl always made mistakes. Claire had covered her tracks. She was sure of it.

She relaxed, letting the pills perform magic on her rattled nerves. She needed to report to the emergency room for her shift. She closed the combination lock and tugged to make sure it was fastened. She was no Abby.

Claire checked her reflection in the mirror over the sink in the section where the toilet stalls were located. Her thirtieth birthday was coming in another month. She touched the corners of her eyes where she had a few laugh lines. Who thought those were funny? She had never been beautiful, but a few men looked at her twice. Not that she looked back. Her husband had been enough man for a lifetime, good and bad. As she walked down the hall, she tightened her ponytail and prepared for work.

She entered the emergency department through the swinging back doors used for transferring patients from the ER to the operating arena or a room for admission. The front door on the opposite side led into the waiting area for family and friends. In between, sliding glass doors opened for patients brought in by ambulances. The room was brightly lit with a few enclosed rooms, but most were curtained bays.

The ER doctor wore a long white coat over jeans and a polo shirt. The casual look was friendlier, but most patients in the emergency room didn't want to make friends. They wanted to stay alive. He didn't notice she was late. He didn't even acknowledge she had arrived.

A central desk allowed nurses to monitor patients and respond if they were needed. She took a deep breath, sat at the desk, and studied the whiteboard listing the current patients. Only three. She hoped it would be a slow night.

Claire returned to her thoughts. She'd have to replace the gun. She felt safer with one in her hand even though she never planned to use it. Some people thought all nurses carried a pharmacy. She'd been stopped more than once by drug users begging for pills. One of the addicts had pulled a knife, but she had batted it away with her backpack and had run. Running had helped her lose a hundred pounds, but no one could outrun a bullet.

With the warmer weather the fairgrounds would host a gun show soon. They had everything a girl could want, and for many, the sales were off the record. It had taken her an hour to find a gun the right size and weight to carry in her bag the first time. She liked the small revolver and would buy one similar. Of course, she'd need cash to buy it to avoid a paper trail. Even with the cash in Edith Merryweather's purse, she'd have to wait for her next paycheck.

She made good money as a nurse. Where did all her earnings go?

Chapter Seven

Vivien Lawson was going to kill her husband. The baby hadn't stopped crying since he left for the drugstore. What was taking him so long? She paced back and forth in the living room, rubbing John-John's back, trying to soothe him. He tugged on his ear and wailed.

She didn't want to call her mother. It would give her an opportunity to lecture her on how she was throwing her life away. She shouldn't have quit college to have a baby. She should have stayed in school and earned her degree. She hadn't told her mother the pregnancy was unplanned, and her morning sickness had been too severe to sit in a classroom.

Jack had insisted they marry, and he had finished his bachelor's degree in engineering last June. He already had a good job, and John-John would be old enough to leave in the college daycare facility in the fall, so she could return to school. It was a good plan, but her mother wouldn't listen. She was inflexible.

Not every man was like her father. He had cheated on her mother, and she had never trusted another man, refusing to remarry. Jack loved her. He would do anything for her. What other husband would go out in the rain to pick up medicine for a sick baby without a word of complaint? She was the worrier, and Jack was her calm. She needed him to return.

The light rain had turned into a deluge but passed

quickly. Jack was dressed for the weather and enjoyed walking in the rain, so what was keeping him?

She checked the internet. Heat might help an ear infection. She tossed a washcloth in a bag and heated it in the microwave. "It'll be all right, John-John. Daddy will be home soon. He's bringing medicine to make you feel better."

She stared at the door, willing Jack to appear. "You better not be talking to an old friend you ran into while our baby is suffering."

John-John rested his head against the warm cloth on her shoulder and quieted. She needed a few moments of peace to gather her thoughts. She could call the pharmacy. She had the number on her phone along with the doctor and every emergency number a mother might need.

Someone knocked at the door. Finally. She headed for the front door but paused. Why was Jack knocking? He insisted she keep the door locked when he was away from home. "Did you forget your key?"

John-John whimpered on her shoulder. "Sorry, baby." She kissed his warm forehead. "Daddy is home. Everything will be fine."

She unlocked the door and yanked it open. "What took you so long?"

The woman on the front porch appeared surprised, and her left eye was swollen and bruised.

Vivien searched around for trouble. "Are you all right? Do you need me to call for help?"

The woman frowned, confusion in her expression. "Are you Mrs. Lawson?"

"Yes, who are you?"

She showed her a photo ID. "I'm Police Detective

Sydney Harrison." She paused. "Do you know a John Lawson?"

"That's my husband." She didn't move or breathe. She fought the panic rising in her chest. Why was a police detective on her doorstep? She looked past her. "Where is he?"

"May I come in, Mrs. Lawson?"

"It's Vivien." She blocked the doorway, searching the darkness. "He walked to the pharmacy to pick up medicine for the baby."

"I have it." The detective removed a small bottle topped with a rubber dropper from her coat pocket. "Please, may I come in?"

Vivien pushed open the door and backed away. Something was terribly wrong. She didn't want to hear the news. The detective stepped across her threshold.

"Is Jack hurt?"

"Why don't we take care of this little fellow first?" The detective looked at the label on the bottle. "Half a dropper full every four hours." She unscrewed the cap. "Why don't you hold him, and I'll put the drops in his mouth?"

She held the baby away from her. "Who are you again?"

"Detective Sydney Harrison. I have two children of my own. I've done this before."

Sydney was a mother, but Vivien examined the bottle. It had her son's name on the label along with instructions. Vivien shifted John-John in her arm so he was cradled in her elbow. His crying had subdued to short pitiful sobs.

Sydney measured the liquid in the syringe, placed the plastic tip far in the corner of the baby's mouth, and squeezed the rubber stopper on the end.

John-John made a face and tried spitting out the medicine, but Sydney had placed it deep enough that he had only one choice. He swallowed and let out a wail. Vivien moved him to her shoulder, patting his back until he calmed. "Tell me about Jack. Where is he?"

"Something happened on his way home."

Vivien's knees buckled.

Sydney grabbed for the baby. "Why don't we put him to bed? Where's the crib?"

Vivien carried John-John to the master bedroom. She had decorated a spare bedroom for the baby, but she liked to keep him close when he was ill. She put him in the bassinette at the end of the bed. He had nearly outgrown it. His bottom lip quivered, but he was exhausted from crying, and his eyes fluttered for a moment before closing. She brushed back the feathering of hair covering his head and placed the single blanket over his legs.

She closed the bedroom door. "How badly is my husband hurt? I told him to drive, but he sits all day at work and likes to take a walk in the evening. John-John and I usually go with him, but tonight with the baby sick, we stayed home. He had already showered and dressed for bed, but the pharmacy called and said the prescription was ready, so he fetched the medicine. Men don't care what they wear in public. He didn't even put on shoes, just galoshes. Did he trip and fall?"

Sydney hadn't smiled or reacted to her light banter. "It's more serious than that."

What had happened to Jack? It had to be bad news for a detective to visit. "I can call my mother to stay with the baby. Did you take him to the hospital?"

"You should call your mother."

Vivien gripped the back of the nearest chair and prayed.

Chapter Eight

Sydney allowed time for Vivien to compose herself. By the lack of care to her appearance, her day had been stressful. Vivien wore stained sweats and fluffy slippers with dog faces on them. Her hair was in a sloppy braid with a few loose strands that framed her confused and frightened face. She was too young to be a widow.

Breaking bad news was part of the job, but was it kinder to blurt it out or prepare her first? "Let's sit in the living room." Sydney waited as Vivien took a seat on the sofa. She sat nearby in a rocking chair. A blanket rested over the back. "Call your mother. How long will it take for her to arrive?"

"She's fifteen minutes away. I told Jack she lived too close, but after John-John was born, I stopped complaining. Free babysitting for date night." Vivien stared at her phone. "What do I tell her?"

"I can talk to her." Sydney wanted to gauge the older woman's reaction. She didn't need someone who would be hysterical and add to Vivien's grief.

After an exchange of pleasantries, Vivien focused on the topic. "Mom, I need you to talk to a detective. Her name is Sydney…" She looked at her, a quizzical expression on her face.

"Detective Sydney Harrison."

"Detective Harrison has something to tell you about Jack." Vivien's voice broke as she said her husband's name.

Sydney took the phone. "Ma'am, is it possible for you to come stay with Vivien?"

"Of course. Is the baby worse?"

"No, he took his medicine and is sleeping. It's about Jack Lawson." No need to be formal. He went by Jack. She turned away from Vivien and lowered her voice. "I have bad news, and I don't think your daughter should be alone tonight."

"What happened to Jack?" Her voice was high and anxious. "You have to tell me."

Sydney kept her voice calm. "I'll give you the information when you arrive."

"Oh, God." Silence.

"Ma'am, are you there?"

"Call me Lucy. How is Vivien? How is my girl?"

Sydney turned. Vivien was on the couch, her legs tucked against her chest and her hands wrapped around her knees as her body shook. "If you can't come, I'll find someone..."

"I'll be there."

What was it about motherhood that took any woman from hysterics to a rock of strength in a breath? When her son had fallen from a slide and broken his collarbone, she had carried him to the car, strapped both children in, and had driven to the emergency room through rush hour traffic to reach a doctor.

"Thank you. I'll stay with her until you arrive." Sydney turned off the phone and placed it on the end table. "Would you like me to get you some coffee or tea?"

"I can't drink caffeine."

"You're nursing," she realized.

"I planned to nurse until John-John turned one, but he's getting teeth. Ouch."

Sydney understood. "Their teeth are like razor blades when they break through the gums. You can train them not to bite."

"I think my reaction of pain and surprise was enough, but I'm anxious each time I put him on my breast." She absently rubbed her chest.

"Do you want a glass of water?"

Vivien refused the offer, but her body spasmed in a shiver. Sydney draped the blanket from the rocking chair over her. She sat across from her, the silence stretching out between them. She wasn't ready to deliver the bad news. She wanted Vivien's mother to be closer. Five more minutes.

"You said you had two children." Vivien gathered the blanket around her. "How old are they?"

"Ethan is six, and Zoe is eight. She already has a boyfriend. He's on her T-ball team. I don't know if I should be worried or dismiss it as puppy love. I wasn't interested in boys until high school and only if dating didn't interfere with my soccer games."

"I decided I was going to marry Jack when I was in the ninth grade. He had no clue what hit him. I sat with him at lunch and laughed at all his jokes. He was such a science nerd, but he loved my artwork." She pointed to a cluster of framed paintings.

One was of a baby sleeping. "John-John?"

"In one of his quieter moments."

Another was of a tasteful nude. "Art class?"

"Jack." She smiled and blushed. "He was so embarrassed when I hung it on the wall, but he's so beautiful. Who would think he has a brilliant mind, too?"

And she had to tell Vivien he was gone. Dead. She steadied her voice. "You're talented."

"That's what Jack's says, but he has to. I think it's written in the rules of marriage." She pointed at the gold band Sydney wore on her hand. "I see you're married."

"My husband is Gordon Blackwood. He's a professor at Newtown College. That's where we met." She didn't usually share her personal life with strangers, but she needed to prevent Vivien from asking questions about Jack. "He was a grad student teaching a beginner forensic class on identifying human bones. He asked me out after class one day, and I told him I didn't date teachers. I'd dated one in my freshman year, and it was a disaster. He wanted to rush things, and I was a wallflower jock. I wasn't ready for a serious romance. But Gordon was different. He waited until I finished the semester and asked me out again. I was going to say no, but he'd been patient. He respected me enough to abide by my rules. I said yes, and two years later I graduated, and we were married."

"Do you have to attend college to be a detective?"

"No, but it helps."

"Do you like being a detective?"

"I always liked solving puzzles and loved shows about cold cases. I wanted to find answers."

"What was your most difficult case?"

This one. She didn't share cases with civilians and deflected her question. "It wasn't my case, but a year ago my husband was run over by a car. Hit and run."

"What?" She paused. "Is he…"

"He's in a wheelchair but getting better. The doctors initially said he might be a quadriplegic, but modern technology is creating miracles. He has full use of his arms and is building strength in his legs. He's teaching a summer class at the college."

"Jack is an aerospace engineer." Vivien's voice was filled with pride. "He's brilliant. He's working on the lunar station. He says he'll make up for not having a real honeymoon by taking me to the moon." She waved her hands as her voice shook. "I'm perfectly happy staying on Earth."

Sydney checked the time. She needed to ask a few key questions before Lucy arrived and emotions took over. She wanted to understand why Jack was on a metal slab in the coroner's examination room. "Does Jack own a gun?"

She frowned and shook her head. "Oh, no. Jack said there were already too many guns in the world. He didn't want to add to the inventory. He talked about getting a dog for protection when John-John was older."

"A dog is a good idea." The facts were adding up. Jack had a sick baby, medicine in his pocket with a location and time away from the robbery, and didn't own a gun.

Vivien crossed her arms. "I've been patient, but it's time you told me what happened to my husband."

It was time to break her heart. Sydney preferred peeling back a bandage, easing it off a wound, but this required ripping it free in a quick jerk. She wanted to give Vivien the bad news moments before her mother arrived. Then Lucy could comfort her.

Leaning forward, she rested her hand on Vivien's knee. "We don't have all the details, but your husband was returning home from the drugstore with medicine for the baby. He was using the alley behind Main Street when we believe an armed robber confronted him."

Vivien's hand touched her heart. "Jack was robbed?"

"He was shot." Sydney choked on the explanation. She took a deep breath and spat the words out. "He didn't make it."

Vivien stared at her, confusion written on her features. "He's young. He's a fighter."

"He didn't have a chance," Sydney said. "He died at the scene."

Sydney caught Vivien before she hit the floor. She pushed her back onto the sofa.

Her head flopped back, and she stared at the ceiling. "It can't be true." Tears flooded her eyes and flowed down her cheeks. She denied the truth with an angry accusation. "You're lying. You're a liar."

"I gave you the medicine. It was in his pocket."

She buried her face in her hands. "No." A pitiful wail escaped from her throat.

"The medical examiner has his body. He'll release it in a few days."

"Body? What do I do with a body?" She let out a short scream. "My husband can't be dead!"

She found a box of tissues and placed it in Vivien's lap.

She grabbed two and blew her nose. "Do you know who shot Jack?"

"It's an ongoing investigation." It was the standard answer, but the lie stuck in Sydney's throat. She sat next to Vivien, pulling her toward her shoulder to comfort her. Life wasn't fair. A good man was dead.

Vivien straightened and blew her nose. "Do you think he knew I loved him? Even when I was complaining?"

Sydney nodded. "Complaining is how we show we care. Men need to worry when we stop trying to improve the relationship and look elsewhere." Like she had done. "He knew you loved him."

Her sobs quieted. "How am I going to live without him?"

Sydney didn't answer. John-John would help. Time would heal some wounds.

Someone pounded on the door. "It's me, Vivien!"

"Momma!" She leapt off the couch and raced to the door before Sydney could stand.

Her mother was an older version of Vivien and engulfed her daughter in her arms.

"Jack is dead."

Lucy led her back to the couch and grabbed the blanket that had fallen to the floor. She wrapped her daughter in it and rocked her in her arms. Vivien let her tears flow freely, wailing in pain. She could be the child now.

Her mother turned. "Who are you?"

"Detective Sydney Harrison. We spoke on the phone." She sat opposite them.

"Tell me what happened."

She shared the basic information and handed her a card. "When we have more details, I'll let you know."

Lucy examined the card. "You find the person responsible for Jack's murder."

"I will." She knew who had shot Jack, but explaining how a police officer had killed him would be easier when she had the armed robber in custody. She needed to find the woman who had set this tragedy in motion, the mystery woman who had borrowed Abby Keller's name. She needed to pay for her crimes.

Chapter Nine

Sydney pulled into the police station parking lot and crossed her arms on the steering wheel. She had driven on autopilot from Vivien's home. All the feelings she had buried surfaced, and she sobbed, tears tumbling down her cheeks. She had experienced Vivien's pain as her own a year ago when darkness had threatened to engulf her, and now she let the memory of sorrow and despair take control until it was spent.

She had been through the valley of the shadow of death more than once. Sydney had experienced her mother's battle with cancer, lost a child to a miscarriage, and had stood by her husband's broken body in the hospital when doctors gave her little to hope for but a bleak future of pain and eventual death from his injuries. The feeling of being utterly helpless and facing darkness without any light was too familiar for her to dismiss the pain and loneliness that accompanied tragedy for others. She could shed a few tears and then focus on her objective.

She took a deep breath and pulled herself together. Vivien and John-John were sweet and vulnerable and innocent victims in this horrible drama. Her duty was to uncover the truth and ease their pain. She wouldn't do that sobbing in sympathy. She lowered the vanity mirror and cringed. The damage was done. She'd have to fix it. She removed a wet wipe from her duffle bag on the passenger seat. It was filled with miscellaneous equipment for any conceivable situation from a first-aid kit to diapers. She wiped her face and let it dry. Then she applied a layer of moisturizer from her personal mini bag and a coat of mascara to restore her customary appearance. Or what was expected with a black eye. The swelling blended with the puffiness from crying.

Sydney would have liked to have called it a night. She was exhausted from delivering the devastating news to Vivien, and now she had to enter the police station and break the bad news that the investigation wasn't over. It was only beginning.

She headed to her desk and finished entering her reports into the computer. She coded Officer Moreno's name. Reports were public record. The press would find out eventually, but it would give Beth time to gather her thoughts and prepare a proper response before the news media demanded an explanation.

In a case involving a shooting, everything needed to be documented for the hearing. Hopefully, it didn't last beyond the review board. Beth hadn't done anything criminal, but the public could be unforgiving when the police shot an innocent man.

She needed to find the woman who had claimed to be Abby Keller. She reviewed Sam's reports and her notes. His description had included a yellow poncho and a hand without jewelry except for a watch. The copy of Abby's driver's license photo only misdirected. She needed a real name and face to go with it.

Like she had told Rick, Chief Kyle Mills had reported to the station when he was informed of the shooting. Sydney made a couple of calls before going to his office. The door was open, but Sydney knocked.

"Come in." His voice was gruff but more as a result of a former nicotine addiction than any angry disposition. Kyle had been on medical leave last year after a diagnosis of cancer. No one knew if he had won the battle. He didn't share his personal troubles with others, but Sydney had been her mother's advocate after a diagnosis of endometrial cancer. Surgery and radiation treatments had left her tired and forgetful. But they had caught the cancer in time because her mother had called about cramps and slight bleeding after years of menopause. No pain. No other warnings. But within a month she was on the surgeon's table. The pathologist report had revealed the cancer had *almost* spread through the uterine wall. Her mother had called it a miracle she had made a phone call to her doctor that set the tests and treatment in motion, and Sydney agreed. Sometimes it was the little things that counted.

She stepped inside and closed the door.

"What happened to your face?"

She'd forgotten about the black eye. "I wasn't on duty when it happened."

"Faris, Moreno, and Wilson turned in their reports," Kyle said. "Everything looks cut and dry. The man had a gun when he turned toward the officers and fired a shot."

Sydney remained standing. "I don't believe the gun was his."

"Most criminals use a stolen gun when they rob someone." He chuckled. "Why make it easier for the police to trace?"

"I don't believe he was the robber," Sydney clarified.

Kyle waved multiple printed reports in the air.

Officers and staff knew the chief hated technology. He claimed the printed page was backup in case of hacking or a computer error. "He was in the alley with a gun, and his victim was begging for her life. He shot at the police."

"I know how it appeared to the officers, but there are some peculiarities I'd like to look into."

"Peculiarities?" Kyle rose, a scowl on his face. "How can they misread a shooting? Not five minutes before, a bus driver reported a passenger waiting at the next stop was robbed of her purse by a man holding a gun."

Sydney was loyal to her fellow officers. People made mistakes. This one had been the perfect storm of errors. "I left a message on Edith Merryweather's phone. I plan to visit her tomorrow, but she's eighty-five years old. She may have been mistaken about her description. I don't think it was Jack Lawson."

"She said a man in dark clothing pointed a revolver in her face." He flipped through several pages. "I have two responding officers stating a man, identified as John Lawson by the medical examiner's office, was wearing a dark raincoat and had a gun in his hand. They heard the woman on the ground begging Lawson not to shoot her." Kyle slammed the reports against the desktop. "What don't I understand?"

Sydney cringed at the exasperation in his voice but squared her shoulders. "I've just returned from Jack Lawson's home. He had a bag of medicine for his baby son and receipt in his pocket that proves he was at the pharmacy during the time of the robbery. I stopped there before visiting Mrs. Lawson and confirmed it. He was traveling from the drugstore in a southern direction to his home. It was the woman in the yellow poncho who was traveling north from the bus stop. Their paths intersected."

"Are you trying to say that neither one of them was related to the armed robbery?"

"I think the woman was the armed robber."

He sat down and leaned back in his chair. "Why?"

She shared her reasons. "The woman was heading north away from the bus stop. The dumpster where we found the purse was along her path."

"Are you sure of the direction?"

Sydney pointed at his folder. "Look at the reports. Jack Lawson had his back to the squad car when Sergeant Faris approached. He had to turn around. The woman was facing the patrol car when it entered the alley from the north."

Kyle ran his hand over his thin hair. "But the woman was wearing a yellow poncho. How could anyone, even an eighty-five-year-old woman, mistake that for black?"

"I can't explain that yet, but she kept her face hidden beneath the hood of her poncho. She never showed her face. Why would an innocent woman hide her identity?"

"But Wilson took her license." Kyle read from a page. "We have her name, Abby Keller."

"The woman in the alley gave Officer Wilson a driver's license belonging to Abby Keller, who reported her purse stolen a couple of months ago. I called and talked to the real Abby Keller, and she's been at Newtown Hospital since three o'clock working second shift. I'm going there next."

He flipped through the reports. "Don't we have any description of the woman at the scene?"

"I have a few details but nothing to identify her."

He gathered the reports in his hands. "That's great! We have a dead man in an alley and a missing witness who may be our armed robber. What was John Lawson doing with a gun?"

"Jack Lawson doesn't own a gun. He doesn't believe in owning a gun," she added. "From what I could determine, a gutter full of water fell and may have knocked the gun from the woman's hand. Two officers noticed an injury to her right hand. Given the situation, they both probably went for the weapon. But Jack Lawson reached the revolver first and had it in his hand when the squad car arrived, and Officer Moreno ordered him to turn around."

"Didn't he hear the siren?"

"Sergeant Faris said they drove in quiet. No siren, no lights. They turned the spotlight on him, and he turned. They saw the gun in his hand and ordered him to drop it."

"He fired it instead."

"The investigative team determined from the entry of the first bullet hole, he likely fired up the alley and not at the police."

The chief looked stunned. "He doesn't know how to drop a gun?"

"He may have hesitated to drop it with the woman so close, or it was cocked and went off accidentally. He was inexperienced with firearms."

He rubbed both hands across his eyes. "You could be wrong."

"I wish I were. I'm giving you the information I've gathered so far."

Kyle stared at the reports. "I asked Faris and Moreno to wait in the squad room until I reviewed all the reports.

I thought you would be bringing good news."

"Do you need me to stay?"

"My job is to inform them we have an armed robber responsible for a man's death out there. Your job is to find her."

"I'm heading to the hospital to talk to Abby Keller."

A single eyebrow rose in a question. "Did you look at the original theft report for Abby?"

"I pulled it up. The purse was never found, and the thief never arrested."

"Newtown Hospital isn't far from our crime scene. Maybe she owns a yellow poncho and took a late dinner break."

Sydney wished it would be that easy. She headed out.

Chapter Ten

Beth paced back and forth in the squad room where officers called a desk home when not on patrol. She had written up her reports, straightened every item in view, and drank two cups of coffee. Enough time had passed for Chief Mills to read the reports forward and back. What was taking so long? She'd done everything by the book. Rick had assured her that she had taken an armed robber off the streets. She'd protected the citizens of the city.

But none of that made it any easier.

Even though Rick had taken charge and prevented her from going near the body, she was responsible for the death of a human being.

She looked out the police station window. It was too dark to see anything but the lights in the parking lot. The rain had stopped, but she kept hearing the pitter-patter on the glass of the cruiser before her future had crashed and burned. Her mind wouldn't stop reliving the details of the shooting. Each movement, each reaction replayed in her head, sometimes fast and other times in slow motion.

Detective Sydney Harrison had interviewed everyone present but the woman in the yellow rain poncho. She had left the scene before Sydney arrived, which was weird. She wished she could remember more about the woman. She'd only had a glimpse of her face, but nothing unusual or distinguishing stood out. She had written white female in her report. It seemed inadequate.

The hard soles of work shoes echoed in the hallway, and she turned to the door.

Rick stood in the doorway. "The chief wants to speak to you."

He gave her a reassuring smile, but she had been raised by consummate liars and had learned to read faces. Rick didn't say another word. No good-bye. No good luck. He walked with hunched shoulders toward the locker room. Something was wrong.

Beth took a deep breath and headed for the chief's office in the opposite direction. She rapped on the door.

"Come in." The chief glanced at her. "Close the door and sit down."

Beth gripped the arms of the padded leather chair. "Is something wrong with my report?"

Her voice shook.

"No, but there were some irregularities in the case you need to be aware of before you leave tonight."

"Irregularities? What does that mean?"

"It means the case isn't as simple as it first appeared. We need to clarify some inconsistencies." He studied the reports on his desk. "The bus driver reported his passenger, Edith Merryweather, had her purse stolen by an armed robber in dark clothing."

Beth leaned forward and touched her hands to the smooth surface of his desk. "The man's trench coat was brown. It probably looked darker in the rain."

"What was the woman at the scene wearing?"

"A bright-yellow rain poncho." She snorted. "It certainly wasn't dark."

"Did you see anyone else in the alley?"

"No. Was there another person involved?"

The chief didn't answer her question. He didn't have to. He was her superior and controlled the situation, any discipline, and her future employment. The same feelings of fear and helplessness she'd experienced in the principal's office during her school years resurfaced and intensified as the silence extended between them. She wiped her sweaty palms on her pant legs.

"Officer Wilson found the stolen purse from the bus stop robbery in a dumpster between the scene of the shooting and the bus stop."

"That proves it was the man in the trench coat. He threw away the purse in the alley." Her chest heaved in relief, and her body relaxed.

The chief raised his hand. "I know, but Jack Lawson was traveling from the north. He couldn't have thrown the purse away."

"Jack Lawson was the name of the man in the alley?"

"Yes." The chief anticipated her next question. "He had no record."

She puzzled over his previous words. "How do you know he was traveling south? He could have turned around when he confronted the woman in the alley."

The chief moved to a map of the city mounted on the wall of his office, and she joined him. He used color-coded pins to mark crimes in the city and placed a green pin on the map. "This is the bus stop where Edith Merryweather was robbed." He pointed farther north. "This is the drugstore where Jack Lawson purchased a prescription for his sick son. The receipt was in his pocket proving he had been at the drugstore during the time of the robbery." He added a red pin in between. "And this is where Lawson was shot."

Beth studied the map but refused to accept the conclusion. Something had to be wrong with the information.

He drew a line with his finger. "Lawson was traveling from the drugstore to his home. Our armed robber was heading north, dumped the purse in a dumpster nearby, and confronted Lawson just before you and Sergeant Faris arrived on the scene. Your report has Lawson with his back to your squad car, which was traveling south toward the bus stop. The woman was the one heading north away from the crime scene."

Beth returned to her chair and gripped her knees. "But Lawson had a gun in his hand. He shot at us."

"You had a right to think Lawson was a threat, but Detective Harrison has collected information that contradicts what you and Officer Faris perceived at the scene."

What was he telling her? Rick had talked plenty about Sydney Harrison. Most of it wasn't flattering, and any praise was laced with sarcasm. Something had transpired between them, but Beth's motto was not to pry. She didn't want anyone looking too closely at her own dysfunctional family. "I don't understand. Did I do something wrong?"

"No, you reacted correctly, but the woman at the scene behaved suspiciously." The chief resumed his seat. "She gave Officer Wilson a phony driver's license. Detective Harrison is talking to more people, but I wanted you to be prepared if it turns out that the woman at the scene was not a victim but the armed robber reported by dispatch."

Beth tapped her foot in a nervous beat. The man had been coming from the wrong direction. Her mind wouldn't accept their conclusion. It had to be wrong. "The man had the gun in his hand. The woman was on the ground begging, '*Don't shoot me!*' "

"From her position in the alley, could she see your approach?"

The headlights had been on. "Maybe."

"Was she shouting the words?"

She closed her eyes. "Yes, she was screaming for her life." Or had she been screaming to an audience? Her family were skilled con artists, and she was a cynic as a result. Had the woman played them? She took a deep breath. "But she wore a *yellow* poncho."

"Do you remember anything else about her?"

She debated whether to reveal what she knew, but the truth won out. "She was in Officer Wilson's car on the other side of the crime scene. I thought it strange she kept her hood up inside the car."

"Why?"

She met his gaze. "Most people take off a hat inside a vehicle. She kept her head lowered. I thought she acted odd when she got out of the car." Why hadn't she stopped the woman? Why had she remained a powerless spectator?

"What happened?"

She took a deep breath and explained. "Officer Wilson left his cruiser and walked to the back of the ambulance. The woman exited and glanced around before heading north."

The chief looked toward the map on the wall. "That's the same direction she was heading from the robbery. Did she go by your car?"

"Yes, she walked past my window."

He leaned forward. "Then you saw her face?"

She shook her head. "Only a glimpse beneath her hood."

Chief Mills removed a photograph from a folder and shoved it across the desktop. "Is this her?"

She stared at the photograph of a young woman with a cheery smile. "I don't know. It could be." But deep down, she knew it wasn't.

"This is Abby Keller. It's the name on the driver's license the woman gave to Officer Wilson. She's been working at the hospital since three this afternoon. Detective Harrison headed over there to talk to her before the woman's shift ends."

The woman had left before anyone realized she wasn't a victim. "I wish I could remember more about her, but I can't recall any details except that yellow poncho. It was so out of place."

"Wilson said her hand was swollen, and you noted a possible injury in your report. Why?"

"She was cradling her right arm when she passed by my car." Beth chewed on her bottom lip. "I asked her if she was all right. She looked surprised, said, 'Gotta go,' and hurried away. Why is her arm important?"

"Detective Harrison believes she may have been injured when a rusty gutter broke off the overhang of a building and hit her in the arm. A piece of the gutter was found on the ground near the body. The impact may have caused her to drop the gun, and Jack Lawson picked it up. That's when you arrived."

Beth leaned forward, her head in her hands. *She dropped the gun, and the man picked it up.* Her pulse raced, but her body and mind were numb. Was he saying Lawson wasn't guilty of any crime? Had she killed an innocent man? The coffee in her stomach threatened to erupt. She searched for a trash can but fought back the nausea. "Why would he pick up the gun?"

"They may have both been going for it. That's one of the unknowns so far. But he had it in his hand when you ordered him to drop it."

"I ordered him to turn around," Beth corrected. "He had his back to me, and I ordered him to turn around. I didn't know he had a gun until Sergeant Faris saw it. He shouted, 'Show me your hands,' then he shouted, 'Gun,' and 'Drop it.' I heard a shot and responded." She paused. "Why would he shoot at me if he was innocent?"

"We don't know. When you heard the shot, you responded correctly. You were protecting yourself and your partner."

Beth couldn't think about herself. Jack Lawson had gone out in the rain for medicine for a sick child. "He had a family."

"He had a wife and son. Detective Harrison informed Mrs. Lawson about her husband's death."

Her heart raced. "Did she tell her I shot him?"

"No, she told her he was involved in a shooting and was dead. She said the case was under investigation, and she'd tell her more when she could."

A wife and baby were now a widow and fatherless child because of her. How was she ever going to make this right? "What am I going to do?"

"You're not to say anything to anyone," the chief ordered. "I have your reports. Officer Moreno, you are on paid leave until the hearing and cleared of any wrongdoing."

She repeated the word *wrongdoing* in her head. What if she had done something wrong? What if she went to jail because she had made a mistake? Perfect

Beth had made a fatal error. "Do you think the detective will find this woman?"

"We'll find her. It's murder. She caused Jack Lawson's death. I want her in jail where she belongs."

She focused on the mystery woman. "She snuck away. She knew what she had done, and she fled before we realized she was the reason for all of this. She played everyone. She pretended Jack Lawson was going to kill her. She's a heartless bitch." She looked at the chief. "Sorry."

He studied her. "Don't apologize for a criminal's behavior. She showed no responsibility or remorse when she left the crime scene. That's what makes her dangerous."

Beth stood. "Promise me you'll find her."

"Detective Harrison won't let her get away. Do you have her contact information?"

"She gave me a card."

"If you remember anything that might help, call her. You probably had the best look at her."

"Nothing about her stood out except for that bright-yellow poncho."

Chapter Eleven

Sydney parked near the emergency entrance to Newtown Hospital but remained in her car. Nearly a year ago she had received the call that her husband had been involved in a hit and run at the college north of town. A student had run him over in the parking lot and left him broken and bleeding on the asphalt.

She would always associate the hospital with the worst day in her life, waiting to hear whether Gordon would live or die. She had spent every free hour within the hospital's walls while her husband recovered from the accident. The head injury had been the primary concern for the doctors, but Sydney had worried about all the broken bones, especially his back. They had warned her he might be paralyzed.

Hospitals were a mystery to healthy people, but she had quickly become educated about medical care. Insurance was a gamble. Young healthy people bet against the odds of needing it, and then when a serious injury occurred, they became acquainted with high deductibles and out-of-pocket costs that added up to thousands of dollars.

She became the primary bread winner. With two young children, she studied for the detective position. The hours were flexible with more freedom to work her assignments. This case had become a test of her abilities. Instead of a cut-and-dried shooting, it was turning into a web of deceit and lies. She needed answers and hoped Abby Keller could provide them.

With an inner nudge to put her worries away, she stepped through the doors and looked around the familiar emergency room. She saw a woman who matched the driver's license photo pouring a cup of coffee from the machine in the waiting area. Abby Keller's straight brown hair was shorter in length, but the features were the same. Her stocky figure was accentuated by the large smock and tight pants.

Sydney displayed her badge. "I'm Detective Sydney Harrison. Are you Abby Keller?"

"Yes." She looked surprised. "How did you know?"

"Driver's license photo. Is there a place where we can talk?"

"Booth two." Abby went through a gate to the back of the booth where a computer allowed her to register incoming patients.

Sydney went around to the patient side and took a seat across from her.

Abby looked around. "I'm the only one on duty, but it's a quiet night. We can talk unless someone comes in, but I don't know what I can tell you that I didn't already tell the police three months ago."

Abby only knew her purse had been stolen. She had no idea someone had used her identification to elude a murder charge. Sydney pulled up the old report on her phone. "You reported your purse stolen here at work."

"They didn't take my purse. Only the wallet."

The report said purse. "Was the wallet in your purse?"

She nodded her head like a bobblehead toy. "Yes."

"What did the wallet contain?"

"Everything important." She sighed, and her shoulders sagged in a slouch. "I had to cancel my credit cards. Which was probably a good thing because all of them were maxed out. I mean I was paying the minimum on them every month, but the totals never went down."

Paying the minimum would barely pay off the previous month's interest. She was digging a hole deeper in debt. Sydney focused on the topic. "Did anyone try to use them?"

"The police told me to cancel them right away. But the credit card companies are making me pay down the balances before they issue new ones. Don't you think they should write it off? What do they expect me to do? Pay cash for everything?"

Sydney told her brain to close her mouth. Not everyone was good with money. She liked numbers and reports and keeping track of details. "It must be difficult."

"You don't know how hard it was to get a new driver's license. I had to ask for a new social security number card, and to get that I had to provide a birth certificate. My mother couldn't find it, and I had to wait for a new one. It took forever to replace everything they took. And the wallet had a photo of my boyfriend in it."

Why was that important? "He couldn't give you a new photo?"

"We broke up, but I liked opening my wallet and letting others see his photo inside. He was mega hot, and they were *so* jealous. I should have known he was seeing another girl. The prime guys always have someone on the side."

Sydney shook her head to clear it. "Let's return to the theft. Any money missing?"

"I told the cops I had a hundred dollars in it, but I can't remember. One time I didn't have enough money to pay for some makeup, and the man behind me paid for it. I thought he wanted something, like he was a stalker, but he was just being nice. It was like that paying-it-forward thing in that movie."

Before Abby could drift off onto another tangent, Sydney reeled her back in. "Anything else missing?"

"I didn't notice it until later, but my pills were gone."

"From your wallet?"

"No, my purse." She twittered in a high pitch that made Sydney cringe.

"What sort of pills?"

"It was a prescription my dentist wrote for pain after removing my wisdom teeth. Why do they call them wisdom teeth? I don't feel any dumber with them gone."

"The pills were in your purse?" Sydney prompted.

"I put the pill bottle in my purse in case my gums started to hurt, but I felt fine, even with all the patients I talk to for registering their information. I must be a good healer. I was planning to get rid of the pills, so I didn't think it was important when I couldn't find them."

Pain pills. Edith was elderly. They often had pain medicine. Was the thief targeting more than cash? "You reported the theft here at work. Where do you keep your purse?"

"In my employee locker." Abby pointed to her left. "It was locked. I had to do the combination to open the door. When I searched for my keys, I saw that my wallet was missing. I went straight to security, and they notified the police. They took my information. I didn't notice the pills until I got home. I didn't see any need to report them missing. Have you found the thief? Will I get my money back?"

"Cash is hard to recover," Sydney said. "How many pills were in the container?"

"Oh, I only took two. I had enough for a pill twice a day for two weeks." She paused to do the math on her fingers. "Twenty-eight minus the two I took."

Was the mystery woman stealing pills? Drug addicts were unpredictable, desperate, and dangerous. Ohio had an epidemic with overdoses from mixtures of cocaine and heroin with fentanyl or the deadlier carfentanil. Dealers didn't care if they killed their buyers. They could always find another addict. Everyone was a victim, from the elderly who were targeted for their medication to the children whose parents could no longer take care of them because they were high or dead. She made a mental note to talk to security next.

Abby's voice intruded on her thoughts. "Is that why you're here? About some missing pills?"

"No. Someone used your driver's license when the police questioned her."

"She pretended to be me? Do I have a twin?" She sounded excited.

"The officer didn't have a clear look at her face."

"Why would someone want to be me? I'm not rich or famous. Should I be flattered?"

"She was hiding her identity." Sydney rose. "May I see your locker?"

Abby stood. "It's just a locker."

"Please show me the way."

Abby looked around the empty foyer and led her to the main hallway. Smaller hallways branched off in different directions with signs listing the various departments. Sydney followed Abby down a short side hallway to a bathroom. Beyond the stalls and sinks was a dressing room with lockers surrounding an open area and wooden benches spaced at intervals. Most of the lockers had combination locks or ones with a key.

"This is it." Abby tugged on a tumbler lock, and it opened. Her eyes widened in surprise. "I thought I closed it."

Abby was a lamb waiting to be fleeced. Sydney offered advice. "You might want to make sure the lock is engaged and tug on it before you leave."

Abby stared with her mouth agape and eyes vacant. The thief didn't have to know the combination. Abby hadn't secured her lock.

"Who's allowed in the locker room?"

She shrugged. "The restroom is open to the public, and there's no lock on the door to the locker room, so anyone can enter. One time I found a homeless woman in here sleeping on the bench. She borrowed a blanket and pillow from one of the patient rooms and made herself at home."

"What about security?"

She lowered her voice. "At night there's only one security guard. If he's making his rounds, he isn't watching the cameras."

Sydney looked around. "Where are the cameras?"

"None in the bathroom and locker area. That would be creepy. Security ran the video from the main hallway camera, and they didn't see anyone behaving suspiciously during my shift when my wallet went missing."

Sydney walked through the two rooms and paused in the hallway. "Is there an outside door nearby?"

"Right there." Abby pointed at the end of the hall.

Sydney opened the exit. The dumpster was to the left and the parking lot beyond. It was a perfect escape route. She made a note of the locker room and door. "I'd like to talk to security."

Abby led her to the main entrance. Hidden behind a wall near the vending machines was a room with an unmarked door. She knocked and introduced Sydney to the security guard.

Sydney showed her badge. "I would like to see footage from tonight."

Abby stood stiffly in the doorway. "I have to get back to my desk. I'm the only one on duty until the next girl comes on shift."

"Could you check to see if a woman came in with an arm injury tonight?"

She nodded up and down several times.

"I'll stop by after I'm done here." Sydney followed the elderly guard into the narrow room and took a seat.

He swiveled in his chair. "What would you like to know, Officer?"

"Detective," she corrected. She needed him to take her seriously. A large screen displayed different entrances and main hallways of the hospital. No cameras were located in the shorter side hallways. "I'm interested in the entrances from nine p.m. on."

"Which one? We have the main entrance, the emergency entrance, the…"

The woman had an arm injury. "Let's look at the emergency entrance first."

A new picture filled the screen in front of her. It was the same entrance she had used. He moved a time bar to nine p.m. "You're lucky you visited tonight. We recycle the tapes every twenty-four hours."

"You don't hold them longer?"

"We send videos to the cloud if something important happens. There's no need to keep everything." He tapped on the keys to start the tape. "What are you looking for?"

"Someone in a raincoat." A woman in a yellow rain poncho entered through the sliding doors. "Stop it."

He paused the display.

Sydney pointed at the face on the screen. "Who is that?"

"I don't know her name, but she works in the lab." He tapped on a keyboard. "I have a list of employees and their photo IDs if you want to try to match them."

She had her. "I need to talk to the woman in the yellow poncho."

"Sure, but if you're looking for women in rain ponchos, I have more."

"What?"

He pointed at the screen. "We had a big storm tonight. She's wearing one of the ponchos the hospital gave out for the chamber of commerce expo." He opened a storage door and pulled out a box. "I keep several on hand for when it rains."

He placed the box on the counter. Inside were small plastic bags of various colors with the name of the hospital stamped on the front.

She unsnapped a yellow bag and pulled out a rain poncho of matching color. "How many colors do they come in?"

"Yellow, pink, blue, black, and camo."

"Black?" She found a black bag in the pile of rain gear and removed it. "I'm going to need these as evidence."

"Go ahead. The hospital had plenty left over from the expo. Employees were allowed to take as many as they wanted."

Sydney stuffed the compact bags into her cargo pants pockets. Edith hadn't been wrong in her description. Changing out of the black poncho and replacing it with a yellow one would have been easy. Then the mystery woman could have walked out onto Main Street without anyone identifying her as the thief. But Jack Lawson had ruined her plans. Now she needed to ruin hers.

The thief could be an employee, but it also could have been anyone wandering around the building in search of drugs and cash.

The rest of the tape showed people dashing through the doors during the scattered showers. For each woman in a rain poncho, she told the security guard to print out her photo and match a name. She needed to check out each one as a possible suspect.

Chapter Twelve

Claire had seen the police detective show her badge to Abby when she joined her in the lobby. She backed into the shadows to make sure they didn't notice her but remained, listening to their conversation in the neighboring registration booth while she pretended to look up a patient's information. Claire straightened the papers kept in the plastic file on the wall as she watched them leave for the locker room the detective had asked about.

Stupid Abby. She was always talking, a regular chatterbox about every detail of her boring life. The most mundane event was a crisis she had to share. For weeks she had complained about going to the dentist about her wisdom teeth. She'd made it into a life and death situation and fretted about how the hospital wouldn't be able to operate without her. Afterward, she had acted as if she deserved a medal for her bravery for surviving the extraction of four teeth in her empty head.

The dental surgeon had prescribed enough pills for two weeks, and Abby didn't know what she was going to do with the extra ones. She asked several of the nurses if it was safe to take them for a headache, and one of the orderlies had offered to buy the extra pain pills. Featherbrained Abby was planning to take him up on the offer.

Claire had saved Abby from becoming a drug dealer

by taking the meds from her locker. She only took the wallet because Abby carried a lot of cash. The girl was begging to be robbed.

She had kept the ID because they bore a slight resemblance to one another. The photo was so generic it could have belonged to a dozen different women. The detective was only talking to Abby because Claire had used her driver's license. That had been a mistake, but she couldn't have given the young officer her real one.

She had a plain face and blended in like a thousand other ordinary women in town. Five hundred people worked at the hospital, and more than three hundred were women. What was she worried about?

The emergency room was quiet, and she moved back and forth to the hallway, stocking supplies, waiting for Abby and the detective to reappear. Nothing connected her to the theft of Abby's license and pills, but Claire didn't underestimate stupid. Tactless people tended to blab and say the wrong thing at the wrong time. Her husband had been king of inappropriateness. He didn't have to tell her not to invite her friends over to their apartment. She was too embarrassed to introduce them to her *charming* husband. He was either drunk or in a foul mood he didn't bother to hide. She had fallen in love with a lie and was too ashamed of her gullibility to admit her mistake. She'd wised up quickly. How fortunate for her Daniel Batton had met his demise in that horrible crash.

Claire stacked cardboard boxes on a plastic tray and added handfuls of packaged syringes and catheters from the medical storage closet in the hallway. Her hand throbbed, so she kept the load light and headed for the emergency room. Nobody bothered her at night while she transferred supplies from stockroom boxes to mobile cabinets and supply drawers. Her job was important. No one wanted to reach for life-saving equipment and find it missing. She set her own pace to keep the clock ticking away the hours of the night until her shift ended.

Her ability to blend in with her surroundings had cost her making employee of the month before, but this month they might finally recognize her. They should. Working in the ER was a lot more challenging than pain management where she had worked for almost seven years. She would still be working there if not for a curious nurse who liked counting pills. Before suspicion fell on her, she'd applied to the ER department. Third shift had taken weeks to adjust to, but she liked fewer co-workers and less supervision.

She had been good at hiding her pill use so far, but the need to feel normal came more often. Replenishing her supply was harder and riskier. She would quit but not yet. The shooting had left her shaken, and she needed to forget what had happened in that alley tonight.

She headed for the storage cabinet in the waiting room with another load of supplies and saw the police detective a few feet away. Who was she waiting for? Had she become a suspect? The tray shook in her hands, and she dropped several packages containing gauze squares on the linoleum floor. She squatted to retrieve them.

The detective knelt on the floor. "Let me help you."

"No need."

The detective handed her two bundles as she restacked the paper-wrapped supplies on the tray.

Claire had kept her latex gloves on to cover her injury. She gripped the tray, and her swollen fingers ached from the movement. She ignored the pain and rose. "Thank you."

Abby dashed from her registration desk and joined them. "Detective, I thought you had left." She stared at the ceiling. "Wasn't there something you wanted me to look up?"

It was just like Abby to cater for attention. The poor child begged to be liked.

"Did you check to see if anyone came in with an arm or hand injury?"

The detective knew. The tray shook in Claire's hands. She adjusted the weight to bear it with her left arm and looked for a way to escape.

Abby snapped her fingers. "That's it. I checked the intake records, but no one came in tonight with an arm or hand injury." She hesitated. "Claire, do you know Detective..."

"Sydney Harrison."

No escape. "I dropped a few things, and she came to my rescue."

"Claire Batton is the best ER nurse we have," Abby said.

"I wouldn't say the best." Claire gave the proper response to a compliment. Modesty was a virtue rarely recognized or rewarded, but she didn't have to brag about herself.

Sydney turned to Abby. "Thank you, Abby. You've been a big help. I'll let you return to your job."

Claire backed up to the ER entrance and used her hip to press the automatic button to open the double doors. She turned and dumped the tray of supplies on top of a mobile supply cart.

"Have you been here all evening?" Sydney had followed her into the ER room.

"No, I work ten at night to eight thirty in the morning." She didn't want to be caught in a lie and told the truth. Her schedule would be easy to confirm. Claire keyed the code to open the bottom drawer of the cart. She needed to look busy so Sydney would leave her alone. She placed the wrapped gauze in the drawer.

"Do you always work the same ten-hour shift?"

She wasn't going away. "Four days on and three days off." The extra day off made the longer shifts worth it.

"I asked Abby if a woman had registered with a hand or arm injury, but she said no," Sydney said. "Did anyone come in through the emergency doors?"

"No, it's been quiet." Officer Wilson must have reported her hand injury. They were looking for her.

"If an adult female comes in with an injured right arm or hand, contact me or leave the information with security." Sydney handed her a card. "It most likely is a sprain, but there might be cuts and abrasions."

Claire took it with her left hand, keeping her right hand hidden. She stuck it in her smock pocket.

Sydney pointed at her wrist. "Do all nurses wear watches?"

"Nurses, doctors, technicians." She touched the stethoscope around her neck. "It's part of our equipment." She grabbed an instant ice pack from her supply cabinet. "Squeeze and shake."

Sydney stared at the bag, but comprehension dawned as she touched her eye. "Thank you."

Had she forgotten the bruise that was darkening? Did her husband beat her? "We have counselors at the hospital." They couldn't keep a secret, which was why she never used them.

"My husband didn't do this. My four-year-old nephew got excited and clobbered me with his new toy truck."

Toy truck? Claire laughed and handed her another ice pack.

"Are you sure?"

"Don't worry about it." Claire had taken half a dozen for her wrist and hand.

Sydney pushed open the doors and left. Claire waited five minutes and grabbed a blank chart. She entered the lobby and looked around. Sydney was gone. Abby was playing on her phone. She joined her in the booth. "What did that detective want?"

Abby paused her game. "Remember when my wallet was stolen out of my locker? Someone used my driver's license and pretended to be me. Can you believe that? Someone wanted to be me. She couldn't tell me why, but my case must be important. Why else would they send a detective?"

Did she honestly think Sydney was interested in the theft of her wallet alone? She needed to know what else Sydney had talked to her about, but Abby might be suspicious of her sudden interest. Or not. "You lead an exciting life."

Abby smiled wide enough to crack her face. "I certainly do."

"Did they find your wallet?"

"No, she was more interested in those old pills I wanted to get rid of. I didn't even think to report them missing to the police, but she asked a lot of questions about them. Do you think that orderly stole them? He wanted me to sell them to him, but I wasn't sure. Someone told me he only wanted the pills to sell to a drug user. I couldn't let that happen."

Abby didn't remember that Claire had been the one to hint at the orderly's motive. The police knew about the missing pills, but they couldn't trace them to her. The orderly was the obvious thief. But they were looking for a woman, someone who had passed herself off as Abby but had an arm injury. She tugged on her sleeve.

Abby frowned as someone signed in at the registration desk. "I have a patient."

Claire left the booth and showed the man where to enter. She removed the card from her pocket and stared at the name. How good of a detective was Sydney Harrison? She'd left no clues to her identity and had covered her tracks by leaving the crime scene. Except for her arm injury. She flexed her fingers. They were stiff and sore. She'd ice them when she finished her shift. She was off for the next three days. Her arm would be as good as new by the time she returned to work.

Claire had enough medicine to keep her happy for a while thanks to Edith Merryweather. Besides, she could quit any time she wanted. She just wasn't ready, yet.

Chapter Thirteen

Midnight had come and gone by the time Sydney finished filing her reports and pulled into the driveway of her home, her haven from the rest of the world. The vision of Jack Lawson's face and the expression on Vivien's features when she had given her the news would haunt her along with all the other memories of a job that saw the worst of mankind.

She opened the door and found peace in the familiar sights, scents, and sounds that worked like a balm on her tortured soul. She secured the door and turned the deadbolt, locking out the rest of the world. The hallway closet had been redesigned for her equipment with a metal liner to prevent any break-ins. She opened the safety box and stored her holster and gun. She emptied her cargo pants pockets and placed the flashlight into its charger.

She checked on the children first. Ethan's room was neat for a six-year-old boy. His action figures were lined up on the shelf in various poses. His dirty clothes were in a pile at the end of his bed, and his latest drawing of an alien monster was on a plastic children's table. He had colored half of it purple and the other half green.

Zoe's room was a disaster with a mixture of items representing her various interests. Dolls were scattered on the floor in stages of undress as if a fashion show had suddenly been halted. Her ball glove hung over the bedpost, discarded after T-ball practice. Books featuring animals, science, and adventure stories were stacked precariously on her desk. Her backpack from school had yet to be opened. She would wait until Sunday evening to do any homework.

Gordon was in his own room, his former study. His desk had been moved to the corner, and the medical bed was the central focus. A stuffed monkey, a gift from the children, wrapped its long arms around the metal railing and was filled with puzzle books and electronic games. His wheelchair was parked in the corner away from the bed. Someone must have moved it. She studied his sleeping form.

When she married Gordon, she'd voiced her concerns about the influx of young female students tempting him while she grew older each year. They had made a pact that if either one of them was tempted to have an affair, they would tell the other before it escalated beyond flirtation.

Because of his injuries, she had been too polite to be honest and too scared to express her fears about their troubled marriage. When Rick pressed her to sleep with him, she'd felt obligated to tell Gordon the truth.

They spent the night talking, sharing the feelings they had kept secret after his accident and making plans for the future even though it was unknown.

She told Rick there would be no affair. Not even a brief conquest in bed. He didn't take the rejection well and pushed her to change her mind.

Gordon didn't like the idea of another man invading his territory. It was archaic, the type of thinking an anthropologist studied and analyzed. She had expected him not to care. But fighting for his marriage, for his wife, had returned the spark to his eyes. For that, she owed Rick.

The fight went further than claiming his wife. Gordon listened to the therapist, and Barry Vespoint had joined their team, first to serve, but more to encourage. He wouldn't let Gordon quit no matter how much pain it took to exercise his wasted limbs.

Now he was preparing to teach again. The summer would be a trial period to see if he had the stamina, but with a goal, he was working harder than ever to build his strength and endurance.

She stroked his arm resting on top of the covers. The dark hairs were soft to the touch, but beneath was hard muscle, stronger from taking his weight when his legs were too weak to support him.

She couldn't explain why she was attracted to her husband. It was more than physical, more than emotional. They had connected with a shared glance and mutual understanding. They were meant to be partners in life. She had almost lost that relationship. Desire welled from deep within, and she leaned forward and kissed his lips. As she pulled away, his hand trapped her, and he returned the kiss, lingering until her breath quickened.

She loved him and had almost lost him. The terror had rushed back when she told Vivien her husband was dead. She pulled away, brushing at the tears that automatically fell.

Gordon touched her wet cheek, his eyes full of concern. "It's late. Did you catch a big case?"

"Too big. I may not be able to solve it."

"That doesn't sound like you, Syd. You're better trained than anyone on the force to be a detective. Follow the evidence."

"I did, and it turned into a whole lot of trouble."

He patted the open space on the bed beside him. "Come tell me about it."

She kicked off her boots and let her cargo pants fall. She lowered the side rail and sat on the bed. Gordon reached under her top and snapped her bra free.

"Hey, that's a smooth move."

He grinned. "I've been practicing on the nurses."

"Gordon!" She gasped in fake outrage. They had always teased each other in the past, and she wanted to recapture the playfulness that had disappeared with trust. "That explains the smiles on their faces after their home visits."

"Let's see if I can put one on yours." He pulled her against his chest and kissed her. He didn't rush, tasting her mouth long and deep before moving to her cheek and neck. He found a warm spot below her ear that made her groan.

"I thought we were going to talk."

He rubbed her back. "We talk better after we're relaxed."

She recognized the tone in his voice. He was in the mood to make love, and she needed to escape from the worries of her job. At least for a little while. She removed her remaining clothes, and he raised the blanket for her to join him. With the long abstinence after the accident and changes to Gordon's body, initial lovemaking had been awkward, like two teenagers discovering sex for the first time. But as they gained confidence, intimacy became more natural. They were finding their old tempo.

She snuggled naked against him, her body molding to his in a perfect fit. Her hand caressed the smooth skin of his wide chest, the rhythm of his heartbeat strong against the palm of her hand. Once long and lean, he was more muscular, the curve and firmness of retrained tissue defined even in rest. She was attracted to his mind but lusted for his new body. She rubbed against him, building a fire of desire between them. Her body reacted to memories of past lovemaking, and she groaned in anticipated pleasure.

His hands moved casually over her body, caressing her in knowledge gained from years of experience, playing a familiar pattern with his fingertips in intimate areas that made her heart race and her body respond with a tightness that demanded release. She returned the favor, using her expertise to tease him until rewarding him with complete submission. Both panted for breath, tensing and clenching every muscle, fighting for the ultimate climax. Sydney cried out for release as her body shook with a final spasm. He moved aside, his hand caressing her as their bodies relaxed. Sex was physically rewarding, but the words shared afterward made their bond special.

"Tell me about the case." He pulled her in close against his shoulder and kissed her forehead.

"I can't." She studied his doubtful expression and raised eyebrow. "It's an ongoing investigation."

Some police officers never talked about work. They didn't think their spouses could handle the graphic horror of the work, but communication was key to their relationship. They shared things on a level that kept any information confidential and private between them.

"Hypothetically, then."

She snuggled closer, resting her chin on his chest. "Are you sure you want to hear this?"

"As an anthropologist I'm always interested in

human behavior."

She stroked her finger along a scar on his chest where a tube had been inserted to save his life. "Hypothetically, a man is walking home through an alley. It's dark and raining. He surprises a woman who is fleeing from a crime. She has a gun in her hand, but somehow the man gains control of it."

He sat, bumping her upward. "Did he shoot her? She was no longer a threat."

She placed a finger over his mouth to silence him. His kissed her fingertip.

"The police arrive. They order him to turn around."

"Wait, does he still have the gun in his hand?"

She stared past his shoulder into the darkness of the room. "Yes."

Gordon ran his free hand through his hair. "Good Lord, they didn't shoot him?"

"He had a gun. He was turning toward them. That was threat enough, but the gun went off."

"He shot at the police?"

"Not sure. He had no reason to shoot. It could have gone off accidentally. That's one of the unknowns I'm trying to figure out."

He pulled her into his chest. "Is he dead?"

"Yes." Sydney choked back a tear.

He grabbed a tissue from the bed stand and offered it to her. "Family?"

"A wife who worshipped him and an eight-month-old baby. I had to tell her he was dead."

His arms wrapped around her. "You were right. It was a bad night."

She kissed him. "Not anymore."

"So what makes it so difficult to solve? Didn't you

arrest the woman?"

"She was gone before I arrived. She gave the police officer a fake ID and walked away when his back was turned. I don't know how I'm going to find her."

"She has to have left bread crumbs, Syd. Follow her trail."

Chapter Fourteen

Sydney compiled a list of people she needed to interview. Even though it was Sunday, she wouldn't take any time off until she caught the mystery woman. One detective covered each shift with their own caseloads. The chief had given her permission to ask other officers to help, and Sam Wilson had volunteered to call hospital employees seen on video entering the hospital wearing rain ponchos and confirm whereabouts at the time of the shooting.

Edith Merryweather returned Sydney's call and said she was happy to meet her. Sydney bumped her to the top of the list she'd written and headed to her home. She parked her unmarked vehicle on the street in front of a beige Cape Cod.

She knocked. The television was turned up and could be heard through the wooden front door. She pounded harder.

"Coming."

The door opened. The woman was barely five feet tall with a mass of white curls surrounding a face lined with life. "May I help you?"

"I'm Detective Sydney Harrison, Mrs. Merryweather." She displayed her badge.

"Come in, my dear." She smiled warmly and ushered her inside from the chilly May morning.

Sydney smiled. It had been a long time since

someone had called her *my dear*.

"What happened to your eye, my dear?"

A rainbow of colors had greeted her in the mirror this morning, and no amount of makeup could hide the damage. "I ran into a truck."

Edith gasped. "How awful."

"A toy truck," she clarified. "My nephew accidentally knocked me in the face."

"Boys tend to break things. I never understood why they enjoyed fighting and going to war." She shook her head as she tottered off.

The front door opened into the living room. The television was still blaring. A lamp cast a yellow glow over a small table next to a recliner. The wooden table was stacked with magazines, books, and mail with a magnifying glass resting on top. Edith was wearing slippers that opened in the back and flopped with each step across the worn rug to the recliner where a colorful crocheted blanket had been pushed aside.

Sydney closed the door. "You have a lovely home." The walls, shelves, and tables were cluttered with knickknacks and personal items Edith had collected over a lifetime, but the room was clean and had a lemony scent.

"Sit down, my dear."

The furniture would be considered antiques by anyone under fifty, and although it was quality, some items were showing their age. A hole in the threadbare rug exposed the wooden oak floor beneath. Sydney sat on the couch and sank to the springs. She moved to the middle cushion and gained some padding. "I'd like to ask you some questions about the robbery, Mrs. Merryweather," she shouted above the religious program where a man in a teal suit preached Sunday's sermon.

She gave her a blank stare. "Let me turn the TV down." She searched for her remote on the table and muted the sound.

Sydney's ears stopped ringing. "I'm here about yesterday's robbery."

"Hobby?"

"Robbery!" Sydney held her hands up and then pointed her finger as if it were a gun.

"Robbery!" She gasped, and her hands touched her lips. "It was awful. I've never had anyone point a gun in my face. He grabbed my purse and ran before I knew what was happening."

He? She was not going to be a good witness. "I'm sure it was traumatic. Are you able to talk about it?"

"It happened so fast I don't remember anything but the gun and a blur of black running in the rain. Did you find the robber?"

"No," Sydney answered honestly. "But we found your purse in a trash dumpster."

Her face wrinkled in a puzzled look. "A jumper?"

Edith evidently wore no hearing aids. No wonder the television had been blaring. "We found your purse in a trash dumpster," Sydney repeated louder and slower.

A smile crinkled her face into well-worn grooves. "Did you bring it?"

"No, we're checking for fingerprints. Do you remember if the robber wore gloves?"

She paused. "I think he did, but I can't be sure. My eyes were on the gun."

Sydney didn't correct her about the sex of the robber. She didn't want to influence any answers. She opened her notebook and made a note. "Do you remember anything else?"

"Why would someone rob me? I'm old. I never carry much money. All I was doing was sitting at the bus stop."

"You don't have a car?"

"Oh, yes, but I don't see very well, and the last time I drove, I hit two mailboxes. That darn cat ran right out in front of me. I would have hit it if I hadn't swerved."

"Did they take away your license?"

"They always pass me. I need identification when I visit the doctor, but I don't drive anymore. My reflexes aren't as fast as they were."

Reflexes? Molasses moved faster than Edith. "Is that why you use the bus?"

"My dear, those mailboxes could have been people. I don't mind if I die in an accident. Who's going to miss me, but I wouldn't want to hurt someone else. What excuse am I going to give if I were to kill someone? I'm a menace in a car on the street."

"That's very insightful, Mrs. Merryweather."

"Call me Edith, my dear." She moved her hand across a stack of mail she hadn't opened. "I don't mind taking the bus. I never go far. I was at the beauty salon, and it took longer than expected. Everybody wants their hair done for Sunday, but I don't go to church anymore. I can't sit in those hard pews. Maybe I should get my hair done on another day, but old habits are hard to break. Afterward I had dinner."

"Who did you eat with?"

"I ate alone. I used to meet up with my friends, but I'm the last one now."

"Then what?"

"I saw the clouds rolling in and was afraid the rain

would ruin all the work the girl did on my hair, so I waited in the bus stop to go home."

"It looks lovely." Sydney pulled out a folded paper. "I have an inventory of the items inside your purse. Could you tell me if anything is missing?" She handed her a printout of the list compiled by Irene.

Edith stared at the paper. "I'm going to need my spectacles." She took her glasses from the side table and put them on. She grabbed a magnifying glass and stared at the list as she ran her crooked finger down the page. "I don't see my money listed or my pills."

Money and pills. The same items stolen from Abby's locker. "How much money did you have in your purse?"

"I had a twenty, two tens, two fives, and three ones. I worked in a bank when I was younger and like to track the bills I carry. I was lucky I keep my phone in my coat pocket. I need to have it handy in case I fall."

The robber had targeted Edith for her cash, but why take the pills? "What do you take the medicine for?"

"Pain." She reached out toward Sydney but stopped short. "I have rheumatoid arthritis." Her fingers were gnarled so that they folded over her palms. "I need my pain medicine. They only prescribe three months at a time. I have to see my doctor at the hospital to get a refill."

"They won't call a prescription in for you?"

"It's part of pain management, my dear." Edith lowered her voice. "They don't want us to become drug addicts."

"Why did you carry your pills in your purse?"

"I don't take them daily like the ones in my pill caddy. I take them when I need them. When I leave home, I put the bottle in my purse. Sometimes I need one after climbing up and down the bus steps or walking around town."

"I'm sorry. Do you have any on hand to take?"

"I keep a few by my bed in case I can't sleep." She sighed. "Do you think I could get a police report? My doctor won't prescribe more pills unless I can prove they were stolen."

"Do you have a copy of your prescription?"

Edith searched in her pile of correspondence and found a white bag with the prescription and accompanying literature stapled to the outside. "Will this help?"

Sydney was going to the hospital next. "I'll see that you get more pills, Edith." She met her gaze. "What can you tell me about the person who robbed you?"

"Oh, I didn't see his face. I was staring at the gun."

"Do you remember anything about the weapon?"

She smiled. "It was a revolver and silver like they shoot in westerns."

Sydney pulled up the picture of the gun Jack Lawson had been holding. "Like this?"

Edith stared at the screen. "That's it. My husband bought one for protection after those commercials."

"What commercials?"

"The ones where burglars broke into your home to rob you." She lowered her voice. "And rape you."

"Do you know how to use it?"

"I put it in a box upstairs after my husband died and haven't touched it since."

"If you want to get rid of it, let me know." Sydney handed her a card. "The police have a buy-back program, and you'll receive a gift card."

She looked at the ceiling. "I'll have to do some cleaning to find where I put it."

Sydney leaned forward. "Do you remember anything else? What was the robber wearing?"

"A huge black cape with a hood." She threw her arms wide. "It billowed as he ran away."

The black poncho she could have exchanged for a yellow one in the alley. The robber was smart and prepared. "Do you remember anything else? Other clothing?"

"He wore sneakers and black pants. He ran beautifully toward the alley."

"Beautifully? What do you mean?"

"Like a track star." She smiled. "Graceful and smooth. My son competed in track, and he ran the same way. He jumped the hurdles like a gazelle."

Could the woman claiming to be Abby Keller be a runner? Edith had provided an important clue. "Do you recall anything about the robber's face or voice?"

"Oh, he didn't say a word. He pointed the gun and grabbed my purse."

For money and pills. "Was your purse open?"

"No. It was fastened and next to me."

Edith's purse had been closed, so why had the robber targeted her? How did she know she would be carrying any pills? Sydney stood to leave.

"Would you like some coffee or hot tea? May is so unpredictable," Edith said. "One minute it's cold and rainy, and the next it's warm and sunny."

"No, thank you." She had another interview, but the look of disappointment on Edith's face changed her mind. "Why don't I make it?"

Sydney played hostess and prepared the tea as Edith

supervised. She pointed at a porcelain cookie jar in the shape of a cat. "Don't forget the cookies."

Sydney lifted the lid. Inside were homemade chocolate chip cookies. "You baked these?"

"Not with these hands. My neighbor loves to bake and brings them over. I don't have to worry about my figure anymore, and you could use a few pounds." Edith laughed as she shuffled back to the living room. "It's so nice to have company. Everyone is too busy to visit anymore."

Sydney liked Edith. In police work she didn't meet too many sincere people, and Edith was exactly the person she presented. Her memory of events collaborated the other information she had gathered and had added important details.

Why was Edith living alone? "Do you have children?"

"Our boy was in the military. He was killed in a helicopter crash." Her hand shook, and she put the cup down. A tear glistened in her eye. "That was so long ago, but the hurt never leaves a mother." Her gaze strayed to a photograph hanging on the wall of a young man in uniform. His medals were in a frame next to it, including a purple heart. Other pictures showed Edith and her husband, a woman graduating, and another of two children.

"You have a daughter?"

"Our girl married a successful businessman, and they run a company together. They live in France, so they can't visit much, but she buys me lovely gifts. The sculptures and artwork are from her. I told her she shouldn't spend so much on me, but she keeps sending things."

She pointed to the last picture. "Are those your grandchildren?"

"Those are mine when they were young. It's my favorite picture of them sitting together in quiet harmony. A brief moment when everything was right with the world." She sighed and sipped from her cup.

Sydney stared at the portraits of Edith's children when they were young and smiling and strayed to the row of medals signifying the sacrifice a young man had made. On the other end of joy was sorrow and somewhere in between was hope to live on. Among the clutter of items were memories that were eternal.

Sydney didn't regret delaying her departure. She said farewell after accepting a bag of cookies and headed for the hospital.

Chapter Fifteen

The hospital was quiet on Sunday with reduced staff, but the president of the hospital had agreed to meet with Sydney. But her first stop was in Pain Management where patients with chronic pain were evaluated and treated. She didn't want Edith to suffer without her medication.

The doctor's office was closed on Sunday, but a receptionist manned the pharmacy where the pharmacist worked limited hours on the weekends. Sydney introduced herself. "Edith Merryweather had her purse stolen. It contained her pain medication. I want to make sure she can receive a refill."

She typed in the name on her computer. "She received one."

"The medicine was stolen," she repeated slower.

"We'll need a police report."

"I can email it to you." Sydney had filled out the form on her laptop in her car and had it ready to send to the email address the receptionists provided. "Where is the office of Phillip Lowell?"

The receptionist chewed on a hangnail. "Up front and to your left, but he doesn't work on weekends. He's the president of the hospital."

She ignored her comment. President Lowell had promised to come in and meet with her. "Don't forget about Mrs. Merryweather's prescription."

"It's in the system, but we're only open a couple more hours. She can pick it up tomorrow."

Edith needed a caseworker, but if she called social services, they might insist she move into assisted living away from her home and memories. That would break her heart. She could put Edith on a list of senior citizens the police routinely did welfare checks on to make sure they were safe.

Phillip Lowell's office was in the corner of the building, secluded from the hustle and bustle of medical traumas. Modern couches and chairs in angular shapes and bright colors were arranged in a small gathering area for guests. The reception area behind a glass window looked vacant. Had he forgotten to meet her? She called his number.

He opened the door and ushered her inside. He was casually dressed.

"I'm sorry I ruined your weekend."

"I was playing golf and on the seventeenth green when you called. Sorry I didn't have time to change."

He won points for making time for her. Someone who ran a hospital could have ignored her call. He offered her a seat in his lavish office. The mahogany desk spanned six feet, and the filing cabinets were made of matching wood. An assortment of photographs decorated the credenza.

"My security chief said you were investigating a robbery where someone was wearing one of our rain ponchos." He opened a drawer and placed several poncho bags on his desk identical to the ones she had taken from security. "We gave away hundreds of these at the last community expo."

"I know you probably don't think a robbery is a big

deal, but this one snowballed into a deadly shooting."

"I talked to Chief Mills and told him I would be happy to cooperate."

She didn't know the depth of their relationship but was glad for his help.

Officer Wilson's search of the employees wearing ponchos into the hospital the night of the shooting had yielded nothing. She had to focus on the injury. "We believe the woman who was wearing your poncho may have injured her arm. She could be local, and this would be the hospital she would visit for medical care. I gave my card to everyone I talked to last night, but she could come in at any time. I'd like the names and addresses of anyone who has cuts or a break to her arm or hand."

"Patient records are confidential."

"It's important I talk to this woman, Mr. Lowell. I don't need any medical information, only her name and address if she shows up here for treatment."

He debated his response. "You said an arm injury?"

"Right arm and hand. It could be bruised or broken."

He typed on his keyboard. "I'll flag our records. If anyone fits that description, I'll notify you, but if the injury wasn't serious, she could have gone to a clinic or other hospital."

Sydney planned to call every place that might provide medical care. Those that weren't open today, she'd call tomorrow. She needed a name. She handed Phillip her card. "Sorry for ruining your Sunday."

"My golf partner wanted to sell me a new scanning machine. I was grateful for the excuse to leave."

Sydney stepped outside to call the bus driver who had reported the crime. He hadn't seen the woman committing the robbery and had repeated the information

Edith had given him. Edith was a regular rider on the bus, and he asked about her.

She checked in with the medical examiner's office, but the autopsy wasn't completed. Irene had news about the revolver.

"One shot was fired, but we didn't find the slug."

"So he definitely fired the gun."

"Not necessarily. If the gun was cocked, it could have gone off accidentally, or it went off when he dropped it," Irene said. "Those old guns don't have any safety features."

"Send me the photos of the crime scene. How far away was the gun from the body?"

"Officer Faris said he kicked it away before examining the body. He had it bagged when we arrived."

Irene had filled in some blanks, but she didn't feel any closer to finding the woman who had stolen Abby Keller's identity, robbed a sweet old lady, and caused the death of Jack Lawson. She headed for the police station.

Chapter Sixteen

Vivien curled up on the bed with Jack's pillow clutched against her face as she inhaled the manly scent of her husband. She had cried out all the tears left in her body on Sunday and into Monday and still hadn't grieved enough. Her body ached with the pain of losing him. She looked toward the doorway, expecting to see him standing there, a crooked grin on his face, but the opening was empty. He was gone. Forever.

Only John-John had kept her from sinking into total despair. She had to be strong for him. But where was she going to find the will to face each day without her husband by her side?

"Vivien!" her mother shouted from the living room. She burst into the room and waved at her. "You have to see this. The police are on the television. It's about Jack."

She wanted to ignore her mother's plea but rolled off the bed. John-John was asleep in his bassinette at the end of the bed for his morning nap. Would he ever realize how drastically his life had been changed two nights ago because his father had done the right thing to fetch medicine for him? She choked on a tear. His forehead felt cool. The drops had worked, and he was returning to his old self. How long would it take for her to feel like herself again?

"They said the chief of police would speak about the shooting." Lucy turned up the volume on the news broadcast and patted the empty spot next to her on the couch.

Vivien grabbed a box of tissues and dabbed at her eyes as she rested against her mother.

Lucy pointed at the screen. "Here it is."

Chief Kyle Mills stood in a room filled with reporters and cameramen. He wore a dark-blue uniform with a name badge above his pocket and a city department patch on each sleeve. Stars on his shoulders declared his rank. Microphones were attached to the podium like a bouquet of black metal flowers. He tapped on one to test it and spoke in a deep, hoarse voice. "Saturday night we had a report of an armed robbery at Third and Main streets. An unknown suspect had stolen a purse from an elderly woman sitting at a bus stop."

"What does that have to do with Jack?" Vivien looked at her mother for an explanation, but all she did was hush her.

"In response to the armed robbery call, police entered a dark alley near the site of the crime. They saw a man standing over a woman, who was on the ground begging for her life. When the man turned, police saw a gun in his hand. He fired a shot, and police responded. The man, John Lawson, died at the scene."

"What!" Vivien jumped to her feet. "The police shot my husband?"

Her mother leaned toward the television. "They said Jack had a gun."

"Jack hates guns. He would never shoot one." She snapped her fingers. "I thought it odd when the detective asked me if Jack owned a gun. They're covering something up!"

"Why would they do that?"

"Mom, didn't you hear what they said? Someone reported an armed robbery at a bus stop, and when the police saw Jack in the alley, they shot him. They're making Jack out to be a criminal when he was the victim." Vivien paced across the floor and turned, retracing her steps. "They made a mistake. I bet they're lying about him shooting first."

"You're getting upset."

Vivien stopped. "You bet I'm upset. I'm not going to allow those cops to dirty my husband's good name and cover up the fact they shot an innocent man. Jack did not have a gun. They murdered him, and they're lying. I'm going to find out the truth and expose it."

Her mother grabbed her flailing arms. "Calm down, Vivien. Perhaps there's a good reason the police said what they did."

Vivien pulled free of her mother's grasp. She hated how her mother denied any feelings. If she wanted to act like a hysterical child, she would. She pointed at the television where the police chief's face was on the screen. "Then he owes me an explanation."

Her mother nodded in agreement. "I can have my brother contact a lawyer."

"What good is a lawyer?"

"They're quite useful when dealing with secrets."

Like cheating husbands. "You call him." Vivien stifled a scream of frustration. If her mother could think of hiring a lawyer, she needed to remain calm and think logically. How could she find out the truth? "I know someone at the local newspaper. They might like a story about lies and corruption on the police force."

"That may not be a good idea. The press is extremely unpredictable, Vivien."

But powerful in the arena of public opinion. Vivien trudged into her bedroom and headed for the bathroom. Her body was stale and dirty from lying around in a cocoon of blankets and misery. The reflection in the mirror staring at her was a stranger. Who was that woman with swollen eyes and blotchy skin? Since hearing about Jack's death, she had done little else but cry. She wore the same clothes she had on when Detective Harrison had given her the news. No more crying. Now was the time for action.

She rehearsed the words she would use when she confronted the chief about his lies.

No wonder good old Sydney had been so kind helping with John-John and waiting for her mother to arrive. She didn't want to tell her the truth. She'd been vague by telling her the case was under investigation, but she must have known. The police always stuck together. Something about a blue line. She found the card Sydney had given her and shoved it into her purse. She'd pay a visit to the tricky detective and ask for details.

She grabbed clothes from the dresser and closet, discarding a few on the bed until she found the right combination to give her confidence. Her mother stood in the doorway.

"What? Don't you think I should do something?"

"I do. This is the first time you've moved since Jack's death. It's put a fire in your belly. But I think you should eat so you don't faint from hunger." She pointed at the black jacket. "That one. It says no nonsense."

She didn't argue but ran her fingers through her greasy hair. "Let me shower first. I need to feel alive again."

"I'll fix something for you to eat while you dress."

"Mom." She waited for her to turn. "Thanks for being here."

She stepped forward and hugged her. "That's what mothers do."

"I'm not doing this for me, Mom. I'm doing it for John-John. I want him to be proud of his father. How can he if the police smear Jack's good name?"

"I agree. I'll support you in whatever you decide."

All she did was argue with her mother. "Why?"

"I know I disapproved of you marrying Jack. I thought you were ruining your life, but my stubbornness made me miss the most important day of your life. I missed my daughter's wedding. I wasn't there when John-John was born. I've learned from my mistakes. Jack was a good man, and I'm proud of you, Vivien, for standing up for him."

She held on a little longer than in the past. "Thank you, Mom."

Vivien let the hot water pour over her head and streak down her tired body. How could she be physically exhausted when it was her emotions that had been battling for a sense of sanity in her upside-down world? She sniffled back a few tears. She would have to be strong for Jack. He wasn't a violent man, but he would want justice for his death. He would want her to defend his reputation and reveal the truth. She let the water revive her, scrubbing her hair clean and preparing for the fight ahead.

Vivien signed in at the front desk of the police station. With her mother's help she had thrown together an outfit of a skirt, button-down blouse, wool jacket, and low-heeled pumps. Casual but powerful. She wasn't going to let the police push her around.

She recognized Chief Mills as he marched down the hall, his hand outstretched. She shook it but didn't smile. She was here on serious business. It wasn't a social call. "I saw the newscast. I have questions."

He waved her forward. "Let's talk in my office."

"I'd like Detective Harrison to be present." Vivien turned to look at him. "I think she owes me an explanation."

He nodded toward another officer. "Have Detective Harrison report to my office."

Vivien entered the chief's office and sat in a padded chair across from his desk, which was covered with folders, papers, and a computer. The calendar blotter contained notes detailing events or meetings in each square.

"You wanted to see me?" Detective Harrison stood in the doorway.

He nodded. "You know Mrs. Lawson."

Vivien turned as Sydney stepped forward and took the seat beside her. The swelling around her eye was gone, but her cheek looked like a sunset. She hoped it hurt. The detective had lied to her.

Sydney smiled. "It's nice to see you, Vivien."

In other circumstances she might have smiled back but steeled her expression. Sydney turned toward the chief, a puzzled look on her face.

"Mrs. Lawson saw the news broadcast."

The broadcast that was a calculated message that said nothing nice about her husband. She should have brought John-John. He would have reminded them a baby was involved. She turned from the chief to Sydney. "Why didn't you tell me the police shot my husband?"

"It was too early to conclude the evidence," the chief

defended.

"Let the detective speak for herself." She used her bitchy voice, loud and angry.

Sydney paused before answering. Her voice was calm but firm. "I had to talk to other people in the investigation after I called on you. I didn't want to misspeak before I had all the facts. I know it doesn't seem fair, but I thought it more important you knew about your husband and why he wasn't coming home."

Vivien rose to her feet. "He was murdered by the police."

The chief stood. "It was an accidental shooting."

"Accident?" she screamed. "He was gunned down by police officers!"

The chief retrieved a folder from his desk. "Your husband was holding a gun."

"My husband never owned a gun in his life." She turned to Sydney. "I told you that."

"We know," Sydney said. "The gun belonged to a robber. Their paths crossed in the alley. We believe the robber was disarmed, and your husband picked up the gun as the police arrived. When they ordered him to turn around, they saw the gun in his hand and ordered him to drop it. The gun went off, and police reacted."

"Reacted?" Vivien's legs weakened. She sat before she fell. "They killed him. Why didn't they fire a warning shot? Why didn't they stun him?"

Sydney leaned closer, pain in her eyes. "When an officer perceives a threat such as a gun, especially if it's fired, the normal response is to shoot until the threat is over."

"Normal? Nothing is normal about this." Vivien fought to compose herself.

"When the responding officers heard the shot, they responded appropriately," the chief said.

Vivien stood and pounded her fist on the chief's desk. "Who are these officers, and what have you done to them?"

"Any officer involved in a shooting is put on leave," the chief said. "There will be a hearing tomorrow on Tuesday, and the officer will testify before a board. It's standard procedure."

"Officer? You said officers responded."

"Only one fired a weapon."

"And your board will exonerate him." Vivien's anger returned. "I know how you protect your own." She gathered her purse. "I want his badge. I want him put in jail for the murder of my husband!" She headed for the door but turned. "You have not heard the last of me. I'm hiring a lawyer, and he'll expose the truth."

Chapter Seventeen

Sydney stood in the hallway as Vivien walked away. She was on a mission for the facts, and Sydney had misled her. She had told Vivien her husband was shot. But she hadn't told her a police officer had shot him. She'd rationalized the lie, but it didn't change it into the truth.

She returned to the chief's office. "I should have given her all the information surrounding her husband's death before you made the announcement."

"That was my call. The press wanted an official statement. They already had too many rumors. I had to respond."

"But the way you said it. An armed robbery. A man with a gun in the alley. The police shot him. It makes it sound like Jack Lawson was the robber. No wonder she's angry."

"Do you want the robber to know we're looking for her? She may not realize she's wanted for murder. If we alert her to the seriousness of the crime, she may panic and flee. How are you coming on identifying her?"

"I have a few clues, but no solid lead on the identity of the mystery woman in the alley." The chief was buying her time before the police would have to reveal all the facts behind the shooting. But there was another problem if a lawyer became involved. "Vivien is going to find out about Beth."

The chief looked tired. "I better contact our city's legal department and let them know about Mrs. Lawson's threat. I wish I could protect Officer Moreno, but she's going to have to learn to deal with this sooner than later. After the hearing, she'll be on desk duty. You can give her some of your cold cases to work on."

"Are you confident the hearing will end in her favor?"

"If it doesn't, I'm hanging up my badge. Police officers are human beings. She acted on the information she had." He slumped at his desk. His illness had taken a toll on his body. His uniform was loose, and his jowls sagged along a once firm jawline. His eyes had bags beneath them. "I worked my way up through the ranks. I took every course offered to be a better police officer. But there's always the unexpected like a man holding a gun in a dark alley and not knowing what to do with it. Nothing can prepare you for that."

"Beth is new on the force."

He frowned. "Should I be concerned?"

"I meant I don't know her. She could have a spine of steel." Any officer would be shaken by the shooting. Everything had been done by the book, but an innocent man was dead. It was one of those incidents that took a toll on everyone involved.

"You're new at this, Detective. I have confidence you'll solve this case, but you need to keep me updated on every detail." He searched her face. Did he find her wanting? "What have you found out from your investigation so far?"

"The gun was registered to a man who died two years ago. He was ninety. The gun was old and lacked safety features according to the ME's office. His son said the guns, knives, and ammunition were bought by someone at the estate sale."

"No name?"

"Not even a description beyond middle-aged man. We know that's not our woman. Could be her husband or boyfriend."

"Where does that leave us?"

She scanned her notes. "I talked to Abby Keller. She comes into contact with a lot of people at her job, but her wallet and pills were stolen from her work locker. She may have forgotten to snap the lock closed."

"A crime of opportunity?"

"That would explain the missing wallet, but I'm leaning toward a fellow employee, someone who knew she had pain pills. Abby admitted she told everyone about her wisdom teeth surgery and the leftover pills she wanted to get rid of."

"You think our thief was after pills and not cash?"

"The pills from Abby's locker and from Mrs. Merryweather's purse were both pain medicine. I think our woman could be an addict or is supplying one. The cash would help buy drugs."

"Did the thief know Mrs. Merryweather?"

"The pain management center is in the hospital, and that would reinforce the idea that the thief worked at the hospital and knew Mrs. Merryweather received pain pills on a regular basis. It would explain why she was targeted even though her purse was closed."

"How many employees?"

"Three hundred fifteen women."

"Narrow it down."

"I talked to the president of the hospital. He's having staff pull information on any patients with an arm injury like the one we think the robber sustained when the gutter fell."

"You better widen your search to neighboring healthcare facilities."

"I already did. If this woman works at the hospital, she wouldn't want her fellow employees to know about her injury and report her."

"When I chose you to be detective, I knew you were capable, but this is a tough case. We need to find this woman. Sergeant Faris is on desk duty until after the hearing. Have him help you."

"Yes, sir." Sydney walked back to her office. The chief meant no insult. She'd only been a detective for a few months, but asking for help, especially from Rick, felt like admitting a weakness. She shoved personal feelings aside and analyzed her information.

She had no definitive description of the woman. No fingerprints. No DNA. The injury was the best way of identifying her, but if she wasn't injured badly enough to seek medical treatment, she might never find her.

She could postpone asking for Rick's help until she ran out of options, but when she passed his office, he was playing trashcan basketball with a stress ball. She paused in the doorway. "Do you have time to make some phone calls?"

"I still have another quarter to play." She stepped back to leave, but he stood. "What can I do?"

"We're looking for a white female with an injury to her right arm or hand. I need you to help call the med centers and doctors' offices in the area. She may not even seek medical treatment, but it's the best chance we have of catching her."

He walked around his desk. "I should have taken the

time to look at her more closely, but she was so ordinary."

"That's what makes it hard to find her."

He walked behind her, closed the door, and blocked her exit.

She crossed her arms. "What are you doing?"

He leaned against the closed door. "It's time we talked."

"There's nothing to say."

"We had an affair."

"We *almost* had an affair." It was a distinction that was important to a woman. Sexual infidelity was harder to forgive than emotional adultery. She'd fantasized plenty about movie stars, which was a lot different from getting naked and intimate with a live person.

He leaned in close. She tried not to retreat.

"You made me believe you were going to leave Gordon. I had plans for us."

Sydney shook her head. "Short-term plans. You asked for a weekend getaway. I drove home and confessed to Gordon about your proposed tryst."

He looked at her as if she were crazy. "You what?"

"When we married, we agree to be honest if one of us was tempted so we could mend the marriage before the deal breaker of adultery. Lies destroy trust, and without trust, love struggles to exist. When he realized he might lose me, he decided to fight."

Rick huffed as understanding dawned. "For your marriage."

"For me." Sydney bit her lip. "I believed Gordon had stopped loving me after the accident. I couldn't remain married without his love. I was scared, confused, and needed someone to talk to."

"And I was convenient." His voice was bitter.

"You were a friend, Rick. And contrary to what you think, men and women can be friends. I still count you as one."

He had a crooked smile on his face. "But you're in love with your husband."

"Yes. And don't forget you're married."

"She filed for divorce a year ago."

"I didn't know."

"It's not final because we're fighting over assets. We barely talk and usually with a lawyer in the room. We were in love when we married. How does it all go wrong?"

"How does a man like Jack Lawson go out for medicine and end up dead in an alley because of a gun he didn't own? Sometimes there are no answers."

Rick sat at his desk. "Send me a list, and I'll start making those phone calls."

Chapter Eighteen

Claire wiggled her fingers and winced. When she finished her shift Sunday morning and reached home, she had put ice packs on her hand and arm and kept it elevated. Then she'd rested all Monday, hoping the pain and swelling would decrease, but her wrist hurt to rotate. She couldn't wait any longer. If the bones were broken and healed incorrectly, she might lose mobility in her hand, and her career as a nurse would be over.

The throbbing pain from her injury had taken a toll on her supply of pills. She didn't want to run out now when she needed relief, but she had no intention of buying from drug dealers. They couldn't be trusted. She had purchased what she thought had been ordinary oxycodone pills, but they were oxycodone fentanyl pills, which could stop breathing. Luckily, she recognized the symptoms of shortness of breath, cold skin, and drowsiness and had inhaled the naloxone nasal spray before she'd lost consciousness. She'd kept the deadly pills as a reminder not to buy from lying dealers again, but maybe it was time to get rid of them. She put the plastic bag of the toxic tablets in the zipper compartment in her backpack. She'd get rid of them at the hospital before she accidentally overdosed.

She poured the remaining pain meds from Edith's prescription bottle onto the table and sorted them into her pill caddy organizer. She calculated how many she would need and crushed the tablets into a fine powder before snorting it off the tabletop. Claire relaxed back in her chair, waiting for relief to flood her body.

Hopefully, enough time had elapsed between the shooting Saturday night and her plan to visit the neighboring hospital today to throw off any searches for a woman with an arm injury. She checked her appearance against Abby's driver's license. Her hair didn't matter. Women changed color and styles often enough not to match an old photo. Even Abby's weight could be explained by a diet, but the age difference might be noticed.

Abby had worn a lot of makeup in her DMV photo to cover her acne. She was always touching her face with her dirty fingers and turning her skin into a field of erupting volcanoes. Makeup would help Claire with her disguise. She searched through her bathroom vanity drawers. Most of the expired powders and liquids should have been thrown away, but she wasn't going to waste money on new cosmetics for a one-time use. She chose a liquid foundation that gave her a fake tan, blue eye shadow, pink blush, crimson lipstick, and green nail polish for her short nails. Strangers would notice colors, none which she commonly wore. Applying the crème and powders with her left hand took patience, but she accomplished the task.

"Do you think I should get my nose pierced?" she asked her reflection in an imitation of Abby's high-pitched voice. She had the painted face and empty-headed persona. Now she needed an outfit. She changed her yoga stretch pants for a pleated short skirt, part of a schoolgirl costume she had bought before gaining weight. Discovering it fit again was rewarding. She buckled on four-inch heels and strolled back and forth in front of the mirror before nearly twisting her ankle. Her legs had been chubby stumps before she began running. Now they were graceful curves of hard muscle. Too bad her plan involved scraping the flesh off them.

She needed to fall, skin her knees, and brace her fall with her hand to provide the perfect excuse for an emergency room visit. She'd have to stage the accident closer to Olde Bend Hospital. She didn't want to drive any distance with bloody knees. Besides, the injuries needed to look fresh to avoid any link to Saturday's shooting.

After packing Abby's license and insurance card in a little pink purse, she counted what little cash she had on hand. She wouldn't need to pay anything at the emergency room, but if the doctor wrote her a prescription, she'd have to pay the deductible. It would be months before the insurance company sent the bill to Abby. She scanned her apartment. It was sparse. She had pawned or sold anything of value to help pay off debts. What remained was necessary or of no monetary value. She had sold her gold wedding band but kept the photograph of her late husband on the table next to her bed. The picture was taken shortly after they were married and was a reminder never to make the same mistake again. Good old Danny Batton. He never refused a drink, a bet, or a chance to beat her.

The first few years had been pleasant enough although the warning signs would have been apparent to anyone not blinded by love. He bounced from job to job, complaining about co-workers or low pay until he decided to start his own business. Claire had cosigned a loan for a truck, trailer, and lawn maintenance equipment. But Danny couldn't find enough customers to cover the bills. He sold the trailer and equipment but kept the truck. Instead of looking for work, he lounged on the couch, drinking and watching idiot programs all day. When she "nagged" him about finding a job, he reminded her who was in charge. Strength equaled power.

She had considered divorce, but the lawyer said she'd have to share his debts, especially the loans she had cosigned. She'd worked extra shifts to pay off one bill only to have two more take its place.

Claire rarely drove her old hatchback car, but Olde Bend Hospital was too far away to walk. Ever since the accident she hated driving and began walking, then running. But she could never run fast enough or far enough to escape the haunting memories of the night Danny died.

They had gone out to dinner to celebrate their wedding anniversary. Five years that had destroyed all her hopes and dreams nurtured by a childhood of princess stories. How had she ended up married to an ogre instead of a prince?

He was so drunk by the time they left the restaurant to head to the theater in Olde Bend he could barely walk to the truck. After he knocked her to the ground to keep her from taking the driver's seat, she crawled into the passenger side and secured her seat belt. Danny had the music cranked to a full blast to avoid any conversation. He tapped the beat on the steering wheel before moving to her thigh and giving her a wolfish grin. He wanted to get lucky.

She was familiar with marital rape in all its variations. He wasn't going to be denied his rights, and she was too exhausted to fight back or care. She couldn't report his abuse. She didn't want anyone to know she was a battered wife. Admitting she had been a fool was too embarrassing.

Claire turned onto the steep winding road where the accident had taken her husband's life. She slowed, looking for the turn he had missed.

The sky was clear today, but that fateful night the rain had been steady, and the darkness blended the road into the ditch and woods that bordered on each side. He ran off the asphalt pavement more than once and struggled to pull the speeding truck back onto the roadway. She'd told him to slow down, knowing he would hit the accelerator in spite.

Claire braked as she approached a familiar turn in the road. This was the place. The tree had been fractured into a splintered web the night of the accident, but during the last three years the top had broken off and was rotting on the ground. Time had passed, but that night still haunted her. She had been prescribed pain pills for her injuries, but no one understood the need for a cure to the joy of being rid of a parasite and the emotional guilt it caused.

Danny had taken the previous turn too fast, nearly losing control. The plan had formed suddenly and clearly in that scary moment. Claire pulled latex gloves from her pocket. She always had a pair handy. She slipped her fingers inside, keeping them low and out of Danny's view so as not to alert him to danger.

She waited until the next turn in the road, took a deep breath, and moved in a fluid motion as if she were watching the action from afar. She hit Danny's seat belt lock with her left hand to release it and yanked the steering wheel hard with her right, sending the truck off the road and into a steep ravine on her side. The heavy vehicle barreled into the tree. She braced for impact, and the seat belt tugged on her chest with a painful jerk. She hit her head, and her right arm smacked against the truck's metal frame as she was thrown toward the side window. She cried out in pain, stunned but alive.

Danny had disconnected the airbags after buying the truck. Too bad for him. He had flown forward, hitting his head against the windshield full force. The safety glass held except for the hole his head had created upon impact. His chest had smacked against the steering wheel, and he fell back against the seat, dazed and bleeding. It should have killed him, but he grunted in pain. How had he managed to survive? Claire felt his pulse with her left hand. Fast. His breathing was labored. Her touch woke him.

He looked at her through dazed and confused eyes. "What happened?"

"You ran off the road."

He frowned, blood dripping from a long gash in his forehead. "You grabbed the wheel."

"You lost control. I was trying to save us."

He patted his coat. "Call 9-1-1, bitch."

"I already did," she lied. "Remember, I'm a nurse." She showed her gloved hands. Her right arm ached, but she could move her fingers. "Let me check you for injuries."

He relaxed back against his seat. The fool trusted her. He had used terror to keep her in line, but fear had turned to hate.

"Where does it hurt?"

"I can't breathe." He coughed and spat out blood

along with a piece of broken tooth. She pressed against his chest. He screamed. His ribs were cracked or broken, and he likely was bleeding internally. Even if his injuries were fatal, he was dying too slowly. Doctors might be able to save him. That would never do. She needed him dead to escape his abuse.

Ignoring any pain, she clamped her gloved hands over his mouth and pinched his nose. Another bruise wouldn't be noticed. He grabbed at her fingers to free her grasp, but his palms were covered in blood and slipped on the smooth surface of her gloves. It took all her strength to hold tight until he slumped forward against the steering wheel. She checked his pulse. Nothing. He was finally gone.

Headlights lit up the truck as a car slowed and stopped. "Hold on!" someone shouted from the road above.

Claire pulled her gloves off and stuffed them deep into her coat pocket. Then she slumped against the side window and waited to be rescued. She had only hastened Danny's death, not caused it. She had risked her own life to bring about the accident, but God had spared her. That had to mean something. But most importantly, she was free of him.

The paramedics and medical staff treated her kindly. They waited to tell her Danny was dead after she was admitted to Olde Bend Hospital for a broken arm and concussion. She cried and played the hysterical young widow to perfection.

People who had once been friends knew she was better off without Danny, but they offered polite condolences anyway. But her late husband had claimed the last laugh. He had let the insurance on his truck lapse and left her with a huge loan to pay off on a pile of junk metal. The drugs had made her forget her past until Jack Lawson crossed her path and caused a plethora of new problems in her life.

The wooded hillside disappeared, and a sign welcomed her to the town of Olde Bend. She was getting close to the hospital and needed to look the part. She stopped at a gas station with a convenience store. The man behind the counter glanced in her direction and went back to reading his magazine. She searched the aisles until the only other customer left. She sauntered up to the counter and paid for a big fountain drink. She glanced back and saw him watching her strut out the door in her short skirt with her purse hanging off her left shoulder and her cup in her right.

The concrete sidewalk dropped off at least six inches to the asphalt parking lot. Claire turned her head as if distracted and took the tumble as naturally as a stunt double. She hit hard, and her injured arm took the blow as her cup exploded across the pavement in a puddle of bubbling soda. Her bare legs skidded across the dirty asphalt, and her skirt rode up to expose her butt cheeks. No one reacted immediately. That was insulting.

A man pumping gas into his car replaced the nozzle and crossed the lot to help her to her feet.

"My arm." Her reaction was sincere. Her injured arm had taken the brunt of the fall, and she spasmed with renewed pain. She let the tears fall.

The clerk made an appearance and offered to replace her pop. She accepted. She asked for ice in a bag for her injuries. The two men saw to her needs. It was nice to be waited on for a change.

"Are you sure you don't want me to call the

paramedics?" the clerk asked.

"No." Too many paramedics delivered patients to the Newtown ER. One of them might recognize her and wonder about her altered appearance. "I can drive to the hospital. It's not far."

She lowered the visor and stared at her reflection in the vanity mirror. Her eyes were circled in black with mascara smeared down her cheeks. The blue eye shadow added a clownish distraction to her appearance. It was the perfect disguise.

She drove with one hand, her right arm too tender to raise. She took every turn at a crawl. Her body screamed at the abuse it had suffered when she moved her legs and exited the car. She looked every inch the victim of a recent accident with brutal scrapes and a streak of blood streaming from an open cut on her knee cap.

She cradled her right arm and sobbed fresh tears as a nurse greeted her in the emergency room lobby.

"Take a seat here. We'll get you registered and cleaned up."

Claire sniffled into a tissue but was careful not to wipe away the streaks of makeup smeared across her face. Because her injuries weren't life-threatening, she had to endure registration. She wailed and complained as the elderly woman processed Abby's identification and insurance card. She couldn't work fast enough to get Claire out of her booth.

An orderly helped her into a wheelchair and pushed her into an empty ER bay. A nurse brought in a package of bandages and antiseptic. "You took a nasty fall. What happened?"

"I wasn't paying attention and missed a big drop-off from the curb."

She grimaced in sympathy. "This is going to burn." She wiped off the blood and dirt with the antiseptic and gently blew on it.

Claire winced and whimpered at every little touch for her role as Abby. Her knees were skinned enough to keep her from running for a few days. She'd miss the exercise. It was part of her daily routine to escape the voice of Danny as he haunted her, accusing her of ending his life too soon.

The nurse bandaged her knee and examined her arm. Claire yelped.

"Did you hurt your arm in the fall?"

Claire nodded, sniffling back tears. "I think it might be broken."

"I'm going to be as gentle as I can, but I need to clean it up. Then we'll take you to radiology and have it x-rayed. Is that all right?"

Claire nodded. She talked the same way to her patients, explaining what she was doing and asking for their permission. She liked this nurse and thanked her before an orderly wheeled her to radiology.

The technician introduced herself as Lydia and asked if she was pregnant.

"No." She didn't want a pregnancy test or anything that could lead to her true identity. The less information they gathered, the better.

"We'll take precautions in case."

She put a lead vest on her, placed her arm on the x-ray table, and told her not to move. Lydia left the area to stand behind a protective screen, and the buzzing of the machine echoed in her ears. She took another x-ray and then sent them to the radiologist.

Dr. Viola Parks explained that the radius was

fractured along with a bone in her wrist. She planned to put a cast on her arm to keep the bones in place while they healed.

A cast would be too noticeable, and she didn't have the tools to cut through plaster. "Can you put on a removable cast?"

It took convincing, but the doctor put her in a plastic removable cast. She told her to follow up with her regular physician. She raised three fingers on her left hand and swore to obey. When she returned home, she'd cut off the hand section and hide the plastic cast beneath a long sleeve. No one would be able to detect her injury and report it to the police.

The doctor gave her orders and a prescription for pain medicine. She filled the script at a drive-through pharmacy using Abby's insurance card and paid the ten-dollar deductible. But buying pain medicine legitimately wasn't as much fun as stealing it.

Chapter Nineteen

Beth put on her uniform. Her belt felt skewed without the familiar weight of her revolver. She stared at her reflection in the mirror. She'd been so proud when she graduated from the academy. She was going to make her life count for something other than shortcuts and excuses, the tenets of her family. Now her dream was in jeopardy.

All her life she'd had to endure the apathetic dismissal of her parents, Fred and Alice, who belittled every effort she made from getting straight As to making the field hockey team. Lacking any evidence of maternal feelings, Alice had laughed at her sensitivity and told her to toughen up like a real Moreno. Her older siblings, Bubba and Angel, had teased and tormented her at every opportunity. She was the least important member of the Moreno family and the scapegoat. No one would come to her defense if she ever was in trouble.

No matter what she achieved, she couldn't be around her family without feeling small and worthless. That's why she had moved out on her own as soon as she finished high school. Making ends meet had been difficult, but she had done it. She'd worked odd jobs before training as a paramedic technician. When she was old enough, she had applied to the police academy and been accepted.

She hadn't chosen her family, but she had chosen

not to be close to them and their toxic environment. If they heard about this shooting, their criticism would be nonstop. How was she going to keep her name out of the news?

The decision to shoot Jack Lawson had seemed to be the right choice at the moment. Rick had shouted, "Gun," and she had heard a shot, firing at the target. Only the male suspect in a robbery had turned out to be an innocent victim.

She would have to testify at the hearing today and justify her actions. She had to be confident. If they detected any sense of error, it could doom the outcome. The hearing board would decide if she would continue her career as a cop. It had been her dream job, a Moreno on the right side of the law.

Beth grabbed her equipment bag and headed for her car. She turned the key and heard the grinding noise that meant it was dead. The old compact automobile had given up the ghost. Now what? She called the police station to let them know she would be late.

A woman spoke in the background, and then her voice came over the line. "This is Sydney Harrison. I can pick you up and bring you to the station."

Beth was dumbstruck. She wasn't used to acts of kindness, especially from someone who barely knew her.

"Where do you live?"

Beth gave her address. She locked her car doors out of habit. She would consider it lucky if someone stole the junker. She should have waited outside, but a nervous bladder forced her back to her apartment and bathroom.

The phone rang, and she jumped. It was Sydney at the apartment entrance. She released the lock and shouted down the stairs. "I'll be ready in a minute."

"Take your time."

Sydney was coming up the stairs. After growing up in a house where trash littered the floor and the smell of ammonia stung her eyes from cat litter boxes that were rarely emptied, she had been resolved to keep her apartment neat and tidy.

What few possessions she had were perfectly arranged from the books on the shelf to the fake silk flowers centered on the table.

"You have a nice apartment," Sydney said after entering.

"I've been cleaning." She'd scrubbed every inch of the apartment twice. She doubted a speck of dust remained on any surface.

"My son keeps everything neat and orderly. My daughter, on the other hand, thinks cleaning is a waste of time. Considering how quickly she creates a mess, she might be right."

"My family were hoarders." Why had she admitted that embarrassing fact? Beth shrugged as she looked around to diminish the impact of her confession. "They never threw away anything. I try not to accumulate too much because I still find it difficult to let go."

"I kept my children's baby teeth. My husband teases me about saving bones. This from a man who has a human skull."

"What?" Did she say skull?

"Gordon teaches courses in forensic anthropology and facial reconstruction. He borrows skeletons and skulls from the Cleveland Museum of Natural History. They have quite a collection."

And she thought her family was weird. Beth searched for her bag.

"Did you lose something?"

"I can't find my bag. I had it just a minute ago."

Sydney pointed to the floor behind the couch.

She retrieved it. "I guess I'm a little nervous." She grabbed her bag and followed Sydney down the stairs. "Have you ever had to testify before?"

"Yes, only answer the questions asked. Don't volunteer any information. Keep to the facts and avoid any emotions. Your decisions were based on the events you faced."

"I'm sorry for what—"

"No," Sydney interrupted. "You're not sorry for doing your duty. Focus on how you felt when you arrived on the scene. Recall your training. He had a gun. You were in danger. You fired in self-defense."

"The chief told me Jack Lawson was out picking up medicine for his baby boy. He was in the wrong place at the wrong time. How can I block that out?"

"You didn't know Jack Lawson. All you knew was a man was standing in a dark alley with a gun pointed at a woman on her knees. When he turned, your partner saw a gun and alerted you to the danger. You heard a shot and reacted."

"I heard his gun may have gone off accidentally." Beth paused in the lobby of her apartment. "Do you think I'm a bad cop?"

"No, you're human. Everyone makes mistakes, but when a cop does, it can mean someone dies. Sometimes it's a bad guy, and sometimes it's a police officer."

"And sometimes it's an innocent man."

Sydney stopped and stared. "Does your family know?"

Her family? They would be overjoyed she was

kicked off the force. "No, I didn't want to worry them."

"I understand. People don't realize how dangerous the job of a police officer can be. We want to protect our family from worrying every time we put on the uniform." Sydney opened her car door. "But sometimes we have to remind them how difficult the job can be and ask for support."

"I'm the only police officer in the Moreno family." She was the first Moreno to graduate from high school, and the first Moreno to earn an honest paycheck. "I'll give my mother a call after the hearing." She delivered the lie with a smile.

"Did you grow up around here?"

She couldn't escape small talk on the drive to the station. It was better than thinking about the hearing. She knew how to reveal some facts while hiding others. "I grew up in a small mining town in Southern Ohio. You don't realize you're poor when you're surrounded by poverty until you attend school and get *those* looks."

"There's always somebody richer, someone with nicer clothes," Sydney said. "My father was a bricklayer. We didn't have much, but we never went hungry. We were content. Maybe that's why I could never understand the drive to accumulate boatloads of wealth. How much money does a millionaire need?"

"My parents spent money as quickly as they got it. They were teenagers when my brother was born. My sister soon followed. I think I was an afterthought." One they regretted.

"You're lucky being the youngest. I bet they spoiled you."

"Spoiled? I always wore my sister's hand-me-downs or something from the church charity drives.

When I first saw the price tag on a new dress, I nearly fainted. I still don't buy anything unless it's on sale."

"I look for sales, too. My husband was in an accident a year ago. He's going back to work part time, but it's been tough financially. We had to sell the yacht."

Yacht? Was she joking? Sydney flashed a wide smile.

"Remind me never to play poker against you."

"Gordon said I would have been a good storyteller in ancient times." She laughed. "But he always knows when I'm lying."

"Is that good or bad?"

"It depends on the circumstances." Sydney pulled into the station. "This is your first year on the force, but you've been doing a good job. Your record will hold up in the hearing."

"All I wanted was to be a cop. It was my dream. I keep wondering what if I had done something differently?"

"You were placed in a tough situation, Beth. You're sorry Jack Lawson is dead, but if you had it to do over, you would have no choice but to fire your pistol for your own safety. The woman who brought the gun to that alley is the villain. She caused Jack's death."

Beth nodded. Sydney was giving her answers to questions the board would ask. She repeated the phrases over and over as they entered City Hall, which was adjacent to the police station. Their shoes echoed on the tile floor in the hallway leading to the mayor's court used for the hearing.

The chief waited outside the door with two men she didn't know. One was in a wheelchair. He smiled broadly and waved at them.

She raised her hand to wave back but realized he was looking at Sydney. "Who is he?"

"My husband, Gordon Blackwood. Most of the police officers have taken courses at the college from him. That's how I met him."

Gordon had enough maturity to make his handsome face interesting. Sydney had mentioned her husband had been in an accident, but she hadn't mentioned the severity. Rick, on the other hand, had shared all the precinct gossip in their recent forced partnership. Leaving his Newtown College classroom, Gordon was injured in a hit and run by a student who fled the scene. Rick said nothing about a wheelchair. He focused on the part of the story where he found the driver cowering in his dorm closet and arrested him.

Rick offered his support to a fellow officer in need. He claimed to be the sort of guy women could count on. He hinted at a romance and Sydney being grateful for his attentions until she was named detective instead of him. He had called it a pity call by the chief. Then she had kicked him to the curb.

How much of it was true? Rick had made himself the hero and the victim. Her family had taught her to trust actions over words. Sydney had been nothing but professional and kind. Rick, on the other hand, bragged about his accomplishments and expected her to be impressed. She recognized a con game for attention when she heard one.

Sydney pulled her forward. "This is Officer Beth Moreno." She waved to the young man standing behind the wheelchair. "This is my husband's aide, Barry Vespoint."

A man opened the door to the courtroom. "Elizabeth

Moreno," he called out.

Beth's feet wouldn't move. Her heart pounded against her chest, and her breathing was ragged. If she ran away, would they find her cowering in a closet?

"Go ahead," Sydney urged.

She took one step and then another. She reached the door and glanced back. Sydney nodded and smiled. It didn't help. The chief had already entered and stood near a table in front of the judge's podium. He waved her forward. She squared her shoulders and entered the courtroom. It had a gallery of three bench seats, a wooden barrier with a gate to an open area, and two tables with chairs arranged facing each other in front of the judge's seat. Three men in dark suits sat at one of the tables. Each had laptops and folders in front of him. One was writing on a yellow legal pad. None of them looked up. The stern group would hear the evidence and render a verdict about her future.

A man stood at the other table with Chief Mills. "This is your attorney."

"I didn't know I had an attorney."

"The union pays for him."

She wouldn't be alone. She sat between the two men. Someone had placed bottles of water on the table for each of them. Beth's mouth was dry, but she didn't dare drink anything. Her hand might shake and betray her nervousness.

"Please raise your right hand and swear that the testimony you are about to make is the truth, the whole truth, and nothing but the truth."

Beth raised her right hand. "I swear."

The judge on the right typed for several minutes on his computer. "For the record, please state your full name."

"Elizabeth Sophie Moreno."

Chapter Twenty

Sydney stared at the closed door. Beth had looked so young and vulnerable. She had been guarded when sharing information about her family. Like any case, she had investigated those involved. Her research had uncovered some disturbing facts in Beth's background, but she respected her privacy and hadn't exposed them. From what she could deduce, Beth was facing this crisis alone.

"You're worried about her," Gordon said.

She turned to her husband. "I'm not worried about the testimony. She made the only decision possible under the circumstances. It's living with what she's done that will be the challenge. Her family doesn't live around here, and she hasn't had time to form a support group. She doesn't have anyone to help her through this, Gordon."

"She has you."

"As investigating officer of the shooting, I'm obligated to perform certain duties. I'm only a fellow employee offering support."

He chuckled. "When have you done anything halfway, Syd?"

Her philosophy was to live each day to the fullest, one day at a time. Partly because she was a cop and death could come quickly. Or a car could hit someone she loved and nearly end his life. "From what I've learned about her so far, she's proud and a perfectionist. She's taking this failure hard."

"We all stumble. If she falls, you can help her up."

"She's not used to accepting help. She won't ask for it."

He stroked the top of her hand. "I know another woman with a stubborn streak."

Rick hurried toward them and looked around. "Has Beth gone in already?"

Sydney rested her hip on the arm of Gordon's wheelchair. His hand exerted a slight pressure on her waist. "She's inside."

Rick stared at the closed door. "How did she look?"

"Nervous, but she'll do fine."

"It's her first time before the review board. I wanted to give her a few words of encouragement."

"The chief said you shouldn't have any contact," Sydney said.

A scowl creased his brow. "I'm not going to tell her what to say. I wanted her to know she didn't do anything wrong."

"Of course, she didn't, but the board reviews every shooting. It's protocol, Sergeant Faris. You know that."

He raised an eyebrow as if to question her lecture. He turned and paced back and forth. "There's nothing to worry about. It was a clean shooting. The fool man fired a gun."

"Jack Lawson wasn't a fool. He was a law-abiding citizen who didn't know he should have dropped the gun as soon as the police arrived. But he didn't want the woman to have it, so he held on, and when he turned…"

"I shouted gun." He slammed his fist into the palm of his other hand. He met her gaze briefly before turning away.

"Walk me out?" Gordon asked as he released his brake.

She broke her gaze from Rick's back and smiled at her husband. "Love to."

Gordon looked at Barry. "Why don't you bring the van around? Syd can push me."

She took over the task as Barry hastened down the hall.

Gordon jabbed a thumb over his shoulder at Rick pacing back and forth. "Are you worried about him?"

She glanced back. "The sergeant can take care of himself, but I've never seen him so defensive." Beth was nervous enough without Rick giving the wrong impression and making the board doubt their version of the events.

"Something about him is troubling you."

Gordon knew enough about the case for her to confide her concerns. "Rick never fired his gun. He said he had a bad angle. He was afraid of hitting the woman behind Jack Lawson."

"Were his feet glued to the ground?"

Rick was no rookie. According to the forensic report, Beth had fired six shots. Three missed the target and two only wounded Jack. If Lawson had been a real threat, Beth or Rick could have been hit. His instinct should have been to protect his partner and himself by moving into position to fire his gun.

Gordon raised an eyebrow as he looked at her over his shoulder. "I've put a bad idea in your head."

"One I had dismissed." Prematurely. "Rick wouldn't put another cop in danger." She couldn't think the worst. "I think he was letting her have the glory. For whatever reason. Only it didn't turn out that way."

After delivering Gordon to the van, Sydney returned to the courtroom. Rick had given up pacing and sat on a bench, tapping his foot in a frantic beat. No one else was around. She sat next to him. Gordon had raised a question she had shoved to the back of her mind, but she knew interrogations began with the easiest questions and built to the most difficult. "Do you know what you're going to say?"

"I'm sticking to the facts. No embellishment. No drama."

"Really?" She should have bitten her tongue to be silent. He had spread plenty of false rumors about her these past few months. "I shouldn't have said that. The past is in the past."

"I don't take rejection easily."

No, he didn't. "Let's focus on the present. I have a question that requires an honest answer." She studied his face, searching for any sign of deception. "You said you didn't fire your gun because you had a bad angle."

His jaw tensed, and his voice was sharp. "That's what I told you. Don't you think it's true?"

She'd been right about him hiding something. "Why didn't you move for a better angle?"

He jumped to his feet, his voice angry and loud. "What are you accusing me of, Detective? Do you think I was afraid to shoot?"

She stood and raised her hands. "Don't get defensive. You're a good cop. But I think it's odd you didn't fire a single shot. I'd like to know why."

"I heard the shot and ducked behind my door. I warned Beth to take cover, but she was already firing her gun." He gripped his head and rubbed his temples.

"She's the rookie, and I'm the one cowering. The more years I'm on the force, the more I worry I won't go home at the end of the day. Does that make me a bad cop?"

"I have children. Do you think I want to leave them without a mother? You did the smart thing when you heard the shot."

Rick ran his hands across his face. "If he was an innocent bystander, why did he fire the gun?"

"I don't know. We can't know if it accidentally went off, but a shot was fired. Beth responded." She pointed at the closed door. "The hearing is about what happened and what you thought in the minutes of the shooting. Hindsight doesn't work for a cop. You make the best decision at the time based on the barest facts. Everything happens in a split second, but you can't afford to hesitate."

"By the time I reached Jack Lawson, he was dead." He groaned. "He had to be the robber, but then the chief said he wasn't."

"He had disarmed a bad guy and was mistaken for one. Everyone is assumed innocent only in a court of law. On the streets, we have to suspect everyone is carrying a gun. Everyone wants to kill us. We can't take chances, or we're on the medical examiner's table."

"I keep thinking if only I hadn't yelled gun, he might still be alive."

"We're required to alert others to danger when we see it. The woman posing as Abby Keller put Jack Lawson and Beth on that fatal confrontation. She's the one to blame, and I'm going to find her."

Rick touched her arm. "I know I've said some things that weren't true. I was mad, but I think the chief made the right decision when he picked you. If I were the better choice for detective, I would have taken a closer look at that woman. I don't want your job. I just want her found. I'll be back on active duty once this hearing is over. I'd like to help any way I can."

"I appreciate that."

Chapter Twenty-One

Vivien had made a mistake. She hated public speaking or being in the spotlight. She preferred sharing her emotions through her artwork. Jack had been the public speaker. But her lawyer had insisted she needed to make a personal appearance. The public needed to put a face to the tragedy of her husband's death. A large picture of Jack was placed on a stand to the side of the steps where her lawyer spoke to a group of reporters standing in the yard in front of her home. They had gathered to hear the truth about her husband's death. She nervously fussed with her hair as she stood on the porch next to her mother, who held John-John in her arms. She was doing this for Jack's son.

The lawyer introduced her and signaled her to step forward onto the upper step. Flashes mounted on cameras exploded in bright lights that blinded her. She attempted to step up on the porch, but the lawyer gripped her arm and pulled her to the bottom step closer to the crowd.

"Talk to them."

She unfolded a prepared speech that shook in her trembling hands. Tears blurred the words on the page she had penned last night, and she relied on memory, jamming the paper into her coat pocket. She dabbed at her cheeks and cleared her throat. "The police lied." Vivien's voice trembled. "My husband was an innocent victim, and the police painted him as the villain in their public version of what happened. He was not an armed robber. He has never owned a gun. He was walking home from the drugstore where he bought our son medicine for an ear infection."

She took John-John from her mother and held him so the reporters and audience could see him. His eyes grew wide, and he clung in fear. She patted his back and cooed in his ear before continuing. "My son lost his father Saturday night. The police have made excuses and promoted lies to cover their mistakes."

John-John cried, and tears rolled down Vivien's cheeks in spite of her resolve not to cry. "The detective who visited my home the night Jack was killed didn't tell me who shot him. The police let me assume it was the robber." Vivien cleared her throat. "I had to hear the truth on the news that a police officer killed my husband. He never had a chance. He was a wonderful man, and I'm here to make sure his good name is restored." She looked at her son. "John-John will never know his father. Jack will never have the chance to teach him how to swim or work on a science project together. I can't give him his father back, but I can make sure he never has to be ashamed of his name, John Lawson, Jr."

Camera flashes captured mother and son. John-John wailed, echoing her own fears. She turned to flee, but her lawyer's hand was on her back, holding her firm.

He handed her his handkerchief. "They'll have questions," he whispered in her ear.

She juggled John-John onto her hip and dabbed at the tears on her cheeks.

"What do you plan to do, Mrs. Lawson?" one of the reporters shouted out.

Vivien didn't know. Her lawyer had talked about suing the police department for wrongful death and defamation. She looked at him for guidance.

"For now, Mrs. Lawson must bury her husband and take care of her son. Alone," he added. "We're asking the police department to right this wrong with a public apology, not only by the department but by the police officer responsible. And then there will be their obligation to provide for John-John's future. We cannot put a price on Jack Lawson's life."

More reporters shouted questions. She hadn't expected so many people to be interested in her story. She sorted through the catapult of questions.

"Is it true you're asking for five million dollars in damages?"

Five million? She looked at her lawyer. He hadn't mentioned a dollar amount.

He raised his hand as if to silence the rumble of questions. "Five million?" he demanded. "Mr. Jack Lawson was a successful aerospace engineer at NASA's Glenn Research Center in Cleveland working on the Artemis program and Moon to Mars initiative. His wife and son deserve to be compensated not only for the salary he was earning, but for the potential earnings of his unfulfilled career."

He warmed to his subject. "Mrs. Lawson is a single parent because of the actions of the police department. She must raise her son alone. And more importantly, they robbed the Lawson family of fulfilling their dreams of another child."

Vivien had mentioned a second child when her lawyer had questioned her to prepare his case. They were going to have two children and wanted them close in age.

She had not thought about the unborn child, but to have the reality spoken aloud brought the possibility to a halt. No more children with the man she loved. Her lip trembled.

"The police didn't just take the life of Vivien's husband. They took her future and the future of John-John. As a single parent she will have to work. She will have to leave John-John in the care of strangers while she earns a living for the two of them. She will miss out on those precious moments between a mother and child as she toils to pay the bills."

Vivien fumbled with the handkerchief she clutched in her hand as tears streamed down her face. Was her future as bleak as her lawyer painted? Not only was Jack gone, but another child. Her family dream was broken. As he spoke, her world crumbled to dust.

Chapter Twenty-Two

Beth munched on popcorn as the local news played on the screen. She was stress eating, but she couldn't help it. She'd already finished off a box of cookies and a small pie. It was Wednesday, four days since the shooting and one since the hearing. Her phone rested on the table beside her couch as she waited to hear the verdict of the board. She knew it was too early for the call, but the waiting stretched into an eternity. The chief had said she had to pass a psychological exam to return to active duty but could return to desk duty after the review board finished their work. But what if they found her guilty of wrongdoing?

She was a cop, and shootings were a part of the job. In order to keep the majority of people safe, bad guys needed to be taken off the streets. Some couldn't be reformed. From her experience, a good person could make a mistake they regretted, but an evil person had a difficult time embracing an honest and moral life. Sometimes religion accomplished it, but too many people were con men like her father. He'd been born again so many times he could claim membership in a half dozen churches. As soon as an opportunity arose to tempt him, he fell from grace. Had her family genes dominated her convictions to be a good person? Was she destined to lie to herself and others to justify the means to an unscrupulous end?

She grabbed a handful of popcorn and popped it into her mouth. She had to remain positive, but the little things in life made it harder to deal with the big looming one. Her car had been towed to the repair shop, and the mechanic estimated six hundred dollars for repairs. It would empty her savings. She needed her job. Work would have helped keep her mind off the shooting and the guilt that gnawed away at the image of perfection she had created for herself in spite of her upbringing. But now, alone in her apartment, she couldn't forget Jack Lawson and his grief-stricken family. She'd researched everything she could about them. They had been an ideal family before her error. She reached for more popcorn and froze.

A familiar face appeared on the screen. It was Vivien Lawson standing in front of her home. She wore her hair in a single side braid with a ribbon on the end. She looked like a teenager. She was young and nervous and in pain.

Beth turned up the sound. Vivien's voice broke with emotion, and her body shook. Anyone with a heart was moved. She held her baby, who was terrified of the ordeal. Poor little guy. She comforted him, and the way he responded to her gentle touch revealed that Vivien Lawson, for all her youth and tragedy, was a good mother. The lawyer took center stage and announced they were suing the police department for five million dollars. Would they sue her? She had nothing of value. The reporters hammered questions in a quick staccato. The lawyer answered a few before turning to Vivien.

"I don't care about the money except for John-John." She kissed the baby's cheek, washing it with her tears. The words didn't matter. The emotion was raw and real behind them.

The fake Abby Keller had brought the gun to the alley, but Jack Lawson had it in his hand when Beth had ended his life. Now she had the image of his widow and son scorched into her brain, a picture she wouldn't forget.

"What do you want, Mrs. Lawson, if you don't want the money?"

"Jack was murdered walking home from a drugstore on a rainy night. He was a good man, a loving husband, and devoted father. Our lives were destroyed by a police officer trying to make a name for himself. I want someone to pay for Jack's death. It's the least I can do for my son."

Vivien broke down, sobbing. The mob of reporters shouted out questions in a barrage of noise, and her lawyer took over.

"The police had a hearing on the shooting, but we all know how that will end. The police officer will be acquitted, and there will be no justice for Jack Lawson. But I swear we will expose the truth, and someone will pay for killing an innocent man."

The police department might find her justified in taking a man's life, but Beth couldn't. She turned off the TV and sat in solitude, contemplating her actions. Jack Lawson fit the description of the robber. The gun in his hand had gone off. It had been impossible to know which way the bullet had traveled.

The rationale of not hesitating was drilled into every police cadet. A bad guy with a gun had the advantage and made it imperative for police officers to act as soon as a threat was evident. Rick had yelled, "Gun," and she had aimed her pistol. As soon as she heard the shot, she'd reacted. She played the scene over and over all night, unable to picture a different outcome.

Beth awoke to knocking. The room was bathed in morning light. She had slept on the couch, and her neck ached from the awkward position the hard sofa pillow had created. She had a piece of popcorn in her hair. She checked her phone. It was Thursday morning, and she had several messages she'd missed. Before she could read them, someone pounded harder on her door. She staggered to her feet and peered through the peephole. The woman on the other side was unknown, and Beth left the chain on the door as she opened it to a narrow slit. "What do you want?"

"Are you the police officer who shot and killed John Lawson?"

Beth slammed the door shut and turned the dead bolt. The woman shouted through the locked door that she was a reporter from the local paper and continued with an onslaught of questions. How had she gotten through the entrance and up to the second floor? Beth's heart pounded in her chest, and she gasped for breath. How had they found out her identity? The chief had said her name wouldn't be released to the press unless necessary. She crossed the floor to the window and pulled the curtain aside. Vans and cars were parked in the street. Men and women with cameras and microphones were gathered on the sidewalk and parking lot below her apartment. She'd been exposed. She sank to the floor and rested her head against her bent knees. *Are you the police officer who shot and killed John Lawson?*

She had been to enough press conferences to know the hostility involved. Once newshounds had a bone, they became rabid dogs. They had her name and her address. If she stepped outside her apartment, reporters, like the one at her door, would press forward, shouting questions and demanding answers she couldn't give.

Even if the board exonerated her, the public would condemn her the same as Vivien had in yesterday's press conference.

Crawling below the level of the window, she snatched her purse and retrieved the card Sydney had given her. She dialed her cell phone number.

"Detective Harrison."

"I didn't know who to call. A reporter knocked on my door just now. Others are camped outside my apartment. What should I do?"

"Beth Moreno?"

"Who else would have reporters stalking her?" She was screeching. "How did they find out it was me?"

"Calm down. I'm at home yet. I'll call the chief and see what he knows and call you back."

Beth gathered empty containers and dirty dishes, carefully avoiding the windows. When the phone rang, she dropped a plastic cup, and pop splattered on the floor. She ignored the mess and grabbed the phone.

It was Sydney. "The good news is the review board released their decision."

Bad news always followed good news. "Shouldn't I have been told? What did they say?"

"The chief copied me on the text he sent you. Didn't you get the message?"

She ran her fingers through her greasy spiked hair. "I just woke up. I haven't had time to check my messages."

"They acquitted you of any wrongdoing."

Beth should have felt happy, but the image of Vivien and John-John prevented any rejoicing. Their lives remained ruined.

"Beth? Are you there? Did you hear…"

"Yes, yes. I'm here."

"The chief wants you to come in for desk duty. He's scheduled a press conference at two."

Standing in front of a hostile crowd was the last thing she wanted. "I wasn't planning on coming in to work until three, and my car is in the shop." She looked toward the window.

"The chief has you on day shift while you're on desk duty. I could swing by and take you in."

Maybe having a friend wasn't such a good idea. "How do I get through the mob of press outside? They're all over the parking lot."

"I'll have dispatch send some officers to move the reporters to the sidewalk."

"The sidewalk? How is that going to help?" She crawled back to the window and peered over the sill. The group had grown. She sat against the wall, her heart racing inside her chest. "If the board found me innocent, why are they here? Why won't they leave me alone?"

"Have you seen Vivien Lawson's press interview?"

Beth squeezed her eyes tight to block the image. "She was very sympathetic."

"Reporters like emotional stories. Her picture is on the front page."

"What if mine is on tomorrow's front page?"

"You can't think about that. News runs in cycles. They'll give up when something more exciting comes along."

"How long will that take?"

"We can't let others influence our actions. We can just do our job. When I arrive, I'll call, and you can let me in through the lobby door."

Getting in wasn't the problem. "How are you going to get me out past all the reporters?"

"I'll think of something. I should be there in ten minutes."

Beth looked at her wrinkled clothes and ran her fingers through clumpy hair. "I'll need to shower and dress. Give me thirty minutes."

Chapter Twenty-Three

Sydney shoved her phone into her pants pocket and turned on the television. A local station was broadcasting the scene outside Beth's apartment. Neighbors and curiosity seekers gathered with the reporters who were setting up their equipment in their quest to capture the news.

Crowds were unpredictable. It only took one rabble rouser to turn the scene ugly. Beth had been acquitted, but the community didn't need to accept the verdict, especially with Vivien Lawson on television to remind them of her loss. She had to think of a plan to rescue Beth from her apartment.

"What's wrong, Syd?" Gordon had been listening to her side of the conversation.

"The papers found out Beth was acquitted in the Lawson shooting and want the scoop. The chief is making a formal announcement at two. He wants Beth to come in to work, but reporters are surrounding her apartment."

"I heard you telling her you would pick her up."

"Her car is in the shop." She pointed at the screen where the crowd was surging outside the apartment. "How am I going to get her past all those people?"

"Aren't there two doors in apartment buildings?"

"For safety reasons, but hardly anyone uses the front doors. The cars are in the back."

"She's not driving," he reminded her.

Sydney smiled as she visualized the internal wheels turning in her husband's brilliant mind. "What do you suggest?"

"I think a little sleight of hand is needed in this situation."

Was he joking? "You're going to do magic tricks?"

"My hands are known for magic." He grinned from ear to ear and raised a knowing eyebrow.

His hands had compensated for other shortcomings when they had resumed lovemaking. He had learned to use them in a way that made her tremble in anticipation and remembrance. The memory made her defensive. "You're not performing any magic on Beth."

His warm laughter rose to his eyes as he studied her outfit. "You should change into sweats."

"But I'm going to work."

"Pack a bag. It's early enough in the day that two women going off to the gym shouldn't attract undue attention."

Gordon was right. Even though she wasn't wearing a uniform, her jacket, badge, and equipment belt shouted police. If she was going to get Beth out undetected, sweats might work.

He removed his phone from the bag on his chair. "I'll call Barry. I'll need him to drive."

"I can drive you."

He wheeled his chair toward the bedroom. "You'll be driving the getaway car for Beth."

She followed behind. "Getaway car? Did you have a previous life as a criminal?"

His face lit up with boyish charm. "I have a few secrets from my youth I haven't shared."

She leaned against the doorframe. "I'm intrigued."

"Good. I wouldn't want to become boring to a woman who leads such a colorful life."

Sydney kicked off her shoes and removed her trousers as Gordon talked to Barry on the phone. His heated gaze stayed on her in silent praise as she changed clothes and packed her bag. "Don't you have a meeting at the college?"

"Later." He snapped his fingers. "I'll need Horatio."

"What?" She followed him to his office. "Why are you taking Horatio to a meeting?"

"I'm not taking him to college. He's going with me to Beth's. Horatio never fails to attract attention." He took a towel-wrapped item from his desk.

"A human skull tends to do that."

He examined the adult male skull and scrunched his face in thought. "How do I introduce him to the crowd?"

"You could toss him in and hope someone catches him."

"I would never treat Horatio with such disrespect." Gordon looked around his room. "I'll need my smaller saddlebag for the side of my wheelchair."

"The smaller one?" She examined the leather tote. "The skull will stick out."

"Exactly." He placed the skull in the bag with the face partially exposed in the opening. "What better way to distract from a police officer than a man with a skull?"

"Sometimes your brilliance amazes me." She kissed him, lingering long enough to cause him to want more. "But don't do anything dangerous."

"I am a college professor on my way to work when I stopped to see why a crowd was gathering. Once I have their attention, I'll tell them about my work in anthropology and the study of man's behavior to draw their attention from the apartment. You and Beth can escape out the front and give me a call when you're safely away. I'll conclude my lecture and head to my meeting."

The plan was simple. It could work. "Are you sure you want to do this?"

"According to a wise saying, *the only thing necessary for the triumph of evil is for good men to do nothing.* My job is to inspire young minds to think. It'll be a nice challenge to see if I can convince older ones to examine and understand their behavior."

"I hardly think the minds in that crowd are doing anything cerebral. They're bored."

"Mankind no longer labors to survive. Our lives are filled with foolish pursuits. It takes a crisis to wake us up to what is in danger." He took her hand. "And what makes life important."

Their kiss was interrupted by the doorbell ringing. She opened the door for Barry. "Come in."

He looked beyond her at Gordon. "I thought your meeting at the college was this afternoon, Professor?"

"We have a mission," Gordon said. "How would you like to rescue a fair damsel in distress and slay a ruthless dragon?"

Barry looked at Sydney. "Do you know what he's talking about?"

She shrugged. "He's a romantic. That's one of the reasons I married him."

Gordon grabbed a coat. "I'll explain on the way."

Sydney looked at Barry. "There's a large crowd. Maybe you shouldn't go."

"Nonsense." Gordon winked. "Barry has faced

mobs before."

Barry looked worried as he pushed Gordon outside to the drive. "Is this about the accident?"

"No, it's about a young woman who needs our help," Gordon said. "Where does Beth live?"

Sydney gave Barry the address and headed out first.

The reporters and photographers were camped in the back of Beth's apartment where tenants entered and left the building to reach their vehicles. A police car had arrived, and the officer was moving people out of the parking lot and to the sidewalk.

Sydney drove around the block and positioned her unmarked car on the front side of the apartment building. A young woman was trying the front door but gave up and headed around the side of the building. Sydney called Beth to let her in. The door's lock clicked open, and she made sure the door was secure when it closed.

She ran up the stairs and knocked. After the sounds of a lock turning and a chain sliding free, Beth opened the door. Sydney stepped inside, and Beth bolted the door.

"I don't see how I'm going to leave unnoticed. I should stay home."

The shower had failed to erase the signs of stress on Beth's face. "The review board recommended your reinstatement." She'd be safer at the police department than in her apartment. Sydney surveyed the wreckage. The room, which had been spotless, was cluttered with empty boxes, tissues, and crumpled food bags. Her uniform blouse was misbuttoned.

"Take off your uniform and put on some sweat clothes and sneakers."

Beth looked at herself. "I didn't realize desk duty

was casual."

"You can change into your uniform at the police station." Sydney looked around. "Do you have a gym bag that doesn't have the police name on it?"

Beth stared at Sydney's workout clothes. "We're pretending we're going to the gym." She disappeared into the single bedroom. "Do you think that will fool them?"

"That's only part of the plan." Sydney looked out the rear-facing window, moving the curtain but not showing herself. The crowd below reacted, pointing and shouting at her shadow.

Good. The first distraction. She had called dispatch, and the police officer allowed Barry to pull the van into the parking lot in front of the door. Gordon was good at small details. The vehicle would block the entrance and any view of the hallway that ran from front to back on the main floor.

Barry lowered Gordon on the lift from the van and wheeled him toward the crowd. People reacted two ways to someone in a wheelchair. They either backed silently away as if the person's disability were contagious or were curious about how that person was injured. Gordon talked to the reporters and spectators. Distraction number two.

What was her brilliant husband saying? He could spend hours lecturing on his favorite subject and never lose the attention of his students. Young people valued muscular bodies and pretty faces, but a sharp mind filled with fascinating ideas was a life-long aphrodisiac. Someone pointed at the skull in the bag attached to Gordon's chair. He removed Horatio, and the crowd gathered closer. He had captured his audience's total interest.

"Is this all right?" Beth stood in her doorway in gray sweats. Her short red hair was messy, and she wore no makeup. She lugged a maroon-and-gold gym bag with a bulldog emblem. "I'm having flashbacks to high school."

"Do you have a ball cap?" Her auburn hair would help others identify her.

She smashed a hat onto her head and joined her near the window. "What's your plan?"

"A distraction."

She took a tentative glance. "Is that your husband, Gordon, holding a skull?"

"That is Horatio. He uses him to teach students how to identify whether a skull belongs to a man or woman."

"I remember you said he teaches facial reconstruction."

"Hopefully, in the future. This summer he's teaching aging techniques for missing persons." It was one of his easier courses. "You should take it if you haven't already."

Beth stared at the crowd. "They're getting awfully close. Aren't you afraid for him?"

"Barry would never allow anyone to harm Gordon. You should ask him about their relationship sometime. I think you two have a lot in common."

"Does he come from a dysfunctional family?" She reddened. "I guess everyone thinks their family is the odd one."

"Sometimes they're right." She didn't press her to share more of her personal life and unlocked the door. She looked around before signaling Beth to follow as they crept down the steps.

Sydney blocked her at the bottom. "Let me check first." No one was in front. She opened the door. "My car is across the street."

Chapter Twenty-Four

Beth had changed into her uniform and was tying her shoes when Sydney joined her.

"The chief needs to know about the trouble."

"It was nothing."

Sydney blocked her path. "The chief needs to know everything that happens to his officers. It could save a life or capture a criminal. I know you're a private person, Beth, but everything you do as a police officer is documented and public record."

"I need to work on being more open," she admitted.

They paused outside the chief's office and knocked.

"Come in." He pointed to his computer. "I saw the broadcast in front of your apartment. I tried calling."

"I was flooded with calls, Chief Mills." Beth scanned the list of unknown callers. "And my number is unlisted."

"How did they find out Beth's name and address?" Sydney demanded.

"A clerk in the courts leaked the information," the chief said. "She's being reprimanded."

"One of the reporters got inside Beth's apartment and knocked on her door."

"I'm all right." Beth felt calmer wearing her uniform and surrounded by people who supported her. "I was going a bit stir crazy waiting for the hearing verdict. She took me by surprise."

"Do you still plan to have a press conference at two?" Sydney asked.

"Yes, I'd like both of you to be there."

"Are you sure?" Beth's calmness turned to panic. "I won't know what to say."

"You won't say anything. But I won't have the news agencies intimidating my officers. I'll make a statement and remind them we're looking for the armed robber."

"I think we should invite Vivien to the press conference," Sydney said.

"Are you crazy?" Beth's voice was an octave too high. "She hates me."

"Officer Moreno is right," the chief said. "Her lawyer is out for blood, and he knows how to garner sympathy."

"We need to reach out the olive branch at some point," Sydney said.

"Not in front of the public."

Beth agreed with the chief. Vivien wasn't ready to heal. Her wounds were raw and oozing with pain like her own. How long would it take Vivien to forgive Beth for taking her husband's life? Never. Beth's hands trembled in her lap. How long would it take to forgive herself? She wished she knew.

Beth followed Sydney to her office. The detective bureau consisted of rows of filing cabinets along one wall and two desks facing another two. Three of the desks were assigned. She took the empty one. "What do you have for me to work on?"

"The chief wants you to review a cold case about a couple found dead in the park ten years ago," Sydney said. "I was working on it before this happened. The file was scanned into the system, but I think DNA evidence may be found with new technology on the clothing from the victims. I need you to retrieve the original box of evidence from the Nile crypt."

"The Nile crypt?"

"That's what we call the basement. It floods every time we have a heavy rain. Don't tell me you've never been down there?"

"I remember it from my initial tour. It was cold, damp, and scary."

Sydney wrote a name and number on a piece of paper. "The case number is 20090054128." She added four numbers. "This is the code to the door. Watch out for the crocodiles."

Beth gasped before she saw Sydney's smile. "I'm new and just gullible enough to believe you."

"I thought a little humor would put you at ease. You looked nervous."

Sydney was good at reading people, which was scary for someone with secrets to hide. She took a deep breath to steady herself. "I'm grateful for the distraction." The case would keep her mind occupied. For a little while.

After going up and down rows of shelving, Beth finally located the evidence box. Her personal phone rang, and she answered without looking. "I found it, Sydney."

"Sydney? This is your mother. You haven't called in so long you don't even know me." The cigarette-damaged voice still had a razor-sharp edge to its coldness.

Beth closed her eyes and counted. She should have looked at the caller's ID. Now it was too late. "It's really not a good time, Mother. Reception isn't good," she lied.

"I can hear you fine. I saw your photo and name on the news, Lizzy. How could you shoot an innocent man?"

"I can't talk about the case, Mother. It's under investigation."

"Are they going to arrest you?" Her voice sounded gleeful.

She paced along the row framed by the shelving, counting down her anger. "No, I'm on desk duty."

"Well, it's only a matter of time before they throw you to the wolves. How could you shoot an astronaut?"

What was she talking about? "He wasn't an astronaut."

"They said he worked for NASA."

Sydney had said Jack Lawson was an engineer working on a space project. "Not everyone who works for NASA is an astronaut."

"Someone is going to have to pay, and Morenos are always at the top of the cops' list. You better come home."

Was she crazy? "I'm not coming home."

"We can hide you."

"I'm not a fugitive."

"Don't be a fool, Lizzy. You can't count on those cops to have your back."

She shouted into the phone, "When did you care what happened to me?"

"We're family."

She only included her in the brood for one reason. "You need money."

Alice exhaled a long sigh. "Fred is in jail. If you could pay his bail, we would gladly hide you in the old cellar."

"Where Bubba cooks meth? I'm not paying Father's bail."

Her voice changed from desperate to angry. "Then I hope they throw you in jail, you ungrateful child."

Beth hung up. She counted to four before the phone rang again. Her mother was calling back. She hadn't finished gloating.

Beth muted her phone and stuck it in her pant leg pocket, trying to block out her mother's hateful words, but they were like daggers into her heart, bleeding any love she could muster for the only family she knew. She had hoped to impress her parents with good grades, a respectable job, and hard work. But they valued shortcuts. She had strived to rise above their sordid life, but what had it gotten her?

She hoisted the box but didn't have a good grip, and it fell to the floor. She sank next to it and let her depression wash over her. She felt like a second victim of the woman in the alley. The mystery woman had destroyed her life.

Beth didn't let her pity party last long. She gathered her emotions into the protective shell where she had learned to store them and hoisted the box. She tromped up the stairs and saw Officer Sam Wilson seated on the top step. She had met him at roll call where assignments were given out to each officer. He had been the driver of the second cruiser to arrive at the scene of the shooting.

"Hello. Are you looking for me?"

"I wanted to talk to you."

Suspicion was her first reaction. "Why?" She passed him. "The review board found me innocent of any wrongdoing."

"You didn't make a mistake." He jumped to his feet

and followed her. "Hey, I screwed up that night by letting the armed robber escape."

"She snuck away," Beth corrected. "At least you didn't kill a man."

"I've killed plenty of men."

She froze and turned to face him. His face didn't look so young anymore. He wasn't joking. "What do you mean?"

"I'm in the Ohio Army National Guard."

She shrugged and started walking. "That's different."

"Not as different as you think." He grabbed the box.

"Careful. That's evidence."

"You obeyed your training as a cop. There was a threat, and you neutralized it."

"Jack Lawson wasn't a *real* threat." She took the box. "I killed an innocent man who made a mistake. I feel like crap."

"Every trial in our life makes us a different person. Sometimes better. Sometimes worse. It's our choice. I just finished another tour. I can never be the Sam Wilson I was before fighting in the war. You'll never be the same Beth Moreno you were before Jack Lawson's death."

Is that why she felt like a stranger? But what if she didn't like the new Beth Moreno?

Chapter Twenty-Five

Sydney had tracked down every woman who had an arm injury in the area. None of them had been the mystery woman. It had been five days since the shooting, and she was no closer to discovering the identity of her robber. Every hospital and medical facility on her list had been contacted. The woman had escaped without any way to find her.

She listened to the messages on her office phone. Lydia, a technician in radiology at Olde Bend Hospital, said she had a case that fit the description of the injury. Sydney called her back.

"A woman came in Tuesday with an injury to her arm and wrist like the one you described," Lydia said.

"Tuesday," Sydney repeated. That was three days after the incident. "Did she say how she injured her arm?"

"The report says she fell in a parking lot. She was scraped up and still bleeding when she came in."

"My woman was injured Saturday." She almost disconnected. "Do you have her name?"

She heard clicking on a keyboard. "Her name was Abby Keller."

Sydney wanted to do a happy dance, but the fake name didn't solve her identity problem. "I believe that's the woman I'm looking for. I'll be over in half an hour."

She didn't take any chances and contacted the real

Abby Keller who swore she was uninjured. The mystery woman had waited to be treated, but she'd made a mistake. She'd used Abby's fake identity again.

Sydney called the hospital's director to clear any red tape. He assured her they would cooperate with her investigation. She left a note for Beth who was still in the crypt and headed for Olde Bend Hospital.

Dr. Viola Parks met her at the main entrance and escorted her through the maze of hallways to the radiology department. A woman with the name *Lydia* and *radiology technician* printed below her picture name tag was searching on her computer.

"I talked to you on the phone," Sydney said. "Do you have the information on a woman named Abby Keller?"

Lydia scrolled through the screens and pointed at the information. "She was treated for a broken arm Tuesday morning."

The robbery was Saturday night, but she'd known not to visit an emergency room right away or seek help at the nearby Newtown Hospital. The woman was clever, but Sydney liked challenges. The information on the screen matched Abby's driver's license. "Do you remember what the woman looked like?"

"She was a mess," Lydia said, looking at the doctor.

"You spent more time with her. I only remember that she'd been crying, and all her makeup was smeared down her face," Viola said.

"I offered wipes to clean her face, but she said the alcohol would dry her skin," Lydia said.

She was worried about dry skin? Officer Wilson had described the lack of makeup on the woman in his cruiser. She was hiding her identity this time behind an abundance of cosmetics. "Can you describe anything about her appearance to help me identify her?"

"Her hair was real," Lydia said.

"Real? How do you know?"

"This is radiology. We do cancer treatments. A lot of the women wear wigs. Her hair was brown, shoulder length with a blunt cut. The color matched her eyebrows, so I'd bet it was her natural color. And her eyes were brown."

Medium-length brown hair. The same as Abby's photo ID before she cut it. "What can you tell me about her injuries?"

"She had a serious case of road rash," Lydia said. "The woman said she'd fallen at the convenience store down the road. She was wearing a short skirt and heels when she did a belly slide across the pavement. A nurse cleaned her up and bandaged her knee."

Sydney nodded. "What did her right hand and arm look like?"

"Swollen, but it takes time for fluids to swell around an injury, and the bruising was yellow and purple like the injury had taken place days earlier."

"I can tell you about the bones." Viola turned to Lydia. "Can you put the x-rays on the viewer?"

The computer image was enlarged on a screen on the wall. "She had a fracture in the wrist and another above it in the radius." Viola showed Sydney where a white line marked the breaks.

Sydney pointed at a mark above her elbow. "What's this line?"

"That's an old break," Viola said. "You can see the calcium build up, so it's been a couple of years since she broke it."

Was she a victim of abuse? "Did she have any other injuries?"

"Just the scrapes on her skin," Lydia said.

How was an x-ray going to help her identify her mystery woman? "Did you notice anything more about her?"

"I think she worked at a hospital," Lydia said.

Abby worked at the Newtown Hospital where her pills and wallet were stolen. Was she right about an employee being the thief? "How do you know?"

"She asked how long it would take the radiologist to read the x-rays. Most patients think I read them. She could have just been familiar with our procedures, though. I'm sorry I can't be more helpful."

This mystery woman could be the person she was looking for, but she had no name. She studied the x-ray. "Is there a way to find out if you treated this woman for the previous break?"

"I could search our records," Lydia said. "It'll take some time."

Sydney looked at Viola. "It's important." She had studied every video taken by the police at the scene of the shooting for any hint to the identity of the mystery woman, but she had kept her head lowered and hidden by her hood. The dash camera inside Sam's cruiser had caught a portion of her face when she turned back, but it was dark, and raindrops blurred the image. Her best bet for discovering the mystery woman's real identity was from the hospital. They kept meticulous records, and hopefully, the woman had used her real name for the past injury.

"Make it a priority," Viola told Lydia.

"I'd appreciate it. Could you send the x-ray to

Newtown Hospital and ask them to check as well?"

"Do you want us to send it to the orthopedic doctors in the area?" Viola asked.

"Yes. I'm desperate for a lead. I need to find out what her real name is." Sydney handed her cards to Lydia and Viola. "Call me as soon as you find anything."

Sydney checked the convenience store on her way back to the station. The parking lot was small with a raised sidewalk that ran the length of the storefront. The curb was high. Someone not looking could step off, stumble because of misjudging the distance, and tumble on the dirty asphalt. It was perfect for staging an accident and close enough to the hospital to drive the distance even with an injury.

But the clerk on duty didn't remember the mystery woman. "I wasn't working the early shift on Tuesday."

"Do you have the phone number of the store's manager?"

She called and asked for the name and number of the morning clerk and any videos from the store.

He agreed to send the videos, but the only camera working was above the cash register. She disconnected. Every lead to discovering the identity of Abby Keller's imposter had been thwarted. She checked the time. She'd be back at the station in time for the press conference. Yeah. Her luck was holding on bad.

Chapter Twenty-Six

Vivien stared at the news coverage as she helped John-John stack colorful rings on a plastic pole. The police were going to make an announcement at a press conference. The camera scanned a crowd of reporters, photographers, and the public gathered outside on the porch of City Hall. Why hadn't she been notified? The lawyer had warned that if the media lost interest in her story, it would be harder to win her case, but her husband's death was still newsworthy. Strangers were demanding justice for Jack while she sat at home, but it was too late for her to drive to the station. She turned up the sound.

Police Chief Kyle Mills stood at a podium. A row of officers formed a blue line behind the chief. Detective Sydney Harrison stood next to another woman. She had seen her photo on the news. The short red hair was badly cut or growing out. It had to be Officer Elizabeth Moreno, her husband's killer.

"She shouldn't be a police officer," Vivien said to John-John, who stared back and babbled a few sounds in response before chewing on a plastic ring. He was getting another tooth. Vivien wiped a long line of drool with the bib he wore. She turned to the television and focused on the chief who was speaking.

"Although many officers were present in the pursuit of an armed robber, only one officer fired the shots that struck and killed John Lawson."

"Wasn't John Lawson an innocent bystander?" a reporter shouted out.

"John Lawson was caught in circumstances no one could have predicted," the chief said. "The armed robber was fleeing down the same alley that John Lawson was using to return home after purchasing medicine for his sick son. We believe the robber was a drug addict looking for cash and pills."

A drug addict? How could they mistake her husband for a drug addict? And where was this robber? Or was it a ruse to give the public a different villain? Vivien grabbed a notepad and wrote down several sentences to remind her what she should ask her lawyer.

"We believe the armed robber pointed the gun at John Lawson and was planning to rob him when the gun was knocked to the ground. John Lawson picked up the gun, most likely to prevent the robber from retrieving it."

Was the chief telling the truth or weaving another story?

"Two officers arrived at the scene. Officer Beth Moreno ordered John Lawson to turn around and face them."

Beth Moreno. Killer Beth.

"Another officer saw a revolver in his hand. He perceived a threat and shouted a warning. He ordered John Lawson to drop his weapon, but the gun was discharged instead. Officer Moreno reacted and fired her pistol."

The chief paused before continuing. "The officers had limited information at the time of the confrontation. They were looking for an armed robber in that area. They discovered two people in a dark alley. One was on the ground, and the other, John Lawson, had a gun in his possession. Officer Moreno responded appropriately to the situation."

"Isn't she guilty of murder?" a reporter shouted.

Vivien pointed at the screen. "Absolutely!"

"What about taking her badge away?" another reporter demanded.

"Officer Moreno and other witnesses gave their testimony in front of an independent board that reviews all officers who discharge a weapon. They came back with a unanimous decision that Officer Moreno is innocent of any wrongdoing and acted reasonably in the circumstances presented when confronted with an armed man. We look forward to having her back on the force."

Chief Mills turned and ushered the other officers to leave ahead of him. The reporters continued to shout out questions.

"Back on the force?" Vivien shouted at the television. John-John shrieked, and she picked him up. "How can they put a gun in her hand after she murdered your daddy?"

She carried him into his room and began dressing him for a trip. She debated whether to take John-John to her mother's house, but she would try talking her out of confronting the police and tell her to let her lawyer handle it. But he was more interested in his share of any money she might be awarded than seeking justice. He should have informed her about the press conference. She had a right to confront her husband's killer.

She put on her jacket and grabbed her purse and a small diaper bag. It was no longer the time for words. She wanted action. "We're going to make sure *Killer Beth* never serves on any police force again."

Vivien's drive downtown only raised her agitation, especially when a driver cut her off. She was in the mood for a fight. Some of the reporters and public were gathered outside the police station, wrapping up their broadcast, when she joined them. "Do you know who I am?"

A reporter waved at his cameraman to move in closer. "You're Vivien Lawson."

"That's right. I'm here to demand justice for my husband. Chief Mills admits Officer Moreno shot and killed my husband, but will anyone pay for his death? This phony board found her not guilty of any wrongdoing, but do you want them to return her gun and badge? This is a mockery of justice. My husband is dead, and no one is at fault? My life is destroyed while she can return to work and continue her life as if nothing has happened. Let's hope she doesn't repeat her mistake. Her next victim may be someone you love." She turned and entered the police station. She strode to the front desk and asked for the chief.

"I'll see what I can do." The clerk talked on the phone and met her gaze. "He's agreed to see you, but the others will have to wait outside." He pointed behind her.

Vivien turned. Some of the reporters and photographers had followed her inside. "Please, wait outside." They didn't budge.

An officer stepped forward. "You'll have to move outside." He waited for the press to leave the building before he turned to Vivien. "Please follow me."

The officer led her down the hallway to the chief's office. He knocked and opened the door. The chief stood and greeted her.

She took a seat and settled John-John on her lap. "Is

Officer Moreno here?"

He hesitated before sitting. "Yes, she is."

She leaned forward. "I'd like to talk to her."

He surveyed her as if he hadn't heard correctly. "I'm not sure that would be a good idea."

"I'm not armed, Chief Mills, and I have a baby." She searched the diaper bag for a toy and handed a set of plastic keys to John-John. "I only wish to talk. I think I deserve that much after what happened to my husband."

He paused before rising. "Wait here."

John-John was fussing. Vivien stood and bounced him on her hip as she walked around the room, studying the photographs on the wall. She searched the faces in the group identified by the year the photo was taken. She saw Beth's face in the last group. She checked the previous class. Beth wasn't there. She had only been on the force for a year. She was a rookie. She searched the other photographs for Detective Harrison. She was in uniform in the previous year's photograph and in plain clothes in the current one. She hadn't been a detective for long. Had she mishandled the case? Was her investigation the reason Beth was innocent of any wrongdoing? She turned at the sound of footsteps.

Chief Mills entered with Detective Harrison behind him. No one else entered. "Where's Officer Moreno?"

"She's unavailable," the chief explained.

"Is Beth Moreno a rookie officer?"

"She graduated top of her class at the police academy and has been on the force for nearly a year."

"She shouldn't be on the force at all." She turned to Sydney. "And you haven't been a detective for long, either. Are there any competent officers in this town?"

"There's no call for that, Mrs. Lawson," the chief

said. "Our officers are fully trained and doing the best they can."

"Your best got my husband killed. My lawyer said the robber walked away. Have you arrested him? I want to know what you're doing about my husband's murder."

"Why don't we update you on the case?" the chief suggested.

"Update? Didn't you say everything at your press conference?"

"We left out some information, and we ask that you don't repeat it to the press. It would make it more difficult to find the person responsible for your husband's death. I said there were two people in the alley—your husband and a woman."

"A woman?" She searched her memory. They hadn't used gender when describing the robber. "The robber was female? How could Officer Moreno mistake my husband for her?"

"The elderly lady who was robbed at the bus stop only saw the gun and a person wearing dark clothing running away into the alley. That was the description from dispatch," Sydney said. "When the police arrived on the scene in the alley, a woman in a yellow poncho was on the ground begging for her life."

"Jack would never hurt anyone, let alone a woman."

"I believe you," Sydney said. "Your husband was a good man."

Vivien hugged her baby, her reply muffled with a sob. "My husband is a dead man."

"We're not sure of all the details, but we know she dumped the stolen purse in a dumpster and likely changed from a black poncho to a yellow one before confronting your husband in the alley."

"Then why didn't the police shoot her?" Her heart raced, and her breathing was labored as her voice rose in volume. "It had to be her gun. I told you Jack didn't own one."

"At the scene I found a broken gutter. I believe the woman was pointing a gun at your husband, possibly to rob him, but the gutter snapped from the rainwater in it and likely hit the woman's arm. We know she was injured. She dropped the gun, and your husband picked it up. It's the most logical explanation for why he was armed."

"He hates guns."

"He couldn't let her have it," Sydney said. "She could have shot him."

She was right. Once Jack had stepped between two rowdy youths and a woman they were harassing. One of the boys pulled a knife, but Jack never budged. He stood up to the bullies, and they ran off. That was Jack. A mild-mannered hero who had picked up a gun to protect himself and others.

"I think she was setting your husband up for the crime," Sydney said.

"How?"

"She was in a position to see the police cruiser enter the alley. They pulled up quietly, and your husband had his back to the car and didn't see it. She shouted, 'Don't shoot me,' and stayed down on the ground, crying and acting as if he was threatening her. When the police ordered him to turn around, they saw the gun."

"But it was her gun." A choke caught in her throat. "It was her gun."

Sydney touched her arm. "We know that now, but put yourself in Officer Moreno's shoes. She's responding to a call about an armed robber. She enters a dark alley and sees a man standing over a woman begging for her life. When she orders him to turn around, her partner sees a gun in his hand. When he's ordered to drop it, the gun goes off."

"We believe the gun your husband was holding discharged accidently, but it was dark, and the officers had no way of knowing he wasn't aiming at them," the chief said. "They reacted to the gunshot."

Vivien fought back the tears. She wasn't going to cry. She jerked her arm away from Sydney's comforting touch. "I understand the excuses, but Jack is still dead. How do I live without him?"

"I don't know."

"I'm sorry." Beth Moreno stood in the doorway.

"You." Vivien struggled to stand, but the weight of John-John made her stumble.

Beth reached forward to help.

She clutched him to her chest. "Don't touch my son!"

Beth froze, a look of horror on her young face. "I'm sorry for what happened. If I could take back that night, I would."

She steeled herself against any sympathy. "I don't forgive you, *Killer Beth*."

Beth said nothing. She looked like a kicked dog. Her eyes had circles beneath them. Good. She hadn't slept either.

"I understand you made a mistake, but you ruined my life. You ruined my son's life. You can't make that right."

"No, I can't." A tear trickled down Beth's cheek.

The chief stood. "Do you have anything else to say

to Officer Moreno?"

Vivien couldn't remember all the words she had practiced in the car, but it didn't matter. Nothing she said would make her feel better. Jack was dead. Beth Moreno had shown remorse, but it didn't dull the ache in her heart. "I'm afraid I've wasted everyone's time. I wanted justice, but there is none."

"Justice is only part of the healing process," Sydney said. "There comes a point when we have to forgive the person who wronged us, or it becomes an obsession of destruction."

Vivien slumped in her chair, clutching her son. "If Jack were alive, I'm sure he'd find it in his heart to forgive Officer Moreno, but he's dead, and I can't show any mercy." She stared at Beth. "I want you to suffer as much as I have. For as long as I will."

"Believe me, I will," Beth said with pain in her voice.

The chief waved at Beth. "You're dismissed."

Vivien gathered her bags as she adjusted John-John on her hip.

"Let me help you," Sydney offered.

She handed her the diaper bag. "I'm not a bad person."

"I know that. Neither is Beth Moreno."

"You don't understand. I can't forgive her for what she did." She pulled John-John close. "I don't even know how this will affect my baby. Our lives are turned upside down because of a bad decision."

"I was in a similar situation."

Her voice dripped with sarcasm. "She shot *your* husband?"

"No, I told you a young man ran over him with his

car."

"But he survived."

"Yes, you saw him on television in front of Beth Moreno's apartment."

She recalled the broadcast. "Who? There was a crowd."

"The man in the wheelchair is my husband, Gordon Blackwood."

"The crazy man with the skull?" Had she called her husband crazy?

Sydney laughed. "He has been called eccentric by a few."

"Was the young man who hit him caught?"

"Yes. He was hiding in his dorm room when the police arrested him."

She sighed. "You got justice, and your husband is alive."

"But he nearly died, so I understand your anger. They say time will heal all wounds, but it isn't time that heals. It's what you do during that time."

"Then I'll use my time to seek revenge."

"I wanted revenge, too." Sydney followed her down the hall. "I wanted that young man to rot in jail. I didn't care who he was or why he had fled. I wanted him to pay for crippling my husband."

She stopped, and Sydney nearly collided with her. "Did he go to jail? Did he pay?"

"He was sentenced to two years' probation. No jail time. It was a lenient sentence for someone who had almost killed another human being."

"Then you understand why I want Officer Moreno to pay."

"The woman in the alley is responsible for your

husband's death."

"Have you arrested her?"

Sydney hesitated. "She gave false information to the officer at the scene, but I'm working on finding the woman and charging her with murder for her role in Jack's death."

"How? She didn't shoot Jack."

"No, but in Ohio it's murder to purposely cause the death of another. She used a gun to rob an elderly woman and then caused Jack's death when he picked up the same gun. I'm building a case against her."

She put John-John into his car seat and took the diaper bag from Sydney. "Nothing against your abilities as a detective, but my lawyer will pursue every avenue to make Officer Moreno and the police department pay for my loss."

"You do what you feel is right, but you can always change your mind."

Vivien sat in her car and watched Sydney cross the parking lot to the station. No amount of money or retribution would bring Jack back. But what would heal her broken heart?

Chapter Twenty-Seven

Claire had made it through Wednesday's shift, but she was struggling Thursday night. Road rash wasn't a serious injury, but the healing process pulled and tugged on her skin with every movement, especially her knees.

She had taken her prescription medicine orally as directed so the time release would help dull the pain, but it wasn't working. She needed to snort some pills to make it through the night. Second shift would leave soon, and she could sneak off to inhale some instant relief.

She pushed a cart into the registration area and overheard Abby talking to a nurse in her booth. "The detective called me at home and told me someone used my insurance card at Olde Bend Hospital."

A new patient interrupted the conversation, and the nurse headed toward Claire. She lowered her voice. "Abby has a new story. She's told it to everyone within ten feet of her. Keep your distance."

"Thanks for the warning." Claire waited until Abby finished registering the man, scanned the area for other staff, and joined her. "You look frazzled, Abby. I bet you can't wait for your shift to end and go home."

"It's been a nightmare. Remember that detective who came in Saturday night?"

"Sydney Harrison?"

"That's her name!" Abby grinned. "How do you do

that, Claire? I'm so bad at remembering names. Do you have some sort of trick you use?"

She ignored her silly question. She needed information. "What did Detective Harrison want?"

"She called me at home to ask if I'd been in an accident. Do I look hurt? I told her nothing was wrong with me. Then she asked if I had gone to Olde Bend Hospital. Why would I go there? If I'm sick, I go here. My doctor has offices on the second floor."

"Why did she think you were injured?"

"Someone used my insurance card at Olde Bend Hospital. Can you believe that?"

"Did I hear right? Someone used your ID *again*?" She added outrage to her question. "That's just awful, Abby."

"I know. I had to go down to the police station and fill out a police report, too. The police officer was really nice, but he asked so many questions. He wanted to know my phone number. I thought he was too old for me, but maybe he'll call."

Did she think the officer was making a date? "They always take your phone number."

"Really? He said I should call my insurance company and let them know about the identity theft. It took me twenty minutes to get through to them. I had to answer a million more questions. When I asked if I would have to pay the bills, they said no. But how do I know they're telling the truth? They said they would issue a new card with a different number, but what if I get sick before it arrives?"

"I'm sure you'll be fine," Claire reassured her. "Did they say anything about the person using your card?"

"Detective Harrison said someone came in with a

broken wrist and skinned knees claiming to be me. I wrecked my bike once and had gravel in my knees, but I was ten. What adult woman skins her knees?"

"Maybe she was drunk," Claire offered.

She gasped. "I bet you're right. I hope she doesn't use my ID again. I thought it was exciting for someone wanting to be me, but now it's scary. I'm glad I live with my parents."

"They'll take care of you." Claire left Abby to her ramblings. She'd have to destroy Abby's ID and insurance card later that night. Sydney was hot on her trail. How much time did she have before she figured out her identity? She'd been treated at Olde Bend Hospital after the accident that had killed Danny Boy. Would they be able to match her old records to the new one? She had used different names, and the injuries were unconnected. She had eluded Sydney so far. She could do it for a few more days.

She couldn't panic, but she needed an escape plan. Her paycheck wouldn't hit her bank account until next Friday, but if she didn't pay her rent or bills, she could withdraw the existing balance in cash.

She was scheduled to work through Saturday and could leave town on Sunday without anyone missing her for several days. But what if Detective Sydney Harrison figured out her identity before that? She'd have to watch the news to keep track of any developments. Reporters didn't care if they revealed sensitive information if it garnered ratings. If the police had a suspect, the media would announce it.

Claire glanced at the clock. She'd never make it to midnight. She needed the comfort of her pills now.

Chapter Twenty-Eight

Beth's image had been broadcast on the local channel and digital online news along with the story of the Lawson shooting. She had avoided going out in public, but her cupboards were bare like in the proverbial Mother Hubbard nursery rhyme. She wore jeans, a sweatshirt, and a baseball cap as she bought her groceries Friday after working day shift. She filled her cart, following her list of items that would last at least two weeks. She reached for the cans of baked beans on the top shelf, but they were pushed back and out of her grasp.

"Let me help you with that." The man was taller and easily grabbed two cans. "Is that enough?"

"Yes, thank you." Beth met his gaze for the briefest moment before taking the cans and putting them with her groceries. When she pushed the cart, he blocked her path.

"Aren't you that cop on television?"

"What?" She backed up and turned her cart in the opposite direction. "You're mistaken."

She increased her pace as she scratched off more items on her list. She had missed the aisle for coffee but wasn't going back and risk running into someone who might recognize her. She glanced around, looking for the man she had seen earlier. He was near the stacks of canned beverages, talking to a woman while scrolling on his phone.

Don't act paranoid. He's probably comparing

prices.

She finished with butter and eggs and turned the corner to head out through the self-service checkouts when she saw the man again. This time he had a group of people around him, and they blocked her path. Had they been waiting for her?

The man pointed his finger at her. "You're Beth Moreno, the cop who shot that innocent man, the one with the young wife and baby."

"It is her!" A woman lifted her phone to record her.

Beth froze. The checkouts and exit doors were beyond them. She moved her cart forward, but no one moved out of the way to allow her to pass.

"Murderer," someone called out.

"That poor woman lost her husband because of you!"

Their shouts attracted other shoppers who turned and stared. She needed to diffuse the situation and disperse the angry mob before the threat multiplied. But without her uniform, she was a lone woman. Without her weapons, she had to rely on words.

"Let me by, please," Beth said in her calmest voice. She sounded scared to her own ears. She prayed they didn't detect the fear.

A burly man stepped forward. He wore a bulky jacket, and she wondered if he was carrying a weapon. Ohio laws were lenient about carrying a gun, open or concealed. He took a stance and brushed back his coat enough to reveal a pistol in a holster under his armpit. "What are you going to do? Shoot me?"

Did he think this was the Wild West? She didn't have a weapon. She wasn't going to engage anyone in a gun battle.

Others gathered to discover what was causing the commotion. "What's going on?"

A woman pointed. "That's the cop who shot that poor man buying medicine for his sick baby. I saw her on television."

"Are you sure? She doesn't look like a cop."

Another person shared Beth's image on her phone. "See. It's her!"

Beth looked around, searching for a friendly face. Even a store employee in a blue apron was siding with the rowdy customers, standing with them instead of breaking up the crowd. Her phone was in her purse, and she debated whether to call the police but didn't want to escalate the tension already sparking the crowd. She pushed her cart forward, trying to find an opening, but the wall of bodies had grown two and three thick, and no one was stepping aside. She no longer wanted the groceries. She needed to get away, to escape to safety.

The group moved closer, surrounding her and invading her personal space. One of them lifted the egg carton from her cart, opened it, and dumped the contents on the floor. "Oops. That was an *accident* like you shooting an innocent man."

Someone else laughed. "She certainly is *accident* prone."

"Be careful, she may *accidentally* run us over with her cart."

"Move aside!" she commanded.

A few jumped backward at the sound of the authority in her voice, but others grabbed items in her cart. Someone threw a can that struck her in the shoulder. She turned to identify the culprit. He threw another, hitting her in the chest and knocking the air from her lungs.

The burly man laughed. "Not so tough now without your gun."

Beth refused to cry. Her family had trained her how to hide pain and emotional abuse. She gathered her purse against her chest where it throbbed from the bruise. An egg hit the side of her face, broke, and slid down onto her sweatshirt. Several people laughed. Others moved closer, their faces grim. She was alone against an angry throng.

"Hey, what's going on here?" demanded an employee in a white shirt and tie. He stared at the employee in the blue apron for an explanation.

"They said she was the cop who shot that man…"

Beth took the distraction as an opportunity to abandon her cart and rushed forward between the two employees and away from the mob. She smacked into a bag-filled cart, spinning away as she apologized to the startled customer. She broke into a run when she reached the sliding exit doors and dashed outside.

She ran all the way to her car, searching blindly with her fingers for the keys in her purse and unlocking the door before she reached it. She slumped into the driver's seat and locked all the doors. She glanced in the rearview mirror and turned her head, wondering if anyone had followed her outside. A few people were heading her way. Were they members of the group that had attacked her earlier? She turned the key, and the repaired vehicle roared to life. She said a quick prayer of thanks to the mechanic who had fixed it and backed out. She turned in the opposite direction, gunning the accelerator.

After circling her apartment building for reporters and finding none, she parked her car in the lot and ran upstairs. Beth fumbled with the keys before finding the correct one and turning the knob. As soon as she was inside, she secured the locks and leaned against the door. Her heart was pounding, but she forced her body to relax by deep breathing. Her apartment looked as she had left it, neat and orderly from hours cleaning last night when sleep had eluded her. She put her purse on the counter and opened the refrigerator. The milk carton was nearly empty. Her bag of bread was down to two slices. Her cupboards were still bare. She would have to ration food until she worked up the courage to venture out in public again. Maybe she could have groceries delivered but not today. Some cops enjoyed danger and excitement, but she had joined to restore peace and order in a world that turned to violence to solve problems. She had wanted to connect with the community and show that police officers were trusted friends in a time of need. No one was going to ask for her help now.

After looking outside for any strangers roaming the grounds, she closed the drapes and checked the door locks again. She sat in the dark, waiting for her heartbeat to return to a steady pace. She had a full laundry basket of dirty clothes in the bedroom but didn't dare go to the basement where she might run into another tenant. Hunger pains forced her to order a pizza under an alias. She let the delivery boy in the building and had the money and tip ready when he knocked on the door. She kept the encounter brief, and thankfully, he didn't recognize her.

She glanced at the card of the psychiatrist she was scheduled to see on Monday, but she didn't want to talk to him before then. He'd ask about her family or the shooting, and both topics made her uncomfortable. She'd have to lie to hide the hurt and pain festering inside. And what if she said something that made the doctor refuse to approve her return to the force? She couldn't risk losing her job. She would have to figure out the right thing to say over the weekend to convince the doctor she was well. But she was a Moreno, and as her mother often reminded her, blood would tell.

After eating a slice of pizza, Beth turned on the television. She was on the news again. The confrontation at the grocery store was playing on the screen. Everyone was laughing at her. How would she face anyone again? She clicked it off. Could her life get any worse?

Her phone rang, and she looked at the caller identification. It was her mother. Perfect. She could let it ring, but her mother was persistent. She'd keep calling until Beth answered. She had probably seen the latest video and wanted to gloat. "Hello, Mother."

"What are you doing home? Shouldn't you be in jail?" Her loud cackle forced Beth to move the phone away from her ear.

"It's good to hear how much you care, Mother."

"You're an ungrateful child."

"When did I have the opportunity to be grateful? Should I thank you for the hand-me-downs from Angel and whatever food Bubba didn't scarf down when you were sober enough to cook a meal? I lived in shame from the poverty I had no control over. I worked hard to escape it."

"Shame? None of us disgraced the family name like you."

The Moreno name? Was she serious? "I didn't do anything wrong."

"That's not what the news video shows. An innocent

person doesn't run out of a grocery store. Why weren't you in uniform? Were you wearing a disguise?" She cackled before morphing into a coughing fit.

Anger made her defend her actions. "I worked all day and changed into something comfortable when I got home before buying a few groceries. If I was in uniform, they'd be in jail for assaulting an officer."

"Why didn't you shoot them like you did that poor man?" Her mother didn't pull any punches.

"It was an accidental shooting. I've been cleared." She knew she'd never persuade her mother of her innocence, so who was she trying to convince?

Beth set the phone on the table after turning it to mute. Her mother would keep calling. She lifted a slice of pizza and dropped it. She'd lost her appetite.

Chapter Twenty-Nine

Sydney headed to the convenience store where the fake Abby had received her injuries. The clerk who had waited on her had finally returned her calls. He was working the evening shift and could meet her at the store. He was seated behind the counter, scrolling his phone. She detected a strong odor of marijuana on his clothes. No wonder he had been hesitant to talk to the police.

She flashed her badge. "We talked on the phone."

He straightened in his chair. "My manager said to cooperate."

"I'm not here about you," she reassured him. "A woman took a tumble off your sidewalk on Tuesday and onto the pavement. Do you remember?"

"Oh, yeah." A smile creased his face. "She did a nosedive off the curb and lost her drink. The supersized one. I offered to replace it."

She placed the photo of Abby Keller on the counter. "Is this the woman?"

He studied the copy of Abby's work photo. "No, that's not her."

She tapped on the picture. "Are you sure it wasn't this woman?"

He shook his head. "There's a resemblance, but this woman was older. Nearer my age."

His receding hairline put him closer to thirty than twenty. "Can you describe her?"

"She wore a lot of makeup. Too much for that early in the morning. But then she was dressed like a hooker."

"You think she was a prostitute?"

"Every town has a few, even Olde Bend. Maybe she was getting off her shift."

Like it was a regular job? No one considered what happened to a woman after a night of exchanging sex for cash. Did she go home to the husband and kids and add her earnings to the family savings? More likely, she turned everything over to her boyfriend pimp who gave her drugs for a reward or a beating if she didn't make enough to satisfy him. Was this woman part of the sex trafficking business? That would explain her addiction. "Can you describe what she was wearing?"

He moved his hands across the front of his belly. "She had on a short, pleated skirt and was wearing a thong." He paused. "I think."

"Why are you uncertain? Do you wear glasses?" A nearsighted witness would be unreliable.

"No, but when she fell, her skirt flew up, and you could see her bare butt." He grinned. "I couldn't see any underwear. Do you think she was going commando?"

He was enjoying his role as a witness. "Let's go with a thong. What happened after she fell?"

"A man at the pump ran over, and I came outside to help. She was crying, and her blue eye shadow and mascara were smeared down her face. She looked like a clown after a rainstorm."

He wouldn't be able to identify her face. "Was she injured?"

"She was holding her arm."

"Which arm?"

"The right. I think she fell on it."

Sydney noted his observations. The fall could account for her injury, or it could hide an older one. "Did the fall seem natural?"

"Natural? It was inevitable. She was wearing a pair of stupid shoes."

"Can you describe them?"

"Narrow spikes that had to be six inches high. How can anyone balance on those? That's why she tumbled off the curb."

"Did she have any other injuries besides the right arm?"

"She had a bad case of road rash on what were nice legs."

"Nice legs?"

"Like a runner's. No flab. I ran in high school. Zero body fat." He pinched his belly and found a handful. His face reddened. "I've added a few pounds since then."

Edith had said her thief had run away like a track star.

He snapped his fingers. "I forgot about the stretch marks."

"What stretch marks?"

"On her butt. When she was still on the ground before I helped her up." He moved his hands up and down along his hips. "She had thin white lines marking her flesh. I had a girlfriend who lost a lot of weight. She had the same sort of stretch marks."

The mystery woman was a runner who had lost weight. A runner had a routine. Someone in the neighborhood around Main Street might have noticed her. She gathered the photo. "Thank you."

The clerk turned his attention to his phone and laughed. "This dumb cop is toast."

Sydney was going to walk away, but instinct made her pause. "What cop?"

"The one who shot that man in the alley. A bunch of people tried to stone her with canned goods and eggs."

"What?" She grabbed his phone. The video played across the screen of Beth being attacked while buying groceries. Her scared face appeared in a close-up before she bolted for the door. Sydney handed the phone back to the clerk and hurried to her car.

She watched the full broadcast of the mob's attack on her computer screen in the unmarked cruiser and called. Beth's phone asked her to leave a message. The attack had been hours ago. She called the station. Beth had gone home at four, and no one had been able to contact her. "I'll go to her apartment and check on her," Sydney informed the operator. "Do you have the code to the exterior door?"

"I'll get it for you."

Beth's car was parked in the lot. Sydney parked next to it. She searched the area for reporters, but they were chasing another news story or had called it a day. She phoned Beth again but no response. She entered the code to the door, took the steps to the second floor, and knocked on the door. "It's me, Beth. Let me in."

A woman exited the room across the hall.

Sydney flashed her badge. "Have you seen Beth Moreno?"

"She ordered a pizza earlier. I heard the delivery boy knocking and announcing who he was."

Sydney knocked again. She was eating. That was good. "Did you see or hear her leave?"

She stepped closer to Beth's door. "No, but I can hear her television. She never leaves it on when she leaves. She's very good about that."

Sydney knocked louder. Had Beth fallen asleep? "Beth! Let me in."

Silence. Her intuition was screaming. Something was wrong. She tried the doorknob. It was locked.

The woman had remained behind her. "I have a key. She gave it to me after she locked herself out a few months back."

"Get it! Please," Sydney added after she realized she had barked the order.

The woman retreated to her own apartment and returned with a key on a leather strap. "You don't think she's in any trouble, do you? She's such a nice quiet girl. I didn't know she was a cop until I saw her wearing her uniform. I thought it was a good thing to have a police officer in the building."

Sydney unlocked the door, but the sliding chain was still in place. She backed up and ran at the entrance, using her shoulder to loosen the screws holding the lock. The door swung open. "Stay here," she ordered the neighbor.

"Beth!" The room was dark except for the screen of the television. A nearly complete pizza rested on the coffee table next to her phone. She picked it up. She had several missed calls. Sneakers were discarded in a path to the bathroom. She followed the trail of a sweatshirt and a tee discarded on the floor.

A low light showed beneath the bathroom door. She knocked. "Beth, are you in there?"

She turned the knob. It wasn't locked, and she entered. Lights on the vanity cast a bright glow over the sink. Her remaining clothes were on the floor. The shower curtain was pulled halfway across the tub, which was nearly full of red water.

Red. The color of blood.

Beth had slid down, her head back, her mouth open as water trickled in. She had Beth's phone in her hand and hit 9-1-1 before placing it on the floor. She grabbed Beth's hair and pulled her above the surface. "Don't you dare die." She reached into the water. It was warm. Beth hadn't been in the tub long. She found the plug and twisted it open. The water began gurgling down the drain.

A voice from dispatch sounded on the line. "What is your emergency?"

"I need an ambulance. Suicide attempt. Officer on scene." She shouted the address as she grabbed several towels.

She laid one on the floor and pulled Beth from the tub. She had cut along the inside of her left arm. The right arm was intact. Blood oozed out of the gaping wound and turned the white towel red. She wrapped another towel around her sliced forearm as tightly as she could. It quickly stained. She had to stop the bleeding. She tugged her laces from her shoe and grabbed Beth's toothbrush to form a tourniquet above the elbow. She grabbed the belt from Beth's bathrobe hanging on the back of the door and tied it tightly around Beth's bleeding arm.

She checked Beth's airway. Water dribbled out. She felt for a pulse but couldn't detect one. She needed to start CPR compressions, but the bathroom was too small. She used the towel to pull Beth into the living room and knelt beside her, using her shoulders and stiff arms to press down on clasped hands to compress her heart.

A siren sounded in the distance. She continued compressions. Beth coughed. She was breathing. "Hang on, Beth. The paramedics are coming."

Her eyes flickered. "Let me go."

"Come on, Beth. You can't give up. Fight. Please don't die." She pushed her into a sitting position and hit her on the back with the palm of her hand.

Beth spat out water, took a deep breath, and coughed again.

A man shouted from the first floor that he was a paramedic.

"Up here!" The neighbor called down the staircase.

The first paramedic carried his oversized bag into the room and dropped it on the floor. "Is she conscious?"

"Yes, but she swallowed some water, and she's lost a lot of blood."

He looked beyond her, and Sydney turned. The tub had a ring of red against the white surface.

"Bring the cot!" he shouted into his radio. He knelt behind Beth and listened with his stethoscope. "Her lungs sound clear."

"I'm cold." Beth shivered.

Sydney wrapped a towel around Beth's chest to form a modest covering.

Two other paramedics carried a stretcher into the room. They loaded Beth and covered her lower half with a sheet.

Sydney stepped back as the paramedics saved Beth's life. Her job was done, but her heart thundered in her chest, and her hands shook from a few minutes of sheer panic when training had replaced thinking. The sleeves on her jacket were soaked, and she removed it.

The first paramedic removed the bloody towel from Beth's arm, replaced it with dressing squares, and wrapped the wound with gauze. He handed Sydney the makeshift tourniquet.

The second paramedic covered Beth with a blanket and strapped her in. She placed an oxygen line over her head and inserted the prongs into her nose.

"Let me get an IV line started, and we'll move her." The third paramedic ripped open the individually wrapped medical supplies and inserted a catheter into Beth's hand. He hooked tubing to a bag of sodium lactate solution to replace the fluids Beth had lost and connected it to the shunt on the catheter. He held it aloft as the other two paramedics maneuvered the stretcher out the door.

Sydney picked Beth's phone up from the bathroom floor. "Are you there?"

"Yes, what is the situation?"

"Paramedics are transporting her to the hospital. Thank you."

"I hope she'll be all right."

Sydney turned off the phone and shoved it into her pants pocket. Her body had stopped trembling, and she took a deep breath. She wanted to scream at the rookie for scaring the heck out of her, but that would pass. She had reached Beth in time, and she was alive.

"Is she going to be all right?" The neighbor stood in the living room, watching her.

"They'll take good care of her. Thank you for your help and being a good neighbor."

She pointed. "You have blood on your clothes."

Sydney grabbed a towel and swiped at the stain. All it did was smear it. Blood was part of the job, but she couldn't leave the apartment looking like an accident scene. Sydney wiped down the tub and packed the bloody towels in a trash bag to take home and wash. She gathered Beth's discarded clothes and placed them on the couch. Beth's purse was on the counter. Inside were her car and room keys, a wallet, and a list of groceries. She retrieved her wet jacket, grabbed the other items, and locked the door.

She handed the spare key to the neighbor. "Can you call the landlord about fixing the chain lock on the door?"

"Does this happen very often to you?"

"No. A cop's life is pretty boring fifty minutes out of the hour. It's the ten minutes of absolute terror that makes our hearts stop."

On the way to the hospital, she notified the chief. Her siren parted traffic, and she caught up with the ambulance as it pulled in to the hospital parking lot.

Chapter Thirty

Claire was waiting for the pain medicine to kick in. She had been called in early because the emergency department was busy and a lazy nurse had called off. The warmer weather had brought out the daredevils and out-of-shape athletes who suffered sprains, cuts, and concussions. The discomfort in her arm was difficult to ignore as she wrapped a patient's sprained ankle. She finished the wrap and told the patient to stay off his foot.

She handed him a set of crutches. "Do you have someone taking you home?"

He winked at her. "Are you busy? I could use a little tender care."

She smiled politely. Male patients thought they could sweet-talk a nurse into private care and fulfilling their sexual fantasies, but this was her job. One that didn't get enough respect. "You need to rest." She patted him on the shoulder. She would have preferred to smack him on the back of the head instead. Stupid pervert.

She ripped off the paper cover, disinfected the padding on the exam table, and placed a new sheet of paper for the next patient to sit on. She needed a break. She looked at her watch. She could slip off to her locker and ease her pain with a few snorts.

"A squad is coming in," the intern announced. He jumped to his feet like an eager puppy about to be given a treat. After seeing blood and guts on a stretcher a hundred times, he'd lose his enthusiasm.

Claire's pills would have to wait. An ambulance pulled up to the double doors used only by emergency vehicles. The paramedics unloaded the stretcher.

Claire grabbed a supply cart and headed for the open bay being prepared for the patient. Although it looked like chaos, everyone assumed their prescribed roles. The emergency staff would seamlessly take over treatment from the paramedics who had stabilized the patient en route. One of the paramedics shouted out the information. "Twenty-three-year-old female with deep laceration on her left arm. Attempted suicide."

Stupid girl. How could someone's life be so awful at twenty-three? What she wouldn't give to return to those years and not make the same mistakes.

They wheeled the patient into the curtained bay and transferred her to the examination table. The overwhelmed intern looked around for the doctor on duty. He was new to the rotation and had shown little interest in learning emergency medicine except to videotape the gore. He planned to specialize in dermatology. At least he couldn't kill anyone popping a zit.

A woman walked through the emergency doors. Her cargo pants were wrinkled and smeared with dark stains. Blood. If she hadn't recognized the chiseled features of her face, the gun on her hip and bulletproof vest gave away her identity. Detective Sydney Harrison concentrated on the patient, standing far enough away for the hospital staff to do their job but close enough to know the patient's outcome. From her disheveled appearance, she had found the suicidal woman.

Claire stayed behind Sydney as the paramedics

wheeled their stretcher out of the way. Hopefully, the detective wouldn't notice her. She checked the sleeve on her long smock and flexed her fingers in her latex gloves. As far as she knew, the police hadn't identified the mystery woman, and she wanted to keep it that way.

The ER doctor took charge and turned to Claire. "Bring that cart here."

She pushed the mobile supply unit into position, keeping her back to Sydney, and handed out equipment as the staff called out their needs.

The doctor examined the gauze wrapping. "What happened?"

"She slit her arm in her tub," the paramedic answered. "She's *that cop* on the news."

That cop? The pale face of the young woman was framed by short reddish hair. She looked like she belonged in high school instead of on the police force. Claire grabbed the information chart the paramedics had started. "Elizabeth Moreno? She's the cop who shot the man in the alley."

"You have a problem with that?" Sydney had stepped forward next to her.

Had she said her thoughts aloud? "No." She cringed, trying to make herself smaller under Sydney's intense glare.

She pointed at her name tag. "Claire. Claire Batton. We met the night of the shooting."

Name tags only revealed the first name, but stupid Abby had introduced her using her full name, and Sydney remembered. "Yes. You're Detective Sydney Harrison." She needed to take the attention off herself. "Is the patient your friend?"

"Yes."

A paramedic smiled at Sydney. "The detective saved her life."

Claire stared at Beth on the table. The broadcast of the shooting had been on every news outlet with follow-up stories throughout the week. The woman had been hounded by the reporters and crucified for killing Jack Lawson, the man she had met in the alley. He should never have taken her gun. Men were nothing but trouble. A wave of sympathy washed over her. "We'll take good care of her."

"I'd think a cop would know a better way to off herself," the intern remarked.

"We're glad she didn't succeed," Sydney said, giving the intern a scathing look.

He had enough sense to look ashamed and lowered his phone. The jerk had been taping the trauma.

"We have strict rules about talking about patients," Claire said to Sydney, but her remarks were meant for the intern. "You never know if a relative or friend is riding in the elevator with you. That goes for posting anything on the internet without permission."

He slipped his phone into his coat pocket and slithered off to a dark corner.

"He's an intern specializing in dermatology." Claire didn't hide the disdain in her voice. She hated working with inept doctors and nurses who made mistakes. Too bad the good ones went unnoticed.

"I'd like to keep the officer's identity on a need-to-know basis. No press and no visitors unless approved by the chief of police."

"Patients have to give approval for the hospital to release any information," Claire explained. "Everything will remain confidential."

The paramedics had started an IV to replace lost fluids and had bandaged her arm to control the bleeding. The monitor recording her vitals showed a steady but slow heartbeat, and her blood pressure was low. "Does she have any relatives that should be notified?"

Sydney stared at the numbers on the screen. "You don't think she'll make it?"

"We'll do everything in our power to save her," the doctor promised. He gave Claire a look that was a silent reprimand for speaking the truth.

She was a realist. Beth could die, and relatives should be notified in case she didn't make it. But the doctor believed in miracles, especially when he was the one saving the patient.

"Did you type her blood?" he asked.

"No."

"Type her and order a toxicology screen." He turned to Sydney. "We usually ask friends and family to donate."

"Don't worry. You'll have plenty of donors."

Claire gathered a rubber hose, two vials, and a syringe for the blood draw. It wasn't easy with Beth's low blood pressure, but she filled the vials and sent them to the lab with an orderly.

Sydney had remained in the room but out of the way. A man came through the doors and greeted her. It was Chief Mills. He had spoken at the press conferences about the shooting. He had thrown on a police coat, but his jeans and sneakers meant he'd been called from home. He talked to Sydney in low whispers, and the doctor joined them.

Claire couldn't hear the conversation.

The paramedics were gathering their equipment.

Their job was done, and they needed to prepare for the next call. "We need to replace our supplies."

She waved them to a large cabinet. "Over here."

She punched in the code to unlock the door and display neatly stacked medical supplies she had stocked. "What do you need?"

One of them handed her a list of what items they had exhausted to care for Beth. She gathered what they needed for replacements, scanned the bar codes, and placed everything in a bag.

The paramedic who took the bag turned to the chief and Sydney. "I saw on the news how the public has been treating Officer Moreno. She had a difficult choice. I hope she makes it."

"Beth is a fighter," Sydney said.

He glanced toward the bay where the curtains had been partially drawn to give Beth some privacy as the medical staff took care of her. "You make sure she fights. I heard how it's that armed robber's fault. Have you found him?"

"I can't comment on an ongoing case, but we'll get him."

Him? Claire locked the supply cabinet. Sydney knew the armed robber was a woman. She had used Abby Keller's identification. She'd asked them to report a woman with an arm injury. Why was she lying? The conclusion was obvious. The police were holding back the information. A reward had been offered, and what better way to weed out the liars than to eliminate anyone who identified the robber as a man? What else did they know that they weren't revealing? Was she a suspect?

Sydney was staring at her. *Say something, stupid, before she sees guilty written all over your face.*

"Claire!" the doctor shouted her name.

She shook herself. "What is it, Doctor?"

"Chief Mills has officers in the waiting room. They want to donate blood."

What was she supposed to do? "I'm not a phlebotomist."

"Then find one," he snapped. "Have the girls register the donors and schedule the blood draws. Nobody goes home until the work is done."

Claire forced a smile. "It'll be my pleasure." She passed through the sliding doors to the waiting area.

A half dozen officers were standing in a group and turned to face her.

"If you're here to donate blood, give registration your information."

"I'm in booth one!" Abby called out as she jumped to her feet and waved her arms. "Send someone over!"

"Is anyone O negative?" Claire asked. O negative could be given to anyone and the most needed. Although none of the blood collected would be given to Beth, it would be used to replace the depleted stock used to stabilize her.

"I am."

"You're first." Claire froze. Officer Sam Wilson, the young officer who had interviewed her, stepped forward. She stared, waiting for him to recognize her.

"There?" He pointed to the first registration booth.

Air escaped her chest in relief. "Yes." She told Abby to page the phlebotomist and headed to her locker for her much-needed pain medicine.

Chapter Thirty-One

Vivien and her mother watched the late news for the weather report. Maybe they would get two days of sunshine in a row. A video showed a woman in the grocery store surrounded by shouting shoppers. The screen crawler identified her as Beth Moreno. A man pulled a carton of eggs from her cart and threw them on the floor, and others followed his example as they emptied her cart. They taunted her and called her names. The same ones she had used. Beth looked scared.

"That man threw a can at her." Lucy stared at the screen. "All she's doing is buying groceries and…"

"I know. They're attacking her because of me."

"No, Vivien." She pointed at the screen. "That's an angry mob."

Beth was struck several times before she broke past the crowd, leaving her grocery cart behind. The video followed her as she hurried to the exit, her steps unsteady. She glanced back, fear evident on her face before she escaped through the door.

"It's my tragedy, but they're using it as an excuse to bully," Vivien said. "I wanted justice for Jack. He would never condone violence."

"She's a cop."

"Not in that store. She was one of us. I don't want more blood spilled. Beth Moreno made a mistake. When Jack picked up that gun, she thought he was a threat, and she shot him."

"You can't be on her side." Lucy was shocked.

Vivien met her mother's gaze. "I know. I should be the last person to feel empathy. I hate her for that. I do, but she didn't shoot anyone in that mob or someone they loved." She pointed at the television screen. "This is my pain, and they have no right to seek revenge in my name."

Her phone rang. Vivien looked at the caller's name. "It's the lawyer."

"Why is he calling so late?"

Vivien ignored her mother and walked into the hallway to answer the phone. "Yes, I've seen the news. I don't agree with the way the crowd treated her. How do we stop it?"

"It may be too late," her lawyer said. "Beth Moreno slit her wrist."

"She slit her wrist?" The phone shook in her hand, and her knees threatened to buckle. "She killed herself?"

"What?" Lucy was at her side, trying to hear the conversation. "Is she dead?"

Vivien fought to listen to her lawyer as her mother hovered nearby. She disconnected and turned. "No, she isn't dead. Detective Harrison found her in her apartment, and paramedics took her to the hospital."

"She must have felt guilty."

"Of course, she feels guilty. She has a conscience. She made a mistake." She brushed away hot tears on her cheek. "And now she tried to kill herself."

Her mother grabbed her arm. "But she survived, didn't she?"

Vivien pulled away and headed for the bedroom. "Can you stay with John-John?"

Lucy dogged her footsteps. "Where are you going?"

Vivien grabbed her coat. "I'm going to the hospital. I want to see her."

"I don't think that's a good idea, Vivien. What will others think?"

She slipped on her shoes. "I don't care what others think. Suicide is a cry for help. Remember when my cousin killed herself? Beth needs a friend."

"She killed your husband."

"I haven't forgotten, but I'm the one who incited them. I stood on a platform and asked for revenge. If they hurt her, if she hurts herself because of me, then I'm the guilty party."

Her mother shook her head. "You owe her nothing."

"Detective Harrison said the woman in the alley is responsible. It was her gun. She was committing a crime. That's where the blame should be, not on Officer Moreno. I have to do this, Mom."

"Be careful. Everyone takes sides in these social battles, and they show no mercy to the opponent. There will be cops at the hospital."

Vivien parked her car near the emergency entrance. She hesitated. Her mother was right. She wouldn't be able to avoid a confrontation. Two police officers entered the lobby. How many more were inside? She should return home and let the situation and participants calm down. The medical staff might not even let her see Beth. She sat in the car, her seat belt hooked and her keys in her hand. Stay or go? Jack always said imagined fears were worse than reality. Face them or flee? She took a deep breath, unhooked the seat belt, and gathered her purse. As she entered the hospital lobby, several police officers turned and stared.

A sergeant stepped toward her. "What are you doing here?" His name badge said *Faris*.

Vivien looked around. "I don't want to cause any trouble."

He stared her down, and his voice was harsh. "That's all you've done."

Another officer moved closer. "What does *she* want, Rick?"

Others moved closer in a wall that surrounded her. She shouldn't have come. These were Beth's co-workers, fellow officers, and friends. She was the intruder and the enemy. "I wanted to make sure Beth was all right."

"Officer Moreno is fine," Sergeant Rick Faris said. "Go home."

Vivien stepped back, her heart racing inside her chest.

"What's going on?" The chief's raspy voice echoed in the lobby. He stepped between her and the men and softened his tone. "Mrs. Lawson, you shouldn't be here."

She stiffened her resolve. "That seems to be the general consensus, but I'd like to see Beth. Officer Moreno," she corrected.

"So you can gloat?" Rick demanded.

"Those people at the store had no right to attack her. Do you think I want her blood on my hands?" Vivien fought back tears. "I came here to make amends."

The chief looked surprised. He turned to the group. "Back down, Officers." He chewed on his lip as if mentally debating something. "Wait here. Sergeant, make sure no one bothers Mrs. Lawson."

Vivien didn't move. The men and women in blue turned their backs to her and shuffled away. The sergeant glared. Why was he angry at her? Her husband was the victim. She was the victim. But the police didn't see it that way. Her mother was right. She had attacked one of their own in a public arena, and now that woman was fighting for her life. She had become the enemy. They were on opposing sides, locked in defending their views. Talking to Beth wouldn't change the way they felt about her. She turned to leave.

A man in a wheelchair blocked her exit, and her purse banged against him. "I'm so sorry."

"You're Mrs. Lawson."

She didn't want another confrontation. "I was just leaving."

He extended his hand. "I'm Gordon Blackwood. My wife is Detective Harrison." He pointed to the young man behind him. "This is Barry Vespoint."

Barry extended his hand and grinned at her, a friendly face among the solemn condemners. She automatically shook his hand, digesting the information.

Gordon looked beyond her. "Were you visiting someone?"

She followed his gaze to the officers. "I came here to see Beth Moreno, but I'm not welcome."

"Nonsense," Gordon said. "I'll take you up."

Was he serious? "Chief Mills hasn't given me permission."

"The chief and I are friends." He lifted a bag. From the smell and grease stains, the food had to be burgers and fries. "Besides, my wife said they closed the cafeteria, and she was hungry. Join us."

Barry pushed Gordon toward the elevator doors, and she walked beside them. "You're awfully nice considering I'm the enemy."

He looked puzzled. "Are you the enemy?"

She glanced toward the police officers who were watching her. "I thought I was the victim, but then I saw the broadcast where those people attacked poor Beth, and my lawyer called and said she had tried to kill herself. Why would she do that?"

"I don't know. Luckily, Sydney found her in time."

"Has your wife been Beth's friend for a long time?"

"I don't think they were acquainted before the shooting, but Sydney never commits half-heartedly to anything or anyone. Beth needed her, and she volunteered."

"My cousin killed herself when she was seventeen," Vivien blurted out. "I was a year older, and it was awful wondering if I could have stopped her."

"Some things are out of our control."

"It's not a good feeling," she whispered.

"No, it's damn scary," Gordon said.

"I don't understand why Beth would hurt herself. The chief announced she was acquitted of any guilt in the shooting."

"It's not that uncommon to hurt ourselves, especially when things go wrong in our lives. I have a theory we all suffer from mental illness to various degrees. All it takes is a trigger. I wanted to kill myself after the accident that left me a cripple in the hospital. The doctors said I would never walk again."

She didn't know how to answer. He didn't appear despondent. "But you didn't."

"No, but I wasn't the charming professor you see before you."

He was teasing, but his smile made her heart flutter. Jack would have matured into someone like Gordon.

"What were you?"

"I was angry and defiant. I didn't want anyone's help." He inhaled, then let his breath out slowly. "I got my wish. Even Sydney had given up on me."

"I find that hard to believe. You said she never committed half-heartedly to anyone."

"I pushed her away. I was like George Bailey in *It's a Wonderful Life.* I had to lose everything to realize how much I wanted to live."

"Now we're taking one step at a time, literally," Barry said.

"You're walking?"

"Like a toddler, but Barry is a task master. He'll have me running marathons before he agrees his work is done."

Vivien pushed the *up* button on the elevator.

The sergeant stepped in front of the doors and prevented them from closing. "Did the chief approve your visit?"

"She's with me," Gordon said. "I'll make sure she behaves herself."

He glared at Gordon before stepping aside. "Whatever you say, Professor. Your wife is running the investigation."

"She is the detective," Gordon said as the elevator doors closed.

The sergeant had been openly hostile. "I thought I was the only person he didn't like," Vivien said.

Gordon smiled as if he had a secret. "He doesn't like losing, and neither do I."

"I'm not here to cause trouble."

"What do you hope to accomplish, Mrs. Lawson?"

"Vivien," she corrected. "It was my husband who

was shot in that alley. I was angry, and I blamed Officer Moreno, but I don't want others to use my husband's death as an excuse to attack her. The police make mistakes, but it would be a whole lot worse if we got rid of them and let everyone take the law into their own hands. I want Beth to know I understand why she shot my husband."

"But you don't forgive her?"

She had to be honest. "I don't think I'm ready for that. Losing Jack is still too painful."

"Pain is part of life. Some of it is physical. Some of it is emotional. It's easier to fix the physical. The way to emotional healing isn't as quick."

"Did you ever forgive the person who put you in a wheelchair?"

Gordon's eyebrow rose along with a corner of his mouth. "Do you know what happened?"

"Detective Harrison said a young man ran you over with his car."

"He was a student at the college where I teach."

"Did he run you over on purpose?" She clamped her hand over her mouth. "I didn't mean that the way it sounded."

Gordon laughed as the elevator doors opened on the second floor. "No, he wasn't even in my class."

"I am now." Barry pushed the wheelchair into the hall.

Vivien remained in the elevator, too shocked to move as she stared at the young man. "You ran him over? Why?"

He held the door so she could join them. "I had finished my final exam and jumped into my car to leave the campus behind. I was texting my friends to meet at

221

the local tavern and celebrate the end of term. I didn't see the professor in front of me. I thought I hit a speed bump."

"I have never been described as a speed bump before." Gordon laughed.

She stared at the two men who seemed to be sharing an inside joke. "How can you laugh about it?"

"It takes time." Gordon searched the numbers of the rooms on the wall. "You go through all the stages of grief. Then you decide to live. By the time Barry entered my life, I was ready to help him by offering a job."

"But he was the one who almost killed you." She stopped walking. "How could you trust him to take care of you?"

"Barry didn't want to hurt me. He didn't even know me. He was young, careless, and in a hurry, all the elements for a disaster."

Barry rested his hand on Gordon's shoulder. "I couldn't say, 'I'm sorry,' enough. I visited Gordon in the hospital to tell him those same words, and he offered me a job."

"I realized he was in more pain than me. I told him I needed someone to help with physical therapy." Gordon patted Barry's hand. "We helped each other."

Barry pushed Gordon into the room while Vivien waited in the hallway, peeking through the open door, taking in the scene. Sydney stood by the bedside, staring at a still figure. Beth's left arm was swathed in bandages, and an IV was hooked to her other hand.

Gordon shook the bag of food. "I hope you're hungry."

"Starving." Sydney planted a kiss on his lips and opened the bag. "Cheeseburgers and fries. You certainly know the way to a girl's heart."

"I wouldn't call this meal heart friendly, but you haven't eaten all day." Gordon wheeled his chair close to the bed. "How is she doing?"

"She'll survive."

"But..."

Sydney's voice trembled. "The paramedics saved Beth's life, but she could succeed next time."

Vivien stepped forward. "You think she'll try it again?"

Sydney blocked her path. "How did you get in here?"

"She came up with me," Barry said.

"Well, she can leave with you."

"Syd." Gordon called from the other side of the bed. "I asked her to join us. She was worried about Beth. She braved a hostile blue line to come here."

Husband and wife stared at each other. Sydney's shoulders heaved and relaxed. She grabbed Vivien's arm to pull her into the room. "You're welcome to stay."

Vivien had wanted blood. She'd gotten it. And now she regretted it. "I won't upset her."

Sydney spread a napkin on the mobile tray positioned over the bed and arranged the food. She shook the empty bag and looked at Gordon. "Aren't you having any?"

He motioned to Barry. "We ate."

She took a bite of her cheeseburger and looked at Vivien. "Take something."

"I shouldn't, but the fries smell great." She grabbed a few.

"I think you're going to have to share with someone else. Beth is awake," Gordon announced as Beth opened her eyes.

Chapter Thirty-Two

Voices whispered around Beth, but she was unable to decipher the speaker. She struggled to open her eyes. The shadows were far away, huddled in the distance. She was encased in a white sheet and blanket. Had she died? Suicide had seemed the only way to escape the constant news stories, the hostile public, and her hateful family. She had been alone emotionally if not physically most of her life. Nobody cared whether she lived or died. Then she had heard Sydney's voice. *Fight. Please, don't die.*

Beth reached out her hand and struck a plastic railing. An IV stuck into the back of her hand burned and throbbed beneath the surface of her skin. A rubber tube ran from her hand to a tall metal stand with a plastic bag. A monitor beeped to the side, and her heartbeat scrolled across the screen in a repetitive pattern. Numbers recorded her blood pressure and pulse per minute.

She was in a hospital. Alive.

Her mother's vicious words had cut deeper than any razor blade. She had listened to a series of hateful messages Alice had left on her phone, and she had played them over and over again, searching for a hint of sympathy. She should have known better than to wallow in self-pity and tears. In a moment of despair, she swiped at her arm in a desperate attempt to end all her troubles. The pain was so intense she screamed and dropped the razor blade on the floor. Blood oozed from the wound, turning the water in the tub crimson.

Panic set in, and she scrambled up the slick tub wall only to slip and collapse into the warm water as strength ebbed from her body. She wanted to regroup but closed her eyes instead. The water had been warm, or had it been her blood?

She examined the heavy bandage on her left arm. She had wanted to escape all the problems that had mounted over the past week. She had thought if she died, people would feel sorry for her and forgive her. They'd realize she was a nice person and not the evil woman portrayed in the press. As soon as she cut herself, the desire to die had faded as she realized the finality of her act. Thank goodness, she had a second chance.

She smelled the salty potatoes and broiled hamburgers from fast-food fare. The smell of fries intensified, and her stomach growled. She reached toward the odor.

Someone grabbed her hand. "Beth, can you hear me?"

She wasn't deaf. "Can I have a fry?"

Sydney and others laughed. Were they going to deny her?

"Here." She pushed the tray table closer to her. "You can finish them."

She shoved two into her mouth. The salt burned the open cracks in her dry lips, but the fry melted on her tongue. She reached for a plastic cup on the tray, tugging on the plastic tubing attached to her hand.

"I bet you're thirsty."

A container with a straw was pressed against her mouth. She sipped the lukewarm water. It was enough to wet her mouth. She shoved another three fries into her mouth and savored the heavenly manna as she pieced together what had happened.

Sydney had been in her bathroom. She had pulled her from the water in her tub and saved her life.

"Thank you." Her voice was gravelly and sounded foreign. Something was blowing up her nose. She tugged on an oxygen line, tucked over her ears and pushed up her nostrils. Her vision was beginning to clear.

Others were in the room. Gordon was seated in his wheelchair with a concerned expression on his friendly face. His aide, Barry, gave her a lopsided grin. He was a good-looking young man, and her heartbeat quickened. She was definitely alive. What were they doing here? They barely knew her, yet they had come to her rescue at her apartment when the press kept her prisoner and were now visiting her in the hospital. They cared more about her than her family. Was this what friendship felt like?

Or had they come for Sydney? Was the food for her? How long had she been by her side? How long had she been in the twilight world between life and death?

Another person stood at the end of the bed, quiet and unmoving. Every muscle stiffened. It was Vivien Lawson. She dropped her fry and pulled back her hand. "You."

"It's all right." Vivien stepped closer. "I'm not here to hurt you."

Tears stung her eyes as guilt welled afresh. She had killed her husband. The sort of man she could only dream about marrying. "I'm sorry."

"No, I'm sorry. I saw the mob attack you at the grocery store. I never meant for events to get out of hand. At first, I didn't care what happened. I was so angry, but now…"

Beth stared at the bandage on her arm. Why had she thought her life would make up for Jack Lawson's life? All she had done was move the guilt to another person. Hot tears stung her eyes. "I can't believe I was so stupid. I regretted it as soon as I did it. My mother called and I…" She fell silent. She didn't want anyone to know about her family, her secret shame.

"We're here to help you," Sydney said.

"How? Have you found the mystery woman?"

"I'm getting closer."

"The woman in the alley with Jack?" Vivien stepped toward Sydney. "Are you going to arrest her?"

"She used a gun to rob a woman and caused Jack's death. Armed robbery and murder. She'll go away for a very long time," Sydney said.

"I want to see her face-to-face," Vivien said. "I want her to know how many lives she ruined."

"What about me?" Beth gasped. Did Vivien consider her as guilty as the mystery woman?

"You're one of her victims, too," she said.

Beth met Vivien's gaze. "You don't blame me for shooting Jack?" Was she telling the truth, or was it a horrible joke like her family played?

"I understand your reasons for shooting my husband." Vivien took her hand. "Jack would have forgiven you right away. It took me a little longer. I needed someone to blame. But this is between you and me. Others have no right to pass judgment."

"I'm pretty helpless. You could do whatever you want to me."

Vivien stepped closer. "May I give you a hug?"

Was she serious? "Really?" Nobody hugged in her

family. They might find a knife in their back if they did.

Hot tears fell as Vivien leaned forward and brushed her cheek against Beth's damp face. Vivien truly forgave her. She looked around for a tissue and used the blanket to wipe her eyes. "When do I get out of here?"

Sydney placed a small box of tissues on the tray. "That will be up to the doctor."

"Do you need anything, Beth?" Gordon asked. "We could stop by your apartment."

She worried about the messages from her mother. "I could use my phone."

"I have it." Sydney thrust her hand into her pants pocket. "I used it to call 9-1-1."

"Thank you for saving my life."

Sydney smiled, and it went all the way to her eyes. "Anytime."

Beth held out her hand. It shook. "Did you listen to my calls?"

"I was going to contact your family and let them know what happened." Sydney handed over the phone.

The last thing she needed was her family coming to the hospital and reminding her of her failures. "Please tell me you didn't."

Sydney turned to Gordon. "How about getting a couple of drinks?"

He exchanged a look, nodded, and left with Barry.

Sydney lowered her voice. "I thought better of it after I heard your mother's remarks. Has she always been so cruel?"

Beth leaned back against the pillow, hot tears rushing to her eyes. "You heard her on a good day."

"Your mother isn't coming?" Vivien asked. "Why not?"

"She's not anything like yours." Sydney turned from Vivien to Beth. "Why didn't you say anything about your family?"

"I was ashamed. My dear old mother and father have been failing *parents of the year* awards since I was old enough to remember." Beth scrolled through her messages.

"They can't be that bad," Vivien said. "The chief told me you were top in your class at the police academy."

"You've earned the right to hear this." Beth pressed a message from her mother.

"Don't you dare hang up on me again. I haven't finished with you, Lizzy. Not only do you shoot an innocent man and disgrace the family name, but you refuse to help your family. What good are children if they don't take care of their parents in their old age? You're a selfish brat, Lizzy. You always act so high and mighty. Look, everybody, I'm a cop. Well, now you've been put in your proper place, young lady. No lofty airs for the princess of the county. And don't expect us to welcome you back with open arms when you're fired. I turned your bedroom into a sewing room."

"Sewing room," Beth repeated. "The only needles she touches are filled with illegals."

"I'm sorry," Sydney said. "Your family is wrong."

"I know, but it still hurts. You know you're missing something in your life that others have, and you hide that void with a hard shell. That's why I never talked about them. I'd admit I was poor but not abused." Beth took a deep breath. "When she called, all that cruelty and loneliness rushed back into my life. I didn't know how to stop the pain." She looked at her arm. "I'm glad you found me."

"I'm your friend," Sydney said. "Don't forget that."

"I'd like to be your friend, too," Vivien said.

"Why? I mean how?"

Vivien stepped close, her hand resting on the bed railing. "Because we are forever linked now. Each of us has changed the other's life, and we can never retrace our steps to a point in the past."

Sam had said something similar. Life moved forward with all the changes acquired from the past. Others found it easy to share their feelings. She struggled to admit them to herself. "I can always use a friend."

Sydney unwrapped a second burger. "Do you think you can eat this?"

"I'm starving." She bit into the burger and decided some things were worth living for. "All I ate was a slice of pizza, and I didn't buy any..."

"I saw your list of groceries in here." Sydney searched Beth's purse, which she had brought.

"Why don't I shop for them?" Vivian volunteered. "You can't return home to an empty refrigerator."

Sydney waved the keys she retrieved along with the list. "I have the key to her apartment."

Kindness was foreign to her. "You guys don't have to do this."

"I like shopping," Vivien said. "What's your favorite snack food?"

"Popcorn and anything chocolate."

Sydney threw away the trash. "The grocery store is open all night. Why don't we run our errands and let Beth rest?"

Beth gave a weak wave. "I feel like I should do something to help."

"Get well," Sydney said.

"I feel better already." After everyone said their good-byes, Beth played the hateful messages from her mother and then deleted each one. She promised herself not to think about them again. She paused on the last one. She hadn't heard the words clearly when she was depressed and scared. Something her mother said hinted at a deeper meaning. She replayed it.

"I had two children already. I wish I had never taken you in."

She played it again. *Taken you in.* Not given birth to you or become pregnant with you. *Taken you in.* Did it mean what she thought? She wasn't *their* child. No one had told her she was adopted. That would explain so much.

Her mother wouldn't tell her the truth. Who could she ask? The only family member she trusted was her aunt Sophie, her mother's half sister. They shared a name but she had only been fifteen when Beth was born. Would she remember anything? There was only one way to find out. She dialed her number.

Chapter Thirty-Three

Saturday's dawn was low on the horizon as Sydney drove to Olde Bend. Lydia, the radiology technician, had narrowed the search for her mystery woman to white females between the ages of twenty and forty with a broken humerus, and had a possible match. Dr. Viola Parks was coming in to verify the x-rays.

Sydney hurried to the radiology department. Both women had smiles on their faces.

Viola told Lydia to transmit an x-ray onto a larger viewing screen and pointed to two breaks near the wrist and another above the elbow. "This is the x-ray of the patient claiming to be Abby Keller we showed you before."

Viola signaled Lydia to display another x-ray next to the previous one. "Lydia retrieved the information from the archived data base. This was taken three years ago. The woman was in a car accident."

Only the fracture above the elbow on the humerus was visible, but it appeared to be the same.

"The assessment from the intake was general. A twenty-seven-year-old female in a single vehicle collision with a tree on the road coming up from the valley. She was the passenger." Viola ran her finger down the list on her personal medical data pad. "The doctor states she also suffered a concussion and a cut to the right side of her head requiring four stitches. She suffered bruising in the chest and shoulder area, likely from the seat belt."

"No airbags?"

"You'd have to check the police report. All we have is the ER medical report."

She was the passenger. "Does it mention who else was in the accident?"

Viola scrolled down. "Here's a note from the ER doctor. He informed her that her husband, the driver, was declared dead at the scene."

"What was the woman's name?"

She scrolled to the top of the page where registration information was listed. "Claire Batton."

"Claire?" The ER nurse she had first met during her interview with Abby Keller? She was working a ten-hour shift from ten p.m. to eight thirty a.m. She would have had time to rob Edith, confront Jack Lawson in the alley, and reach the hospital for work. She also knew Abby.

Claire had worn long sleeves and gloves every time she saw her. Most nurses removed their gloves if they didn't need them. They didn't want to build up a latex allergy, but Claire had always worn gloves even when stocking supplies. She was hiding her injury.

"Here's the information she gave to registration." Lydia printed a page. "Daniel Batton was listed as her husband and emergency contact. I was right about her being a nurse. She was employed at Newtown Hospital in the pain management department."

Pain management where she'd have access to drugs and know the patients who received them like Edith Merryweather. "This is what I needed."

"We were glad to help," Viola said.

Sydney pointed to the current x-ray on the screen.

"How would you treat a break like that?"

"We'd put a cast on it," Viola said.

She didn't see a cast on Claire Batton's arm yesterday when she saw her in the ER. "Did someone put a cast on the woman who claimed to be Abby Keller?"

"She insisted upon a removable brace," Lydia said. "No plaster cast."

"Do you have a brace like the one you put on her?"

Viola opened a drawer and removed a plastic sleeve. "This fits over the break and fastens in place. That's what we put on her."

The brace fit closer to the skin and was easier to hide beneath a shirt. Claire knew they were looking for a woman with an arm injury. Sydney had revealed that information on their first meeting. Claire had been one step ahead of her in the investigation. She handed Lydia her card. "Send her file to my email address."

Lydia transferred the files with a few strokes on the keyboard. Sydney paged through Claire's record for anything helpful. "Is this right? It says she weighs 220 pounds."

"The woman I treated was a hundred pounds lighter," Lydia said.

Sydney let out a breath. "Then it's not the same person."

"Bones don't lie," Viola said. "It's the same woman." She pointed to the older x-ray on the larger screen. "The edge of the skin shows lighter against the dark background. See how her arm bows out around the bone in the old one. The newer one shows a thinner arm. She was a lot heavier three years ago."

Her mystery woman had runner's legs and stretch marks. Claire must have taken up jogging after her husband's death. She was the woman who had posed as Abby Keller. Sydney thanked Viola and Lydia and headed to her car. She called the chief on the way back to Newtown. "The mystery woman is Claire Batton. She's an ER nurse at the Newtown Hospital." Her shift was ending. "She may still be at the hospital, but I have a home address." Sydney read off the street address. "Double-check with the hospital to make sure it's current. She may have moved. This address is three years old."

"Where are you?"

"I'm coming from Olde Bend and heading to Newtown Hospital. Have officers stop her if she's still there." She needed to learn more about Claire's history. What was she capable of when cornered? "Chief, could you ask for the accident report from three years ago involving Claire and her husband Daniel? He died in it."

"An auto accident?"

"Yes, near Olde Bend." Claire's life of crime didn't begin Saturday at the Third Street bus stop. Sydney contacted the medical examiner's office while driving along the winding road to Newtown. The same stretch of road had claimed Claire's husband. What had happened that night?

"This is Irene. Is that you, Sydney?"

"Yes, I need a favor. Do you have the records for Daniel Batton?" She spelled the name. "He died three years ago in a car accident. I want to know cause of death."

"If we did the autopsy, we'll have electronic records of our findings and the official statement from the medical examiner."

"I need the information as soon as you find it."

"What's going on, Sydney?"

"Our mystery woman in the alley is his wife, Claire. She's an ER nurse and probably a drug addict. I'm going to transmit her medical records from the accident. I want to know why her husband died and she escaped with a broken arm and a few bruises."

"I'll send it to you as soon as I find it."

"Thank you, Irene. It's important."

"You said Claire is an ER nurse. She isn't in the same hospital as Beth, is she?"

"Yes, she was in the ER when they brought Beth in. You don't think Claire would harm her?"

"Geez, Sydney, a lot of things can go wrong in a hospital."

Irene had voiced her worst thoughts. Beth had seen Claire leave the alley. What if Claire perceived her as a threat? She called dispatch. "I need a welfare check, and give a status report on Beth Moreno at Newtown Hospital. Send an officer to her room."

She hit her siren and lights.

Chapter Thirty-Four

Claire needed to leave town, but first she had to cover her tracks. Work last night had been a nightmare with police everywhere. Officer Wilson hadn't blinked when he saw her in the lobby. He didn't remember her, but Beth Moreno had stared long and hard when she made her escape from the alley. It was the same look Beth had given her in the ER before they wheeled her upstairs to her room. She knew. Too bad Beth hadn't been successful in her suicide attempt. That would have been one loose end neatly tied up in a bow.

Her shift was over, and Claire clocked out. She was dead tired from working the extra hours and bought a large cup of coffee from the cafeteria before going to her locker. She needed the extra jolt to keep her wits about her. She hadn't done anything wrong, but she had heard the police officers talking about making the woman in the alley pay for the crime. The police needed someone to blame for Jack Lawson's death besides one of their own. As long as they didn't know her identity, she could make her escape. They couldn't put her in jail if they couldn't find her.

She loaded everything on the locker shelves into her backpack. She wasn't coming back. She took inventory of her pills and found the fentanyl-laced ones in the small zipper compartment. She had meant to dispose of the dangerous pills, but now they might serve another purpose. Beth already looked guilty. She should take the full blame for Lawson's death. They would stop looking for her then.

A nurse came out of Beth's room, and Claire hid behind the tall metal rack holding breakfast trays that had been collected from patients. "I just came from her room. She's fine. She ate a good breakfast and could be discharged tomorrow," the nurse said to someone on the other line of the phone at the central station.

Claire closed the door to Beth's room and placed her backpack on the counter. Injecting fentanyl into Beth's IV line would be easy. She put the fentanyl-laced pills in her crusher and ground them to a fine powder. After transferring it to a vial, she added saline solution and shook the container to mix them together. All she had to do was insert the deadly mixture into the drip line.

By the time the monitor signaled Beth's distress, she would be in her car heading to a new life. If Beth died, it wouldn't be her fault. The woman was hooked to a monitor. The inept staff would be at fault for not knowing Beth was reacting to an overdose of drugs.

"Are you taking out the IV?"

Beth was awake.

Claire kept her head down as she turned to face her. "Not yet."

Beth scratched at the clear tape holding the tubing in place where the catheter was inserted into the top of her hand. "It's really uncomfortable."

Claire pointed toward the metal stand with the saline solution hanging on a hook by Beth's bed. "Is it? Once you finish that last bag, I'm sure they'll take it out." A dead woman wouldn't need fluids. She removed a syringe from a drawer and unwrapped it.

"What are you giving me, Claire?"

Claire dropped the empty syringe on the counter and turned. "How do you know my name?"

She pointed at her chest. "It's on your badge. I like the name Claire. It's strong and pretty."

She was being paranoid.

"I know you."

Claire's body tensed, and her hand shook. "You know me?"

"You were one of the nurses in the ER who saved my life. I don't know how to thank you."

She relaxed and shrugged. "It's my job."

Beth grabbed Claire's hand. She winced, and Beth released it. "Are you hurt?"

She flexed her fingertips. She didn't want Beth to figure out who she was and lied. "My hand was smashed between a doorway and a patient's bed when I was pushing it. They don't make the openings wide enough."

Beth stared at her hand. "I'm sorry. I hope I didn't hurt you."

"I'm tough." Beth was being too friendly to know her identity. She left the syringe on the counter and grabbed her backpack. Beth had cheated death a second time. "Gotta go."

Beth gasped. "You're the woman in the alley!"

Claire spun around. Beth remembered her. Stupid girl. She dropped her backpack.

Beth searched for the call button.

Claire found it first and tossed it over the head of the bed out of Beth's reach. "I'm doing you a favor. Do you want to be known as the cop who shot an innocent man? You won't have to worry about being hounded in grocery stores or view the tear-streaked faces of that baby boy and his mother."

Supplies were organized the same in every room so nurses and doctors didn't have to search. She pulled open the drawer for restraints. Beth kicked beneath her covers and tried to lower the rail, but Claire knew how to handle unruly patients. She had the strap around Beth's wrist and attached the other end to the rail. She leaned over her body and restrained the other one before Beth realized she was a prisoner.

She screamed, but Claire clamped her hand over her mouth. She grabbed a wad of gauze and stuffed it in her mouth. "Breathe through your nose, Beth." Her heartbeat was accelerating. If a nurse was at the station, she might notice.

She attached the gauze in place with several strips of medical tape. "You made me do this. I was ready to leave, and you had to recognize me. This is not my fault."

Claire inserted the syringe into the vial to withdraw the mixture of lethal drugs.

Beth's eyes widened as Claire injected the needle's contents into the port at the base of the saline bag.

"I was going to let you live, but how will I escape if you tell them I was the woman in the alley?" She looked at the drip. The fatal drug wouldn't take long to reach the IV catheter in her hand. She had to hurry.

Beth struggled to free herself.

"Relax, Beth. You won't feel a thing with fentanyl. Just close your eyes and go to sleep."

She dropped the syringe into the red sharps container along with the vial she had used to mix the drug.

Claire grabbed her bag and closed the door before heading down the hall. A nurse came out of a room on the opposite side of the nurse's station and looked her way. Claire lowered her head and barreled through the ward door.

She stopped in a bathroom near an exit and changed out of her scrubs into leggings and a sweatshirt. It was a necessary delay. They would be looking for a nurse. She tied her sneakers and stuffed her uniform into her backpack. No code had been announced, so she had time. She needed a fix to calm her nerves.

She checked to make sure nobody was around and went into the bathroom stall. She calculated the milligrams she needed and dropped them into the crusher, grinding them into a powder. She snorted the pain killer, repacked her supplies, and headed outside.

She should have driven her car to work, but she hadn't run since the shooting, and she'd noticed her weight going up. She couldn't let that happen after all her hard work to regain her slimmer figure. She broke into a run. Her apartment wasn't far.

She would pack and find another job in a different town. The aging population needed nurses, and she was one of the best. She had excellent references from the pain management department. She could create a couple from the ER doctors. She'd have no trouble starting over.

A siren echoed in the distance. Had someone checked Beth's room and found her tied to the bed? Claire dashed up the steps to her apartment door. This had been her home for eight years, but she felt no fondness for the place. It wouldn't be difficult to leave.

She grabbed a suitcase from the closet and plopped it on the bed. She packed everyday clothes, underwear, and scrubs. She added toiletries. She removed the cash she had withdrawn from the bank from under the mattress and hid it in her bra. Too bad she hadn't had time to replace her gun. She grabbed the photo of her late husband from the nightstand. His smug expression taunted her. She had worked hard to be a nurse and build a career. But now everything was unraveling. "It's all your fault." She threw the photograph across the room. The glass shattered on the floor.

She strapped on her backpack and gripped the side handle on her suitcase. With a final glance, she closed the door and dashed down the steps. She crossed the parking lot and headed for her car in the canopy garage shared by other tenants. A police SUV turned in, and she hid behind the nearest vehicle. The officer parked the cruiser in front of her car and got out. He looked at the license plate and headed for the building door.

The cop was the one from the hospital, Officer Sam Wilson. The same cop who didn't remember her from the night of the shooting or the blood drive. But the police were looking for her. Had Beth somehow told them? That narrowed her window for escape. Because her car was blocked in, she had to leave on foot. She headed for the duplex behind her, cutting through the yard, and made her way to Main Street.

Claire sat on the bench in the bus stop. She felt light-headed and had trouble reading the bus schedule. Her heart was pounding in her chest, and her breathing was labored. What was wrong with her? She could run ten miles with ease. She'd felt like this once before.

The fentanyl. She'd crushed the toxic pills in her personal pill crusher, the same one she had used to get high on oxycodone. How much fentanyl had she snorted? She had naloxone hydrochloride in her bag. She frantically searched through the backpack until she found it.

She inserted the nasal spray. The tightness in her chest began to ease. She could breathe. She couldn't board the bus now. She might have another attack and draw attention. She needed time to recover. Where could she hide for a few days?

Chapter Thirty-Five

Sydney pulled into the first empty spot at the hospital and shoved her car into park. She dashed through the sliding glass doors to the lobby outside the emergency room. She stopped the first nurse she saw. "Is Claire Batton here?"

"Her shift ended at eight thirty. Can I help you?"

Sydney pushed the button for the elevator, but it was too slow. She ran up the steps to the second floor.

Rick was strolling slowly toward the room with a cup of coffee in his hand. "Dispatch called the nurses desk and said Beth was fine."

The nurse at the station looked at Rick. "Did you call about Moreno?"

"Yes," Sydney answered. "Have you visited her room?"

"A little while ago. She had a hearty breakfast, and her vitals are good."

No alarms had been sounded. Perhaps Beth was fine. She tried to calm her pounding heartbeat. Her instincts had been wrong, and Claire had left without visiting Beth.

Rick took a sip from his coffee cup. "What's up?"

"The mystery woman is a nurse in this hospital. I thought she might have harmed Beth." She pushed open the closed door. Beth was tied to the bed with cloth restraints, and her mouth was covered in gauze taped to her face. Her eyes were wet with fear-filled tears as she kicked at the covers.

"This is going to hurt." Sydney ripped the tape off and pulled out a wad of wet gauze.

The oxygen line was still stuck up her nose, but Beth coughed as she tried to fill her lungs with a deep breath.

Sydney removed one of the restraints. Rick ditched his coffee in the trash and went to the other side of the bed to unhook the other restraint. "Where's the call button?"

Sydney stuck her head out the door and shouted for the nurse. When she turned, Beth was using her teeth to tug on the tape securing her IV catheter to the top of her hand.

Rick released the other restraint, and Beth reached over and yanked the catheter from her bruised flesh. Blood spurted over the white sheet.

A nurse stood in the doorway. "You can't do that!" She grabbed a wad of gauze and pressed it against Beth's hand and clamped the IV line. "I'll have to put a new catheter in."

Beth pulled her hand away. "You're the woman in the alley. Your name is Claire."

The nurse stepped back and looked at Sydney and Rick. "My name isn't Claire."

"She's confused." Sydney patted Beth's shoulder. "You're safe, Beth. You need to calm down."

She grabbed Sydney's arm, but her clasp was weak, and Beth's hand trembled as it hung in mid-air. "She was here. The woman in the alley. A nurse."

She stroked Beth's arm as she gazed into her eyes. "Yes, her name is Claire Batton. When was she here?"

"I can't remember. I'm so weak." Beth relaxed back

against the pillow. "I feel tired."

Sydney shook her. "What did she do to you?"

Beth's hand went to her chest. She panted and struggled to breathe. The machine monitoring her vitals beeped a warning as her heartbeat slowed and her blood pressure dropped. She pointed at the access port beneath the drip chamber of the saline solution. "Claire. Fentanyl." Beth dropped her hand and closed her eyes.

The nurse was searching through the supply cabinet but turned. "Did she say fentanyl?"

Claire had drugged Beth. Sydney grabbed the tubing dangling from the saline bag. "She put fentanyl in Beth's IV line."

The nurse stared at the monitor. "That could kill her. How long ago did she inject the drug into the port?"

Beth didn't answer. Her body relaxed against the mattress as the machine's alarm went off. Her heart rhythm went flat.

"She's going into cardiac arrest." The nurse searched the cabinet. "I can't find the naloxone."

"I've got some." Sydney reached into her pants pocket for a canister of nasal spray for opioid overdoses, removed the oxygen line in Beth's nose, and replaced it with a dose of the lifesaving antidote.

Medical staff filled the room in response to the code to save Beth's life. The antidote had restored Beth's heartbeat, and her blood pressure was rising.

The doctor had her stethoscope pressed against Beth's chest. "What happened?"

"Someone gave her a dose of fentanyl." Sydney gathered the rubber tubing hanging from the saline bag. "We need the IV for evidence."

The nurse grabbed a plastic bag used for storing

clothing and put the saline bag and line inside. "Why is someone trying to harm this woman?"

"Do you know a nurse named Claire Batton?"

"No, but I saw a nurse in the hall right after I checked on Beth."

Sydney handed the bag to Rick. "Send this to the medical examiner and get someone to guard Beth's door."

Rick kept pace as Sydney hurried down the hall. "I'll keep Beth safe, but where are you going?"

"Dispatch sent a patrol car to Claire's address. If we got lucky, she's been arrested."

"I didn't understand what Beth was mumbling about. Why would this nurse try to harm her?"

"Claire Batton is the woman in the alley who pretended to be Abby Keller. Beth recognized her, and she tried to kill her with a fentanyl overdose."

Rick shook his head. "Why? She may have caused the death of Jack Lawson, but a good lawyer could get her out in a few years. An attempt on a cop's life could get her life."

"I think Claire Batton has dealt with life and death long enough to become judge and jury. She set Jack Lawson up to look like the robber and pretended to be Abby in order to escape. Now she gives Beth a fatal overdose because she recognized her." Sydney ran her hand through her damp hair. Her heart rate had yet to return to normal. The elevator door opened, and she pushed the button for the first floor.

"This woman sounds like she's crazy, Detective. Be careful."

"You do the same, Sergeant."

Sydney pulled into the back of the apartment

complex. It was similar to Beth's four-unit building, but this one was neglected by the landlord with peeling paint on cheap wood siding and weeds growing in the barren yard.

Officer Sam Wilson's cruiser was parked behind an old hatchback in the open-air garage. She parked and hurried inside.

"Did you touch anything? We need a warrant to search the place."

"I called for one, but the door was unlocked," Sam said. "As first responder, I announced myself and opened a few doors to see if she was hiding, but the place is empty. She left in a hurry."

"We'll have to wait for the warrant, but she's gone." Sydney backed out of the apartment and headed down the stairs. "Did you look outside?"

"I had a license number for a car she owns and saw it in the garage when I arrived. I parked behind it and hurried inside."

"Good thinking to block her escape." She tried the door of the car. It was locked. "I'll ask for the search warrant to include her vehicle."

"She could have slipped out the front while I was in the back. Dispatch sent out a BOLO on her, and officers are searching the neighborhood. She couldn't have gone far."

She kicked a discarded bottle in the parking lot and sent the plastic container flying. Claire had gotten away. She finally had a name to the mystery woman in the alley, but she had slipped through her fingers.

"Who is this woman, Claire Batton?"

"She's your mystery woman in the alley," Sydney said.

"You found her." His smile turned to disappointment. "And I let her get away, again."

"She's clever. She's been one step ahead of me the whole time. I met her Saturday night in the hospital. She was an ER nurse who had come on shift right after the shooting. She was so cool and calm I never would have suspected her of anything."

"An ER nurse," Sam repeated. "The paramedics might have recognized her. She didn't want any of them to treat her. That explains why she snuck off." He snapped his fingers. "Hey, there was a nurse at the hospital named Claire when I gave blood."

"That was her."

"I didn't recognize her. Am I blind?"

"She's ordinary. She's not the type of woman who makes an impression. No one could remember anything about her, but Officer Moreno recognized her as the woman in your squad car who had pretended to be Abby Keller. Claire tried to kill her by injecting fentanyl into her IV line before she came here."

"Fentanyl? Is Beth all right?"

"She's stable. Claire didn't try to hide the fact that she had been in her room. She had her tied to the bed and gagged. If Beth hadn't told us about the fentanyl, she might be dead."

Sam ran his hands through his hair. "Why would she want to kill Beth when you know her identity?"

"Claire doesn't know I figured that out."

"I'm glad you reached Beth in time."

"Not before she went into cardiac arrest." Sydney paced between Sam's car and her own. "Sergeant Faris is guarding the room and sending me updates." She looked at her phone. "I really hate this bitch."

"Put me on the list."

The chief called with a verbal approval for a search. Sydney headed for the door. "We can go inside. They'll send a K9 crew to search for drugs."

"She probably didn't leave any of those behind."

Sydney silently agreed. Claire was an addict. Drugs would be a priority. "Bag anything in the bathroom medicine cabinet."

She looked around with the eyes of a detective, searching for clues. A picture of Claire in a bikini was stuck to the refrigerator. It had been taken when she was heavy. Maybe it was a reminder never to gain weight again. The bedroom had been ransacked with clothing discarded on the bed or floor. An empty space in the closet was next to a smaller travel bag. "It looks like a suitcase is missing."

"If she's on foot with a suitcase, she should be easy to spot."

Sam was optimistic. Claire hadn't left much behind to track her. Something had been removed from the bed stand, leaving a clean mark in the dust. "I wonder what was here." She glanced around. The drywall was dented on the opposite wall. She picked up a picture frame with broken glass.

"What is it?" Sam looked over her shoulder. "Who's that?"

Sydney had seen the same face on the accident report the chief had sent her. "Daniel Batton, her husband."

"She's married? Where is he?"

"He died in a car accident." Why did she throw it against the wall instead of taking it with her?

"Losing someone you love can mess you up." Sam

turned toward the window. "Looks like the crew is here to search the car."

Sydney stared out the window. "Claire could have seen you arrive. She had to flee on foot."

"We have a face now. The chief can release her picture and name to the media. Everyone in town will be looking for her."

If she was still in town. Claire was on the run. She would stay in hiding until she felt safe to reappear.

Where would she hide? She'd have to interview her co-workers, family, and friends. It would take time, and Claire was slipping away. She found empty pill containers in the trash and bagged them. She would talk to every person listed on the labels. One of them might provide a clue to Claire's whereabouts.

Her phone rang. It was Rick. "How's Beth?"

"You're on the list for sainthood, Sydney. You saved her life, twice. The doctor is flushing out her system, but she's asking for something to eat." He lowered his voice. "Tell me you have this psychopath in handcuffs."

"No, she slipped away just as Officer Wilson arrived, but we'll find her. She's ruined enough lives."

"The chief is here."

His voice came over the phone. "What can I do to help?"

"Get her photo out to the media."

"The hospital is sending her employee headshot. Anything else?"

"It might be good if Claire thinks she's succeeded at the hospital. Do you think we can keep Beth's survival out of the news?"

"You want the hospital to report Beth died?"

"Not that detailed. Report an overdose of a patient."

"The truth without the outcome," he said. "Do you think she'll return to the hospital?"

"Not if she thinks she succeeded." Sydney recalled something Abby had said. "Sometimes people sneak in and sleep in the hospital. You might want to add security in case she returns. It's her comfort zone."

"I'll keep an officer on duty outside Beth's room. Her new room," he added.

"I think we should put an officer on Vivien's house, too. She's been in the news and has ties to Claire."

"You think she'll target Vivien Lawson?"

"This woman is searching for a place to hide. Vivien is alone with a baby. I don't want to risk a hostage situation."

"I'll call in some officers from other communities for mutual aid. We could use help on this one."

"I met Claire the night of the shooting when I interviewed Abby. I should have known sooner."

"Don't beat yourself up, Detective. You followed every lead. Did you find anything at her apartment that's useful?"

"We found pawn tickets and empty pill bottles but nothing to indicate where she's heading."

"We'll find her."

Sydney stared at the photograph on the refrigerator. Claire had no distinguishing feature to set her apart from anyone else. Her greatest asset was the ability to blend in and fool others.

She called Gordon and alerted him to the danger. Her family was her vulnerable spot, and she didn't take chances with their safety. Everyone Claire knew needed to take precautions. This was no time to let her guard down. Claire had been in possession of a gun when she had robbed Edith Merryweather. It was a good bet she was armed again.

Chapter Thirty-Six

Sydney spent the rest of the day talking to hospital staff who knew Claire and handing out her contact information so they could call her if they saw her. None of them considered Claire a close friend. She had always been a lone wolf. Those who had met her husband hinted at abuse, but Claire never talked about him in a negative way. Her grief had seemed genuine when he died. She had withdrawn and turned down invitations for drinks or socializing. A few admitted they had suspected her when Abby's pills went missing. Claire had mood swings and had an inflated opinion of her abilities. She always had an excuse when confronted about an error or neglect of her duties.

The next day Sydney called every person listed on the discarded bottles of pills to make sure they were safe. Some knew Claire and admitted she had access to their purses or medications. She had two more names on her list. One was Edith Merryweather. The lab had finished dusting her handbag and personal items and had placed them in a clear bag, which was on Sydney's desk. She planned to return the items when she interviewed her. She had left a message, but Edith hadn't returned her phone call. She dialed again, and the call went to voicemail. "Edith, this is Detective Sydney Harrison. I would like to return your purse we recovered. Please call me."

"Hey, you look worried about something." Beth stood in the doorway. She was dressed in civilian clothes, and only a weariness in her face revealed the trauma she had experienced. She looked older, but the smile was reassuring. "Can I help?"

Sydney jumped to her feet and hugged her. "I heard you were discharged. You should be home resting."

"They flushed the fentanyl out of my system, my arm is healing, and my aunt Sophie took me home this morning." Beth shook her head as a low chuckle escaped her throat. "I mean my mother. I have to unlearn everything I knew about my family."

What was Beth rambling about? "Your aunt Sophie is your mother?"

She sat in the chair across from Sydney's desk. "You've been too busy for me to tell you about my family drama. Remember those phone messages you listened to?"

"I remember." Sydney sat on the edge of her desk. "I hope you don't think I was being nosy. I thought we should contact your family in case something…"

"You couldn't know how ashamed I was of my family. I never talked about them because I didn't want anyone to realize how awful they were. Fred is in jail for selling drugs to an undercover cop. Alice is working on another internet scam to raise donations to her favorite charity—herself. My vicious former sister Angel brags about recruiting young girls to work for her in her *business*, and her brother Bubba calls himself a cook because he brews illegal drugs."

"But you succeeded in spite of them."

"I always knew something was wrong. Most parents don't abuse someone they love the way I was treated. It turns out Sophie became pregnant when she was a teenager, and Alice was pressured to take me in. Everything made sense. I'm not a Moreno." Beth smiled from ear to ear.

"If you're not a Moreno, what is your name?"

She giggled like a schoolgirl. "Fitzsimmons. Can you believe it? A cop named Fitzsimmons? I could have a long line of cops in the family tree. I'm not the odd duck. Law and order are in my blood."

"You sound happy about it."

"I was going to quit the force. Sophie wants me to make a career change and offered to pay for college."

Beth was a good cop. Claire had fooled everyone and forced Beth to make a mistake. "Is that what you want?"

"I'm not sure. Vivien and I have been talking about taking classes."

"Vivien Lawson?"

Beth's brows knitted in confusion. "She brought groceries to my apartment. I ruined her life, and she's being nice to me. I can't do enough to return the favor."

Vivien had been sincere in the hospital. "She's forgiven you."

"I don't know how, but yes, she's forgiven me, befriended me, and even let me hold John-John. Can you believe that?"

"I didn't forgive Barry for nearly killing Gordon until I saw the way they interacted. When Gordon first met Barry, he saw a broken young man filled with guilt and pain for a stupid accident. They helped each other heal."

"Barry? His personal aide?" Beth's mouth dropped. "He's the heartless man who ran over your husband and left him in the parking lot? You didn't say anything."

"It isn't my place to out Barry," she explained. "He's the only one who can reveal his mistake, but he talks about it when he sees it as a way to help others heal. He said he was going to tell you."

Beth snapped her fingers. "That's why he stopped yesterday at the hospital to visit me. Sophie was there, and he didn't stay long."

"Before you make any life-changing decisions, you should talk to him."

"He said something about believing in second chances. I wouldn't have a future if you hadn't arrived at my room and rescued me." Beth's eyes filled with tears. "Claire was leaving and said, 'Gotta go.' Those were the same words she used when she passed my cruiser. It clicked in my brain, and I knew. Stupid me. I blurted out that she was the mystery woman. She turned, and I saw the cold, hard look in her eyes. She wanted me dead."

"And if she's willing to kill a cop, she'll be willing to kill anyone."

"She put fentanyl in my IV tube."

"You told me that."

"I don't remember. I think I tore the catheter out of my hand, but the whole episode was surreal. They told me you gave me the antidote." She stood. "You saved my life. That's why I had to come by today. I couldn't wait to say thank you."

"Do me a favor and be careful until we find Claire," Sydney warned. "She's dangerous."

Beth rubbed the top of her hand where a bruise outlined the scab from the catheter. "What have you learned about her?"

Sydney handed her a medical examiner's report.

"Something disturbing. This is the autopsy on Daniel Batton."

Beth scanned the pages. "He died in a car crash three years ago."

"He was dead when the emergency services arrived. The coroner ruled his death from blunt force trauma to the head and chest from sudden impact. He hit the windshield and steering wheel."

"No seat belt?"

"That was the reason for the severity of his injuries, but he had bruising on his left bicep."

Beth frowned. "That wouldn't kill him."

"No. But think about a seat belt. If you're wearing it, you have bruising across your shoulder and chest. If you're not wearing it, no bruises. But if someone unhooks it, the strap gets caught on your arm."

"Bruising on the bicep. Someone unhooked the seat belt before the crash, or it malfunctioned."

"A new truck makes a malfunction unlikely. Claire wore her seat belt and suffered minor injuries."

"She was lucky and he wasn't."

"Maybe she helped her husband's luck. The road from Olde Bend curves in and out around the hills. When you're sliding off a curve, you turn back into the curve, but in the report, the wheels of his truck were turned the other way like someone had jerked the steering wheel."

"Unhook the belt and yank on the wheel. She caused the crash." Beth shook her head. "Why would Claire kill her husband?"

"She tried to keep it secret, but he was a drunk, abusive, and drove them into debt. Any one item would be a motive. All three add up to murder."

"No wonder she didn't hesitate to try to end my life.

How did you arrive in time to save me?"

Sydney handed Beth the old police report from the crash. "Claire was transported to Olde Bend Hospital and diagnosed with a broken arm. The radiologist used the x-ray taken of the fake Abby Keller and matched it to Claire's old x-ray. That's how I identified her."

"It all started out as a theft. How did it spiral out of control?"

"It started small. Most of Claire's thefts were crimes of opportunity. Abby left her locker unlocked. Others on my list left their purses unattended. She saw a way to feed her addiction."

"How long has she been an addict?"

"From the history of thefts, Claire has been abusing drugs since the accident. She had help picking her victims. She worked in pain management where doctors prescribe opioid medication. Edith was one of the patients. Claire had access to their prescriptions, personal information, and scheduled appointments. Someone noticed pills missing from inventory a few months before Claire transferred to the ER. The doctor said there haven't been any shortages since. Claire inhaled pain pills, but she was one step from moving on to stronger meds. She had fentanyl in her possession."

"I remember." Beth shuddered. "Why do you think she turned to drugs? As a nurse, she had to know the dangers."

"Sometimes a prescription to pain meds will trigger the addiction. When she broke her arm, she was given a prescription for opioids."

"How did she hide her addiction, especially from hospital staff?"

"She worked night shift, and as a nurse, she knew

the signs of addiction and how to mask them in herself. Others said she kept to herself and attributed her strange behavior to grief."

"She sounds shrewd."

Sydney tapped her fingers on her desk. "Claire is, but her brain is rewired from the drugs she takes. Who knows how paranoid or illogical she is?"

"Have you found out where she is?"

"Not yet, but her face is all over the news. We've sent her information to every police force across the country, but until she's found, you should stay with Sophie or have her stay with you."

"What about Vivien?"

"Her mother is staying with her. I have an officer checking on them as well."

It wasn't enough. Claire was making them prisoners, afraid of her next move. She sorted through the items on her desk. She needed to find a clue.

Beth examined the purse inside the plastic bag on the desk. "This is so retro."

"It's Edith Merryweather's purse. Evidence said I could return it. She's on my list of people to talk to."

"Isn't she the little old lady robbed at the bus stop?"

"Yes. I've contacted everyone Claire stole pills or money from. I've left two messages for Edith, but she hasn't returned my calls. I was planning to visit."

"I'd like to meet Edith. Vivien and I are thinking of forming a Victims of Claire's Club."

Sydney laughed. "You and Vivien sound like a dangerous combination, but Edith loves company, and she has a jar filled with delicious cookies. I'll introduce you."

"I'll follow in my car. I don't know what the

mechanic did, but it purrs like a kitten."

Sydney gathered her equipment. She put on her bulletproof vest and jacket.

"You said it was a friendly visit."

"I made a promise to Gordon to always wear my vest outside the office. We keep our promises." She grabbed the bag with Edith's purse. "If it makes you feel better, you can wear one, too."

Beth rubbed her chest. "I wish I had one on when that guy hit me with a can."

"You kept your head. I would have been tempted to throw the can back at him."

"The guy had a gun. I didn't want to escalate the incident."

"It takes a lot of self-control to be a cop. You've got that."

"It takes persistence to be a detective. Most people would have given up solving this case a long time ago."

Sydney headed down the hall. "I'm on a mission to find Claire. The sooner the better."

Chapter Thirty-Seven

Sydney parked on the street across from Edith's home. She grabbed the bag and the receipt Edith needed to sign for receiving her purse and the contents. Beth parked behind her.

Sydney knocked on the front door a second time as Beth joined her. "I wonder where she is." She dialed Edith's number.

"I can hear the phone ringing," Beth said. "Would she leave home without her phone?"

"She told me she always kept her phone in her pocket in case she needed it." Sydney turned the knob. The door was locked. "Let's check the back door." The gravel drive crunched beneath her feet. She stopped in front of the garage. The door was open.

"What's wrong?"

"It's empty."

Beth shrugged. "She drove somewhere."

"Edith doesn't drive. She's nearly blind and has arthritis. That's why she was at the bus stop." Sydney called dispatch on a BOLO for Edith's car. She tried the back door. It was unlocked. She pushed the door open. "Do you hear something?"

"What?" Beth frowned. "I don't... Oh, I do hear something. Someone must be in distress."

Beth needed to work on her acting skills. "I'm doing a safety check on an elderly woman," Sydney reported into her radio. She gave the address.

Beth closed the door and looked around. "Is she selling the place?"

"No." Sydney pointed to where darker shadows against faded wallpaper marked where an object had decorated the walls. "She had antique glassware and other expensive gifts from her daughter in here. They're all gone." She gripped her gun and advanced into the next room. "Stay back."

Beth slapped her hips. She gave Sydney a worried look. "I haven't been cleared to carry. You better call backup."

She handed Beth her stun gun. "You're my backup for now."

Edith's side table by her recliner was cleaned of all her medications. Family photographs were still on the wall, but a collection of her husband's sports memorabilia and her son's medals were missing. Like the kitchen, the living room had been pilfered of valuables. Probably pawned. Claire had been here. But where was Edith?

"Edith! It's Detective Harrison. Edith!"

Sydney entered the hallway. All the doors were closed. The first one opened to a staircase to the upstairs. "Don't move," she warned Beth. She dashed up the steps. It was one finished room used for storage. Boxes had been overturned or tossed aside while others remained stacked. She returned. "Someone searched the upstairs."

Beth had opened the next door. "Bathroom."

"I told you not to move."

"I'm on medical leave, not fired."

"Stay behind me. I'll take the next one."

The door opened into a small bedroom that had been converted into a study. An open suitcase was on the floor. Sydney searched through the contents. "Nurses scrubs, clothing, and personal items." She found a prescription bottle with pain meds. "She's been hiding under our noses. I should have checked on Edith sooner." She leapt to her feet and opened the remaining door.

Edith Merryweather was in bed with her wrists strapped to the headboard posts with similar restraints Claire had used on Beth. The stuffy room smelled of urine.

"Is she alive?" Beth asked.

Sydney holstered her revolver and felt for a pulse at Edith's neck. "She's alive." She gingerly stripped away the medical tape covering a few squares of gauze over her mouth, but her lip still bled. "Get a washcloth."

When Sydney unfastened the restraining straps, Edith's arms fell limply to the mattress.

Beth returned with the damp cloth and placed it on Edith's torn lips. "She's a helpless old woman. Who would do something so vile?"

Edith's eyes were crusted with dried tears, and she had trouble opening them. Sydney used the damp cloth to gently wipe Edith's eyes clean.

Edith blinked several times and reached her hand toward her, her gnarled fingers touching her hand. "You came, my dear."

Hot tears stung her eyes as anger boiled within. She looked at Beth. "If I had any sympathy for Claire, it's gone. This is unforgiveable."

"That nurse was so mean," Edith said. "I told her to leave, but she tied me up."

"I'll call a squad." Sydney spoke into the radio,

updating dispatch on the situation.

Beth held Edith's hand, comforting her.

Sydney examined Edith for any injuries. Thin flesh crossed with fine lines hung loose from her bones. Bruises marred her pale skin. She was frail and defenseless, and Claire had violated every rule of decency. She had to bury her emotions and do her job. "Do you know where the nurse went?"

"She took my precious memories and left in my car."

Claire had left clothing and pills behind. She'd return. "Do you know when she's coming back?"

"No." Edith wept as her body trembled. "Don't let her hurt me again."

"Not while I breathe," Sydney vowed.

"I'm wet."

Beth helped Edith sit on the edge of the bed.

"Do I know you, my dear?"

"I'm Beth More…Beth Fitzsimmons."

She squinted. "You look familiar."

Beth shrugged her shoulders. "I've been in the news lately."

"I'll need to get this diaper off. It's soaked. She likes to leave me in it when she's gone. It must be hours since she left."

Claire would be returning soon. Edith stood, but she had been in bed too long.

Sydney caught her before she hit the floor. "She's dead weight."

"I'm not dead," Edith said.

Beth grinned at Sydney. Edith had fight left in her.

"Let's put her back in bed and change her."

"I saw diapers and wipes in the bathroom," Beth

said.

"We'll get her ready for transport." Sydney searched for a clean nightgown. "She can wear this to the hospital." She opened the bedroom window to air out the foul odors.

Beth cleaned Edith while Sydney replaced her gown with a clean one. Edith bore their jostling without complaining.

"Was that a car?" The driveway was on the other side of the house, but she had heard tires on gravel.

"The paramedics must be here," Beth said.

"Stay with her. I'll let them in." Sydney walked through the small house. She looked out the window for the ambulance but saw a sedan. Claire was behind the wheel. She ran back to the bedroom. "It's Claire."

Edith grabbed Beth's arm. "She has a gun."

Sydney looked at Beth and then Edith. "How do you know?"

"It was my husband's gun. The one I told you about. The nurse found it when she went through our belongings upstairs. She stuck it in my face just like the robber." Edith's eyes widened as the memories collided. "She was the thief."

"Yes. She had your address from your prescription," Sydney said.

"She said she was my home health nurse."

"We need to get her out of here." Sydney pointed to the window. "Climb out, and I'll hand Edith to you. Our guys should be here soon."

She pulled Edith to the edge of the bed like she did with Gordon when he was transferring to his wheelchair. "Put your arms around my neck."

Sydney dragged Edith across the carpeted floor and

positioned her in front of the window. She leaned Edith forward and lifted her legs, and she fell into Beth's arms. "Get Edith to safety."

Beth's eyes widened. "You can't stay in there."

Sydney heard footsteps in the hallway and reached for her gun in the holster.

"Drop it or I'll drop you!" Claire shrieked as she pointed a revolver at her.

Sydney dropped the gun to the floor and raised her hands.

"Kick it to me."

Sydney knew every delay gave Beth and Edith time to escape. She gave the gun a kick.

Claire bent down and retrieved it with her left hand. She had bleached her hair blonde and wore a low-cut blouse that would distract any male over fifteen. She looked out the window. Sydney stole a glance. Beth and Edith were gone.

"I have the better deal, a cop instead of an old woman. Put your hands on top of your head." She shoved Sydney's gun into the backpack hanging on her shoulder and waved her weapon at her. The revolver shook in Claire's injured hand. "Head for the other bedroom." She followed. "Put my stuff in the suitcase."

Sydney pressed her radio's emergency button as she bent over Claire's belongings. It opened the microphone to dispatch so they could hear everything going on. She packed the bag, taking her time. "I like your new look, Claire. Every woman should be a blonde once in her life."

"You had my face all over town. It was this or a redhead like your friend, Officer Moreno. I heard she didn't make it."

"Why did you have to kill her, Claire?"

"She recognized me." She ran her hand across her brow. "That's enough packing. Zip it."

Sydney ran the zipper around the suitcase and stood. She pulled up the handle. "How much money did you get from pawning Edith's belongings?"

"That junk was hardly worth the effort." Claire waved her forward. "Go ahead of me."

Sydney was wearing her bulletproof vest, but it only protected her chest. If Claire shot her in the back of the head, she might not die, but she'd be a shadow of her former self. She had to do as Claire ordered until an opportunity provided an advantage.

A siren screamed closer. Another echoed farther away. Claire moved the curtain aside, and Sydney studied the perimeter through the small opening. A police cruiser blocked the end of the driveway. Another squad car replaced an ambulance that pulled away. Edith was probably inside. She was safe.

Claire let the curtain drop and waved the gun to the recliner. "Sit."

Sydney sat on the edge of the seat, her feet planted to respond when the time was right. "You need to surrender."

"Why? If they shoot me, it's murder. I haven't done anything wrong."

Was she serious? Claire had robbed Abby and Edith for their drugs. She had pretended to be the victim to cause Jack Lawson's death. Her husband's death was suspicious, and she had tried to kill Beth. This woman took no responsibility for the havoc she had caused and denied any wrongdoing. But if Sydney pointed out that she was facing prison, it would remind Claire she had nothing to lose by shooting a police officer.

Sydney wanted to stay alive. She had to talk Claire into surrendering. Gordon admired her storytelling ability. Now she needed to shine. "You're right, Claire. None of this is your fault. You had no control over what happened to Jack Lawson."

Claire nodded in agreement. "He shouldn't have picked up my gun."

Sydney leaned forward. Every word Claire said would be recorded. "We know Jack Lawson didn't own a gun. How did he get yours?"

"A gutter fell and hit my arm." She shoved up her sleeve to expose the edge of the plastic brace. Claire jabbed the gun toward Sydney's face. "But you figured that out. You were looking for a woman with an arm injury."

"We knew Abby Keller wasn't the woman."

She snorted. "You got that right."

Sydney had to keep her talking. "So the gutter knocked the gun out of your hand."

"The man reached it first. I thought about running, but the fool cocked the gun. All it takes is a slight touch on the trigger to go off. He could have shot me." Her voice was filled with outrage. "I saw the cops arrive. They lit him up with a light, and he turned. I heard the gun go off, and Officer Moreno shot him dead. Now she's dead. Debt paid."

Gravel crunched outside the window behind her, but Sydney stared ahead. The police were moving into positions around the house. They wouldn't fire and put a hostage in danger without trying to negotiate a surrender. "It takes a cool head to handle a situation like that. The officers told me how you were on your knees begging for your life when they arrived. They thought you were the victim."

She laughed. "Nobody makes Claire Batton a victim. I didn't cause any of this. I was going to leave town. Start fresh somewhere else. And all of this would have gone away, but I forgot about the fentanyl left in my pill crusher. I got sick."

"It can all be over if you surrender. You're an addict. You'll get the treatment you need."

"I'm no addict!" She jabbed the gun in Sydney's face. "I can quit anytime I want."

"I'm sure you can." Her voice shook. "You run. You lost all that weight. That takes a lot of self-control."

"You're damned right. No sweets, no breads, no pop. Men don't understand all the sacrifices a woman makes to meet their approval."

"I'm sure your husband would approve of you now."

"Danny Boy? He's the one who made me fat. He wanted me ugly so other men wouldn't want me. He couldn't lose my paycheck. I didn't do this for him or any man. I did this for me." She jabbed her thumb back at her chest. "I wanted to look in the mirror and be proud of me."

"You can be proud. You're a good nurse."

"I'm up for employee of the month. They don't give that to anyone. You have to earn it."

"How long have you been a nurse?"

"Eight years. I was fresh out of nursing school and working as an RN in pain management when I met Danny. He'd hurt his back at work. He asked me out. I thought he was my Prince Charming. I'll never make that mistake again."

"He wasn't nice to you?"

"He was a bum. He couldn't keep a job, and when I helped him start his own business, he saddled me with the loans. I'm still paying them off."

"Then you didn't escape him when he died in the crash."

Claire's eyes were cold and hard. "He won't let me, but the pills help."

"Do you blame yourself for his death?"

"He was drunk. He wouldn't let me drive. I didn't kill anyone."

"What about Beth?"

"I did that police officer a favor giving her fentanyl. She felt guilty about shooting that young man in the alley. She wouldn't have slit her arm otherwise. She wanted to die."

Claire was justifying her actions and talking freely. "I was ready to leave, but she recognized me. She knew I was the woman in the alley and knew what I looked like."

"She was a witness. She could have identified you," Sydney agreed. "You didn't have a choice, but you do now."

They were playing a cat-and-mouse game with the truth. She held out her hand. "You need to give me the gun, Claire."

"Here it is!" Claire stepped forward and smacked her across the face with the barrel.

It was the same cheek her nephew had bruised, only Claire hit ten times harder. The blinding pain radiated across her face. She fought back a scream. When the stars cleared, she spoke to update the officers listening in. "Hitting me with your gun wasn't necessary."

"You think I'm a crazy woman." She rubbed her

forearm. The assault had hurt her injured arm.

"No, I admire you, Claire. You've been one step ahead of me the whole time. You're smart."

"You bet I am." She jabbed the gun in her face. It shook, and she had to use both hands to hold it steady. "How did you know I was here?"

"I was checking on all your victims. Edith was on my list."

"Victims!" Claire's face was scrunched in fury. "I'm the victim. No one has ever given me a fair chance. Nobody understands my pain, my misery."

"All you have to do is surrender, Claire." Sydney stood and held out her hand. "Give me the gun, walk out the door, and your problems will be over. A good lawyer will make it all go away."

She stepped back. "I don't have any power without a gun."

"If they see you with a weapon in your hand, the police will shoot to kill."

She laughed. "Your trigger-happy police officer is dead."

"Not yet." Beth stepped into the living room. When Claire turned and the gun was no longer directed at Sydney, Beth tased her.

Claire's body arched and shook in a tremor as the electrical current traveled through her body. The gun fell from her hand, and Sydney dove for it. Beth stopped the current to the wires attached to the two prongs stuck in Claire's clothing, and Sydney cuffed her.

She pulled Claire to her feet, who stared at Beth.

"I thought I killed you."

"You need to stay off the drugs, Claire." Beth grinned. "They're messing with your mind."

Sydney looked toward the hallway. "They let you back in?"

"Being off duty, I didn't ask. As soon as the paramedics took Edith, I climbed back in the window. You left it open."

Sydney contacted dispatch on her radio. "All clear. You can send a team in."

Sam was the first in the door. "We were listening in. I thought you were going to become her new best friend."

"Negotiations require a little creative dialogue to make a connection with the hostage taker."

Sam laughed but sobered when he stared at her face. "I'll send in a paramedic with an ice pack."

Sydney touched her tender cheek. "I started this case with a black eye. Great way to end it."

Sam escorted Claire to the door. "I'm going to remember what you look like this time."

Claire had left her backpack next to her packed suitcase. Sydney put on gloves and removed her gun.

Beth handed her the stunner. "Thanks for letting me play cop. It may be the last time."

Sydney holstered the stun gun. "You're not going to quit the force."

"Why are you so sure?"

"I saw the smile on your face when you sent Claire to her knees."

"The woman tried to kill me." Beth's eyes darkened. "But I did it for Vivien, Jack, and John-John."

"And that's why you'll stay on the force." Sydney dumped the contents of the backpack on the floor and searched through the money and pills.

"What are you looking for?"

She gathered a bundle of pawn tickets, receipts for the items missing from the house. "Edith's memories. She deserves to have them back."

A word about the author…

Laura Freeman was a reporter for sixteen years for local papers and the Gannett national papers in Northeast Ohio. She won the Press Club of Cleveland's Ohio Excellence in Journalism award twice and the Ohio Newspaper Association award several times. Her novels include "Impending Love and War," "Impending Love and Death," Impending Love and Lies," "Impending Love and Capture," "Impending Love and Madness," and "Impending Love and Promise," and holiday novella "Tackling Molasses Crinkles."

~*~

Find Laura online at:
https://twitter.com/laurafreeman_rp
https://www.facebook.com/laura.freeman.5648
https://authorfreeman.wordpress.com/

www.ingramcontent.com/pod-product-compliance
Lightning Source LLC
Chambersburg PA
CBHW050020070726
47506CB00015B/538